Imperfectly Perfect

TRACY GOODWIN

sourcebooks
casablanca

Published by Sourcebooks Casablanca, an imprint of Sourcebooks
P.O. Box 4410, Naperville, Illinois 60567-4410
(630) 961-3900
sourcebooks.com

Cataloging-in-Publication Data is on file with the Library of Congress.

Printed and bound in the United States of America.
SB 10 9 8 7 6 5 4 3 2 1

Dedicated to Major,
for being the most loving, kind, and loudest beagle I could have ever asked for.
And for answering to the name Bailey as I wrote this novel.
With love.

Chapter 1

CASSANDRA BENEDICT BELIEVED IN HAPPILY EVER AFTER; HOWEVER, as she limped along the uneven pavement clutching her mangled Aquazzura heel in her right fist and cradling her precious tricolored beagle decked out in a Tiffany-blue tutu beneath her left arm, she began to question her usually unswerving belief.

"What am I doing, Bailey?" she muttered to her precious canine, pausing to lift him higher against her hip as she studied the desolate road in front of her.

The dog was getting heavier with every step she took. To top it all off, he seemed to be on maximum overdrive when it came to generating heat in his sturdy little frame. It was one of his many qualities that she found endearing: his ability to generate heat, especially when he slept beside her. She'd lost count of how many times Bailey had awakened her from a sound sleep as he cuddled with her, causing her to overheat with him. But today, beneath the beating sun, Bailey's stout body felt more like an industrial-sized furnace.

Beads of sweat pooled beneath her custom floor-length ivory gown, and at the back of her neck, while her long golden hair, which had once cascaded in waves and curls down her back, was now frizzy and damp—never a good combination.

Given her present circumstances, Cassandra silently cursed her hairstyle decision as she blew a few damp strands of blond hair from her forehead. So much for her vision of sophisticated elegance. That was supposed to be her vibe today, just like they were supposed to have been indoors, inside an air-conditioned Hamptons mansion. She had no way of knowing that fate was a witch with a capital B and an axe to grind.

Everything had gone to plan, down to the flowers—calla lilies and roses in shades of cream and white—which were her and Jeremy's favorites. Add to that the perfect weather—sunny with a glorious ocean view. Then there was the mansion—she couldn't have asked for a better venue, or one with more sentimental significance.

It was Jeremy's family home, after all…

Jeremy. Every time she thought of him, her heart shattered into sharp fragments. He had been the man she'd trusted beyond measure. Until he proved that she never should have trusted him in the first place. If her father had been there, he probably would have decked Jeremy. Instead, she was alone, handling things erratically at best and in full-on epic disaster mode at worst.

Again she scanned Dune Road, squinting in the sunshine, as her pulse hammered against her temples. Cassandra's desperation for a ride was at war with the unfathomable dread that had settled in the pit of her stomach at the mere thought of seeing a passing car. One would come along eventually, of that Cassandra was certain as she plodded ahead, wishing she'd grabbed her cell. And her purse, with her wallet and her keys. And her dog's leash.

What was I thinking?

The truth is, she hadn't been thinking. Not logically, at least. The only thing on her mind had been escaping as fast as she could, and not looking back.

Mission accomplished.

Given her shock and embarrassment at being so publicly humiliated in front of the crème de la crème of New York society, it wasn't surprising that all Cassandra wanted to do was get as far away as possible from the Roth estate in record time. It was too bad that her stupidity left her trudging down Dune Road with a broken heel and a hot dog.

"I know it was ridiculous of me to bolt like that, Bailey." She leaned down and kissed the top of her beagle's head. "I'm sorry I put you in this position."

Running was not in Cassandra's nature. She never ran from anything, never even jogged. She faced her problems head-on until…today. Yes, today was the day that her firm resolve went out the nearest window.

She stood to adjust Bailey one more time, tossing her heel onto the side of the road. Beneath the sign that stated clearly in all caps: NO LITTERING. Her bad. She took several steps forward, then paused. NO LITTERING. With a loud groan, she limped back to her offending heel, scooped it up, and proceeded forward.

Cassandra was anything but a rule breaker.

Especially not here, where she grew up.

With the ocean on one side and the bay on the other, Westhampton Beach was one of the Hamptons' most elite zip codes. Mega-mansions spanned the coastline along with their large decks, which gave way to private waterfront docks where luxury yachts awaited their owners' every whim. Cassandra had always loved it here, though today the salty air mingled with her very own heartbreak, and her humiliation had eroded the bright, sunshine-filled luster of the clear day.

A loud squawk from a seagull soaring above the nearby ocean dunes triggered Bailey to bay in immediate response—it's what beagles do, after all. And her canine bestie had a tendency to bay in the most spectacular fashion even on the most mundane of days. On this particular day from Hades, his high-pitched, bellowing howl sent tremors down her spine.

She rocked Bailey in her arm. "It's okay. We'll be fine." Who was she trying to fool? Even Cassandra didn't believe her own encouraging words. She doubted her beagle did either.

For someone who'd prided herself in her unwavering belief in happy endings, for someone who had built a business by crafting her clients' storybook dream weddings, even Cassandra would be forced to admit that she had let her client down in astonishing fashion this time around. As for her client, well, Cassandra herself had pulled that short straw. Surely, it must be a near impossibility for a wedding planner to be jilted at her own altar.

If not, then it should be.

Tears welled in Cassandra's eyes, and she blinked past the annoying translucent pearls of emotion. Sure, she wanted to cry, but she was fighting that urge with all her might. Because Jeremy didn't deserve her tears.

Clutching Bailey tighter as she swallowed hard against the emotion choking her, Cassandra muttered aloud, "Why did he dump me?"

That was the multimillion-dollar question. Though it should be simple enough, the answer eluded her. Cassandra's fiancé—ex-fiancé now—Jeremy Roth of the Westhampton Beach Roths still hadn't told her why he called off their wedding. Instead, he'd waited until their wedding day, until he was standing beside her at the altar, in front of one hundred of their nearest and dearest plus the Manhattan media to tell her that he couldn't marry her.

Jeremy—in his Dior suit and the white poplin bee shirt he'd insisted on wearing—*God, that shirt!* It had sparked an argument for the ages. Cassandra had presented the case that with his suit jacket open, the bee would look like a yellow stain in their wedding photos. Pictures of Prince Harry at one of his London appearances was all the proof she'd needed, though Jeremy wouldn't budge. He had insisted on that shirt, and Cassandra had given in, knowing full well that their wedding photos would be forever blemished with the yellow bee.

At least *that* minor disaster had been averted. No wedding meant no wedding photos.

Maybe he dumped me because of our fight over that shirt.

If so, that just might be the worst reason for someone to be dumped ever, in the history of the world. Seriously, though, had Jeremy dumped her because of a damned Dior bee shirt? A giggle bubbled up from her chest and turned into a full-on burst of laughter, inspiring Bailey to bay in response as he regarded her with his wide black eyes.

"I hear you, Bailey," Cassandra said, hugging him close.

Cassandra was officially losing it and she hadn't yet reached the one-mile marker.

It truly was laughable. As was the fact that here she was, hobbling along Dune Road in a wedding dress that cost more than many used cars. Meanwhile, she didn't have a penny on her. Her feet began to throb as she limped along. So much for her favorite heels—or heel, as the case may be. Her remaining stiletto snagged on the hem of her pristine white wedding gown, and she tripped. With her yelp, Bailey barked as she almost toppled to the ground. While clutching him tighter, Cassandra managed to lift the hem of her dress and steadied herself.

As she shifted Bailey to her other hip, she barely registered the sound of a car engine purring behind her until the blare of a horn sent her already-jarred nerves into overdrive, causing her heart to race. Then Bailey began to bark, bay, howl…all of it, all at once, as she cuddled him closer and turned to see the car that could save her…

Cassandra's heart skipped several beats as a Mercedes Roadster pulled up beside her. She knew it well because she'd seen it described on social media, of all places. Selenite Grey Metallic, with the soft top down; the driver had a serious scowl on his face as the wind whipped through his thick, dark hair. That man…

You must be kidding.

She glanced at the man again as he pulled to a stop on the road beside her. Her shaking hands and raw nerves told her that this was no joke.

It wasn't the sight of the car that rattled her, it was the sight of the man sitting behind the wheel of the car.

Andrew Steele.

The billionaire bad boy owner of The Steele Dailies, a hugely popular entertainment and celebrity news site. The tall, arrogant, and broodingly handsome Andrew Steele was as much of a celebrity as the stars splashed across his successful pop culture site. He was known for exposing scandals.

He was also her ex-boyfriend.

And, of all the people in the world, *he* was the one to find her. Of all the people who could have driven past, he was *the one*?

What had she done to deserve this karmic punishment?

As if reading her thoughts, Bailey let out a howl. He was preaching to the choir, as far as Cassandra was concerned.

Her first thought was to make a run for it through the knee-high beach grass bordering the road, and if not for Bailey's safety, she might have tried. Instead, she stiffened her shoulders and put on her haughtiest RBF, also known as (resting bitch face).

It was time for her to keep walking.

"Imagine finding you here." Andrew stepped out of his car and sauntered toward her in that cocky way of his. Tall and broad-shouldered with thick, wavy dark hair that no man had a right to possess and rich brown eyes with long black lashes that were almost criminal, he smiled that crooked grin that melted hearts the world over.

Though she'd seen him pop up in her social media feed almost every day over the years, coming face-to-face with him for the first time since their breakup years prior was a shock to her system, one that caused every nerve to ignite at the sight of him.

She shifted Bailey again, struggling to keep her voice controlled. "Andrew. To what do I owe the honor? No, let me guess. You're seeking snapshots of the jilted bride. Or, better yet, you'd like an enraged quote or two. Or do you just want to gloat at how far I've fallen?"

"None of the above, Cassie. Besides, if I'd wanted to gloat, I would have done it when you started dating that loser Roth." His smooth baritone was unusually sharp and biting. "You should know by now that rebound romances never end well. And he had a tough act to follow. You had been dating *me*, after all."

He winked at her. As if that would soften the blow to her already fractured ego.

She opened her mouth to argue, but given her current situation, Andrew had her there. Nevertheless, he had no right to lecture her, let alone call her Cassie. Jeremy had never called her by her nickname, but Andrew had from the start. She'd loved that about him, once upon a time.

The nickname Cassie had sounded so normal, so approachable. *Cassie* was a girl you could have a laugh with or share a future with. The name *Cassandra* sounded too formal and dramatic—like a soap opera diva. Which, in her case, wasn't far from the truth.

Cassandra's mother, Julia West, had been a soap star on the long-running soap *Meadow Lane*, until its cancellation. As the resident diva on set and off, Julia had named Cassandra after her daughter on the show. Yep. Cassandra was named after the same character who cheated on two of her husbands, set fire to her fictional sister's cabin, and faked her own death at least three times. In other words, Cassandra was named after a not-so-perfect role model.

Long before meeting Andrew, she had tried to go by Cassie in high school and had even succeeded for a while, but her mother had found out and nipped it in the bud. From then on, it had been Cassandra and only Cassandra until Andrew began calling her Cassie when they met in college and started dating.

At the time, Cassandra didn't understand her mother's attachment to her much-too-formal first name. But now, hindsight had brought clarity and she understood at last why her mother had insisted upon her using that unapproachable first name.

Julia West was and always would be a diva of the first order both on screen and off. She was also a control freak, while Cassandra had been the complete opposite of her mother. She'd lived most of her life attempting to appease the hard-to-please woman, and Julia had taught her daughter early on never to push her buttons.

Andrew, on the other hand, had no problem with defying the well-known actress. Cassandra had admired that about him. Way back when, before he broke up with her. Their breakup, his rejection after they graduated from NYU, was nothing in comparison to today's rejection from Jeremy.

Her bruised, battered, and broken heart now ached at the memory of Jeremy discarding her so publicly and at the thought of her mother, who had been too busy filming an independent movie with husband number four in Toronto to attend Cassandra's debacle of a wedding.

As it turned out, her mother's no-show was actually a good thing, because Cassandra wouldn't have been able to withstand her judgment. It was bad enough that she had to put up with Andrew's.

"Come on, Cassie. By now you must be calculating the time." Andrew tapped his watch with his forefinger, surveying her with dark, hooded eyes. His gaze traveled from her mop of blond hair sticking to her face to her once pristine dress, which was now undoubtedly wilting. Though Cassandra was certain she looked frightful, that was no reason to relent.

"No, I'm not calculating the time because I don't have a cell, or a watch. I don't have anything but Bailey, and he's all I need." She wasn't sure why she took that particular swipe at Andrew. Perhaps it was because he'd just reminded her of her poor choice in men, of which Andrew was the first of two too many.

Two failed relationships—Jeremy and Andrew. Each with their ups and downs. The first dumped her at the altar and the other one just mentioned her poor decisions on the side of a posh beach road.

Or perhaps it was because he used her nickname, which was far too personal, and they were anything but that now. "If you've gotten what you wanted from me, I must get going."

"You can't walk to Manhattan, Cassie. What's your plan?"

There it was again. *Cassie.* Was he trying to irritate her? If so, he was doing an excellent job. "Darned if I know. Right now, the only plan I have is to get away from 'the loser,' as you called him and get away from you. Where did you come from, anyway? Were you lurking in the bushes outside the windows of the Roth estate?"

"I didn't need to lurk, I was invited."

"Invited?" Cassandra swayed. She didn't invite Andrew. "Who invited *you*?"

His eyes roved from hers to Bailey. "What's the reason behind the dog in the tutu? It was supposed to be a wedding, not a circus."

"While it was supposed to be a wedding, it wound up being a circus." She laughed. Funny, but oh so true.

"You're doing it again—"

"Doing what?" she huffed, her impatience with him mounting.

"Deflecting with self-depreciating humor. It's what you used to do when things got tough." Andrew was always razor sharp in his ability to analyze her.

Darn him.

Cassandra focused on Andrew's question. "If you must know, Bailey is my bridesman and I couldn't have him walk me down the aisle showing his man part, now, could I? The tutu covers it." She rolled her eyes. She'd have thought that this would have been obvious.

Andrew threw back his head and laughed. It was a laugh she knew all too well. Deep, resonant, and robustly engaging. God, how she'd once missed it.

Do not go there, Cassandra. Just. Don't.

She focused on Andrew's chest, on his crossed arms tugging at his jacket just enough for the fabric to stretch over his broad shoulders as he leaned against the hood of his luxury auto. "Did you just say 'his man part'?"

"What if I did?" Cassandra stood with her shoulders straight, her posture proud.

He shook his head and grinned. "You're still the quirkiest woman I've ever known."

"And you're still the most annoying man I've ever known. No—I take that back. I find you more annoying now." She smiled at him as Bailey whimpered and flailed his paws. Cassandra cuddled him close. "It's okay, buddy. I know you want to explore but I don't have your leash and I don't want you running off and getting lost."

Her dog had been sniffing the salt air ever since they'd begun their hike. Since he was a hound, she knew where his nose could lead him—on a one-way trip. Hounds were notorious for following scents wherever they led, even if they got lost following a specific scent.

"Oh, for God's sake." Andrew yanked off his tie, then knotted the slip of fabric through Bailey's faux-diamond-studded collar. "Allow this poor dog some dignity."

Snatching Bailey from her arms, Andrew placed him on the pavement. Never did Cassandra ever expect her ex to walk her puppy, let alone while said puppy was sporting a Tiffany-blue tutu, but here they were, and Andrew was indeed walking the hound with his makeshift silk leash.

Bailey had never quite taken to Jeremy, which had been a source of tension in their relationship for the past year—ever since Cassandra had adopted the beagle as a puppy. Was *that* why Jeremy dumped her? If so, she would have gladly chosen Bailey over her former fiancé each and every time. Not only was the dog her ride or die, as it turned out, Bailey also had excellent taste, at least when it came to one ex.

Cassandra watched as Andrew stroked Bailey's head and spoke to him in a low, soothing tone then removed the tutu and tossed it onto his back seat. Bailey, in turn, meandered about, sniffing and scratching until he found the perfect place to pee, making Cassandra feel even guiltier. Okay, she shouldn't have left Bailey's leash behind, but she certainly didn't need Andrew accusing her of undermining Bailey's dignity.

Dignity. Andrew's poor choice of words wounded her.

"I'll have you know, Andrew, that the only person stripped of their dignity on this gorgeous day is me."

Andrew studied her through hooded eyes and Cassandra wondered again what he was doing here.

After limping toward the hood of his car, Cassandra leaned against it as she kicked off her remaining shoe. Her feet throbbed, and she ached for a shower followed by her comfortable bed, which was currently being hauled on a moving truck heading to a storage facility. She had planned to move in with Jeremy after the ceremony and had given notice not to renew her lease. The memory sent a searing pain through her temples.

God, the mess that was left behind.

"Are you okay?" Andrew's voice sounded distant. "Cassie?"

She refused to answer, choosing instead to examine her scuffed and broken white bow Aquazzura heels with an exaggerated sigh. They'd been her dream shoes. Shoes she'd associated with opulence ever since she'd seen them on a member of the British royal family. She'd finally given in, telling herself that it was her wedding day, after all. So, she splurged, and oh, how she'd loved them. They made her feel like a duchess. Heck, they made her feel like a princess. For a brief moment. Until her entire world had gone off the rails. Now they were battered, just like her spirit.

Tears threatened to spill again, and she squeezed her eyes shut against the onslaught in the hopes that they'd dry or that her swell of emotion would pass.

Not in front of Andrew.

I can't fall apart in front of Andrew.

"We have a complicated history, don't we?" he asked.

Cassandra's eyes flew open to find him standing beside her, with Bailey now sitting calmly at his feet. Her legs trembled at Andrew's nearness. *Close. Much too close.* She straightened and reclaimed her righteous anger in the hopes that he'd fail to notice her shaky voice. "To say our history is 'complicated' would be putting it mildly."

"I'm sorry." Two words, dripping with emotion.

"Don't. You don't get to pity me. I won't give you the satisfaction." She met his eyes, those rich brown eyes that looked amber in the sunlight.

His expression may have softened, but she refused to. Her anger, her desire to fight someone, anyone, were the only things that would get her through today's indignities. Since Andrew was the only one to stop, Cassandra had her target.

"What would Andrew Steele write of this situation? Oh, I know. 'Celebrity wedding planner Cassandra Benedict sells happily ever afters for a living. But this disgraced socialite was discovered in tattered heels stranded on the side of a road after her fiancé jilted her at the altar in a swanky oceanfront Hamptons mansion. Worse? The whole humiliating experience was witnessed by the crème de la crème of New York's elite and her ex-boyfriend, who owns this very online rag.' Oh, Andrew, how you must be dying to publish this."

Tears rolled down her cheeks. "And I'm crying, too. Quick, get your cell and snap a picture. Or even better, film it for social media. No doubt it will go viral."

Why didn't she think before running out of Jeremy's family home without any of her things? If she hadn't left her cell behind, she'd be in an Uber heading home instead of being stuck here with Andrew, of all people.

"Hey, you didn't deserve this." There it was…more of his unwanted pity. Cassie wiped her eyes, refusing to fall apart in front of him.

Andrew had been her first real boyfriend. They met at NYU and quickly became friends first, then they dated. They'd each come from different economic backgrounds: she was rich, and he was anything but.

She'd always admired the fact that Andrew grew up on what was considered the wrong side of the tracks in the opulent Hamptons. He was motivated to succeed and determined to escape his situation. So determined that he majored in both business and journalism. They dated until graduation, when he fully transformed into the bad boy gossip publisher who always seemed to have something to prove and a perpetual chip on his shoulder. Looking back, Cassandra was certain that Andrew had crafted that view of himself to make himself look more appealing to the public.

Who doesn't love a bad boy, let alone a bad boy billionaire, or so he was rumored to be?

As their relationship progressed, the only thing he wanted more than publicly humiliating the rich and the nepo babies was to become richer and more powerful than them. Andrew eventually dumped her, though not in the same public fashion as her ex-fiancé. Their breakup came after graduation, right before she met Jeremy. Since then, Andrew had written a few articles about Cassandra, whom he dubbed *the celebrity wedding planner* after she was hired by a popular actress. Much to Cassandra's surprise, Andrew's articles about her had been positive, which, considering their history, she'd taken as wins. It'd been a long time since he'd written about her.

What *was* he doing here?

Andrew had admitted to receiving an invitation, Cassandra recalled as spindles of dread inched up her spine. Who invited the premier gossip teller to her wedding?

"Why are you here, Andrew?" She searched the depths of his dark eyes, hoping for an answer. "Who invited you? Or did you get an inside tip?"

With a curt shake of his head, Andrew frowned. "I got an invitation. I thought it was from you."

"An invitation? To *my* wedding?" Cassandra sucked in her breath, swallowing hard. "I handled the invites, and I can assure you that I didn't invite you. Oh no! You did get a tip."

The realization hit her hard, like a punch in the gut, winding her. Andrew had witnessed her utter humiliation because of some tip. Cassandra's mind worked furiously, trying to process what she'd so desperately been hoping to avoid. "Who would tip you off and why? Were they trying to humiliate me?"

A wave of disgust washed over Cassandra as her mind rattled off the possibilities in rapid succession. "When this gets out, and news of this will get out if you haven't already sent the story to publication, the only thing that will dominate the celebrity gossip sites will be that I, the wedding planner to the rich and famous, can't even plan her own wedding. My business will be ruined. My brand will be destroyed."

Though she was no fairy-tale princess, Cassandra believed in happily ever afters. She also loved love. That's what led Cassandra to start her own business. Named A Perfect Wedding, it was her very own wedding planning and coordinating venture. Afterward came her lifestyle site and vlog befitting romantics just like her. It was called A Perfect Happiness because she believed that everyone had a different definition of *perfect*, and because everyone deserved some form of happiness.

Reality hit Cassandra hard. "How can anyone expect me to run a business called A Perfect Wedding when I crafted a perfect wedding disaster for myself? I'll be a laughingstock."

"It doesn't have to be that way," Andrew countered as Bailey tugged on his makeshift leash.

"Here, let me walk him." She reached for the tie, but Andrew backed away with her dog.

"No, you're barefoot and you could twist your ankle or hurt your foot or something."

Did she just hear concern coming from Andrew's mouth?

"I'll be right back. Don't go anywhere." He turned his back on her.

Cassandra crossed her arms over her chest. "Where would I go? You have my dog and I'm not leaving him behind."

"Shush, I'm thinking." With Andrew deep in thought, Bailey began trotting down the side of the road again, clearly ready to mark more territory. Together, he and Andrew proceeded forward while the hound sniffed the ground incessantly.

Like clockwork, each and every time Bailey veered off or became distracted, Andrew would whistle until the dog raised his leg and marked the ground. As ridiculous as it looked, for Bailey it was normal.

Was this Cassandra's new normal? She shuddered at the thought as Andrew's last statement echoed in her ears.

"What did you mean when you said, 'It doesn't have to be that way'?" She knew this man, and his ability to tell a story was second to none.

In a world of celebrities, where reality TV stars and social media influencers were a dime a dozen and real-life drama intersected with art, Andrew was a king- and queen-maker or -breaker, depending on his mood.

Andrew had become successful in part because he didn't care what people thought. Smart and determined to make it without anyone's help, he'd succeeded in record time. Gone was "the nerd from working-class roots," as Andrew had once categorized himself. No, he'd transformed into a powerful man—mentally, physically, and financially. And with power often came popularity. Andrew was living proof of it. Those were the ripple effects of a successful man with a successful career.

It's what eventually broke them up.

Andrew's power and influence came from the one thing Cassie detested more than anything else—the gossip site he created, and the paparazzi that he employed.

His was the one profession she couldn't stomach, not since paparazzi had crashed her father's funeral and had secretly taken photos of her crying beside his casket before publishing them for all the world to see. Of course, Andrew hadn't published those photos. He didn't have a business back then, but she still couldn't stomach his profession or fathom why that's what this brilliant man insisted on doing with his life.

Enough reminiscing!

"Do you have a plan, Andrew? What am I asking? Of course you have a plan. You never say anything unless you've thought it through."

Normally, Cassandra would never consider anything Andrew had to say; however, in her current predicament, what choice did she have?

"Time's ticking, Andrew. Talk. Now. *If* you have a plan, that is." When issued as a challenge, how could Andrew possibly resist?

He flashed her that crooked grin again.

"Oh, Cassie…" Andrew paused for dramatic effect. "I don't think you're ready for my plan."

She shoved her hair away from her face, and Andrew grasped her left hand. "What's the deal with your lack of an engagement ring? Did you give it back already?"

"No, I didn't have time. I ran out of there too quickly. Besides, Jeremy took it yesterday. He said that he wanted to place it on my finger with my wedding band after we exchanged our vows." Cassandra pulled away from him and glanced at her hand, which had worn the cushion-cut one-carat diamond in white gold for the past year.

Her hand looked empty. It felt empty. Moaning, she shook her hand as if that one action would help her forget today's events. "Just tell me if you have a plan. Please."

Right now, she'd agree to just about anything.

"Get in. We've got to get out of here before someone sees us and ruins everything. I'm surprised no one's driven past yet."

Andrew was well within his wheelhouse, plotting who knows what. Meanwhile Cassandra was deeply entrenched in her worst nightmare. With no plan in sight, she was left to rely on Andrew's ability to craft a narrative for her. Was that what he was plotting?

Suddenly, she needed Bailey more than ever. "Give me my dog."

"Fine." Andrew picked up Bailey and gently placed him in Cassandra's arms. Once she was situated in his passenger seat, he then shoved the wilting fabric of her wedding gown into the car haphazardly before closing her passenger door and jogging to the driver's side, then sliding behind the wheel.

Cassandra petted her tricolored beagle's head in an attempt to calm her erratic heartbeat. Whatever scheme Andrew had come up with, she hoped it would work. Her business was dependent upon him. But not her heart.

Never her heart. Never again.

All she needed was her dog, and her career. And a place to live. And her things from storage. The list kept growing…to the point that it seemed insurmountable.

Concentrate on what you can control.

Cassandra inhaled a deep, calming breath, then exhaled. In through her nose, out through her mouth. She repeated the process until her erratic heartbeat began to slow.

First things first. It was time to save herself and salvage the small remnant of pride that remained. She must put herself first, put her business first. Now and always, and if anyone could teach her how to do just that, it was Andrew.

He was an expert at putting himself first.

There was a lot Cassandra could learn from him, and she was ready and willing to do just that—learn from him. Especially if he could help salvage her reputation and her business.

Help me, Andrew Steele. You're my only hope.

Chapter 2

"THIS WILL DO." ANDREW PARKED IN A DESERTED OCEAN PARKING lot several miles away from where they once stood. One of the joys of a springtime Westhampton Beach meant no crowds—at least not the size of those that plagued the Hamptons after Memorial Day.

He handed his cell to Cassie after unlocking the home screen with his fingerprint. "Call whoever you need to and get your things. I assume you packed an overnight bag with your phone, at least."

"Of course. And Bailey's things." She reached for the phone, then paused in the process of dialing. "But don't think I'm agreeing to anything, because I'm not. Not yet. You've got to convince me."

"Right. Because you're in a position to negotiate." He arched his brow in challenge.

Cassie met his eyes with her own determined gaze. "I have nothing left to lose. That's what makes me powerful. Ever heard of the phrase 'what doesn't kill me better run'?"

She suspected he had. After all, the phrase was coined by none other than a popular reality television star. She, too, had been wronged by her man, and Cassandra was channeling some of her strength.

"Do I really need to answer that?" Andrew's drawl was pronounced, conveying that he was bored with such insulting questions.

If Cassandra knew one thing about him, it was that Andrew lived and breathed pop culture, celebrity, and the elites. He perpetually wanted to outdo everyone and out-scoop his competition. That hadn't changed since they'd broken up. It was obvious in his tone.

With an exaggerated sigh, she made her call. To her best friend.

"Cassandra! Where are you? Are you all right?" Cassandra fought back more tears at the sound of her best friend's frantic voice. "I can kill him for you. Or at the very least I can hurt him. Badly. Just give me my orders."

"Lauren, it's kind of you to offer but I need you to bring my stuff to me. Can you find my carry-on, and my cell—it's in my clutch. Bailey's carry-on has his leash, food, toys, you name it, it's in there. And my laptop bag."

"I've already got everything. Just tell me where you are. I'm finally on the road. It took forever because none of the valets were ready for the wedding to be over so soon—" Her friend moaned. "Sorry. That was insensitive. What kind of bridesmaid am I?"

"Nope. It's fine. It's true." Even Cassandra couldn't deny that she wasn't the only person inconvenienced by Jeremy today. But she couldn't think of them right now.

Just herself.

Only after giving Lauren detailed instructions did Cassandra hang up. She then turned to her ex-boyfriend. "You've got five minutes before Lauren arrives, and before I need to figure out my next move. So, what's your idea?"

"Walk with me." Ever the gentleman on this day, he opened her door and escorted her and Bailey to the beach several feet away from where he'd parked.

The warm sand was coarse beneath her bare feet and between her toes. Bailey tugged at his makeshift leash, which was still knotted around his collar, then began sprinting toward the waves.

Cassandra gripped Andrew's tie tightly. She remembered buying Andrew his first designer tie when they were dating. Now here he was, discarding an expensive tie by tying it around her dog's collar and using it as a leash. All the while Andrew wore a designer suit and plotted a PR coup, or so she hoped.

But therein was the problem: if Andrew did come up with some scheme, and Cassandra agreed to it, she'd be putting her trust in someone she no longer trusted. She didn't know what would be worse: being forced to trust him again or having no plan at all.

Bailey's nose led them to the waves crashing against the shore. Cassandra wouldn't let her dog off his makeshift leash, lest he run away. "Andrew, do you have a way out of this for me or not?"

"Oh, I do." He smiled at her. "The way I see it, you have two choices: allow the fact that Roth dumped you to define your life or take control of the narrative and craft a more powerful one of your own. I can make the public forget what happened today. Hell, I can make them believe a whole different chain of events actually happened, while promoting you and your business in a positive light. You just need to trust me."

Cassandra tilted her head to the side, her eyes wide. "Trust you? Really? That's *all* I need to do? You make it sound so simple."

"I deserve that. We didn't end on the best of terms, did we?"

"No, we didn't." He'd dumped her and never looked back, which led her straight into Jeremy's arms. "But unlike my fiancé, you didn't humiliate me in public. So, there's that."

"True. I should get extra credit for that." Andrew's rich baritone was teasing yet decadent. How he had changed. In the years since their breakup, he'd evolved into this sophisticated man standing effortlessly in a designer suit.

When she first met him, Andrew didn't know what designer was. She'd liked him that way. No, she loved him just the way he was. This him—this new Andrew—was one she didn't know. She had to remind herself of that.

"Do you really think you can make people believe that I dumped Jeremy?"

He arched a dark brow. "You doubt me? Come on, Cassie. I can make them believe anything. Besides, you escaped from a guy with a mustard stain on his shirt today. If you ask me, you dodged a bullet."

Cassandra couldn't hold back her laughter. "Mustard stain—it was a Dior bee, but thank you! I knew it would look messy in the wedding photos."

"A Dior bee?" Andrew narrowed his eyes, contemplating that statement. "Okay, that makes sense, but it definitely didn't translate at the altar."

"I told him it wouldn't." Cassandra smiled, happy that at least she'd been right about something today.

Andrew studied her, his brown eyes darkening with intensity. "What you need is a fake relationship…with me. And before you argue against it, hear me out. You need a very public relationship that will look legit. It's *because* we have a history, you and I, that no one will question us getting back together."

"I want to believe you. I do. But I was left at the altar. In front of witnesses. Nothing will change that."

"*I'll* change it. The moment you agree to be my fake girlfriend. And move in with me. That'll protect you from the vultures."

Cassandra squinted in the bright sunlight. "You mean the press? Like you?"

"No on both counts. I'm not the press, and those vultures to whom I refer are far worse than me. Unlike them, I check and double-check that what I'm publishing are facts." Andrew raked his hand through his hair. "This will be my one exception, because Roth hurt you, and because I never liked him to begin with. I'm going to convince the world that you never needed Roth. In fact, I'll convince them that you didn't even want him. I'll make the public believe that *you* ditched him."

"They'll never buy that. Like I said, there's a room full of witnesses who saw what happened." If only it were as simple as Andrew was making it out to be.

Looking off into the horizon, Andrew's eyes narrowed, his brow furrowing as if he was deep in thought. "I couldn't hear what was said…or by whom."

"But the sheer shock on my face was a sure sign that I wasn't doing the dumping…"

"No," his gaze met hers, holding Cassandra in place with his sheer force of will. "That's where you're wrong. I couldn't see your expression. You were whispering and so was he…until you ran back down the aisle. I watched you. There were no tears."

He recited his recollection of the events in a quick staccato, one that was completely devoid of emotion. "No one in that room knew who dumped who. If Roth said anything after I left, I can spin it to make it seem like he was trying to save his wounded pride. Oh! This is good. This is a narrative I can craft. If Roth fights against it, I can paint him as a jilted groom who has no problem lying to save his fragile ego. I'd love selling that."

"I'm sure you would." Sticking it to Jeremy would no doubt be fun for Andrew, since Jeremy was born with a silver spoon in his mouth—just the type of person Andrew used to despise.

A wide smile swept across Andrew's tanned features. He always spent time outdoors, and at the beach. That hadn't changed from the looks of his sun-kissed features.

"By taking you with me to all the society functions you used to hate—starting tomorrow—we will sell our shiny new relationship. Between that, and you moving in with me…"

"I can't move in with you. I won't." She was quick to argue against his proposal, but really, Cassandra had nowhere to go.

It could be a temporary fix…

"For this to work, you'll need to move in with me. I'm in a secure building with doormen, most of whom are built like linebackers. It's safe there, and no paparazzi will get in on their watch. Besides, a lot of what I do is done from my penthouse in Brooklyn Heights. I'll need you to be there, unless you're giving me carte blanche to write whatever—"

"No. I'm not giving you complete authority to do anything. Let's get that straight right now." Cassandra didn't trust him enough to warrant her relinquishing that level of control.

Besides, the apartment that was akin to her freedom wasn't hers anymore. She'd let her lease expire. And she wasn't about to give up her freedom without a fight—at least not permanently—but temporarily… well, temporarily, she had no choice. Did she?

Cassandra's mind began sorting the pros and cons in rapid succession.

Pro: She'd have a place to stay.

Con: It would be with Andrew.

Pro: She'd be protected from the outside world and the paparazzi.

Con: That protection meant that she'd be beholden to Andrew.

"How big is your apartment? And how many bedrooms do you have?" She could feel herself giving in to the safety that Andrew's proposition would offer her.

He smiled again, a dazzling smile that she was certain disarmed many an eligible female. "My penthouse is large enough. Trust me. There are four bedrooms, and two are primaries with private baths. One of those en suites is mine. Another bedroom is my office. Which leaves an entire en suite and an additional bedroom for you. There are three and a half baths in total. And did I mention that I own a penthouse with both western and southern exposures of the sweeping Manhattan skyline and New York Harbor views?"

"Are you actually giving me the Realtor pitch? Are you trying to impress me?" It sure sounded like it.

"That depends. Is it working?" Andrew glanced at his feet, as if suddenly shy or self-conscious. That was the Andrew she remembered…

Cassandra's heart swelled as she studied the man she once loved. There were a few more lines around his eyes and etched in his forehead as he squinted in the bright sunlight, but his brown eyes were familiar, as was his voice. Was it possible that pieces of the old Andrew—of the Andrew she'd once loved—lay dormant beneath his sophisticated charm and self-assurance? If so, was that boyish man she once knew seeking her approval?

"The size of your penthouse doesn't impress me…" She let that sink in. Cassandra was never impressed by money or influence. "You never needed wealth to impress me, Andrew."

Why did she just admit something so personal to him? To make Andrew feel better? He had enough confidence to fill a football stadium, didn't he?

His eyes met hers, holding hers in their mesmerizing gaze. "Spoken like someone who grew up wealthy. Funny, isn't it? To those who fought for every dollar they earned, wealth becomes the only way to impress people."

"You've grown even more cynical." The warm breeze blew several strands of her curls into her eyes, and Andrew reached for them, tucking them behind her ears, as one of his palms rested against Cassandra's cheek.

He remained stock-still for a few seconds, and she held her breath as waves of static electricity coursed through her veins. This man was magnetic, pulling her toward him with an invisible current. Strong and steady, it beckoned her to him until she leaned forward…

Before she could stop herself, she leaned into him. The motion was slight, but Cassandra wondered if Andrew noticed. Did he feel it, too?

His gaze held hers, the corners of his lips upturned into a wry grin. "Did I mention my view? It's quite the sight at night, if I do say so myself."

Andrew was teasing her. Deliberately and unashamedly.

He was mocking her.

That realization was all it took for Cassandra to break free from his heady gaze. "Your wealth isn't attractive to me." That was the truth. She preferred the real Andrew, the down-to-earth Andrew. The way he used to be. Not this version of him.

Never this version of him.

"There's nothing wrong with financial security. I've learned that the hard way. Besides, with my wealth comes my influence and that is what you really need right now." One statement spoken with such nonchalance that she was certain Andrew himself believed it to be true.

"It's sad that you think that your wealth defines you." Cassandra searched for her true north—Bailey. He was hopping back and forth from the waves, his paws wet and sandy, looking just as disheveled as she probably did.

"What makes you think anyone will believe you?" Cassandra's heartbeat quickened at the mere question. Surely, she wasn't still considering Andrew's proposal after he had just mocked her, teased her?

"Regardless of what little you think of me and my profession, people do believe me and believe what I reveal. That's what happens when you deliver the truth more often than not." At Cassandra's scoff, Andrew stiffened his shoulders, and his voice took on a steely edge. "I know scandal, Cassie. I expose it. And I'll be with you, on your side of this non-wedding fiasco. My readers will buy it if we make it look convincing."

Was it even possible for Andrew to pull it off?

Oh, how she wanted to believe him. Cassandra could only imagine the damage that her business would incur if news got out that she, the poster child for fairy-tale weddings and romantic lifestyle content, had been left at the altar. Her monetization would suffer, too, as would her endorsement deals. They were contingent upon her success as a brand, contingent on her personal life being the visual expression and representation of her brand. It was in everything she did, every wedding she crafted, every event she attended, her website, her blog, her vlog, her social media feeds…

And regardless of what Andrew thought of Cassandra's privileged background, she'd built her business all by herself. With a small business loan and a whole lot of blood, sweat, and tears. Sure, she could have used her inheritance from her dad, but she had decided against that. She'd chosen instead to hold on to her inheritance and invest it, put it aside for her future. Because Cassandra had wanted to succeed on her own, and to make her dad proud.

Everything she'd built, all she'd worked for, was now under threat because of Jeremy.

"There's no way this will work," she muttered aloud as Bailey barked, then bayed at a seagull passing overhead. At least he wasn't chasing the seagull.

Cassandra whistled and drew Bailey's attention. He trotted over to her and looked up at her with those large puppy dog eyes.

"I could lose everything." She bent down and petted him before smoothing one of his floppy ears that had folded backward.

"What will you lose if you do nothing?" Andrew stood over her, casting her in shadow.

"Everything. I understand what's at stake, Andrew. It's my life." She narrowed her eyes, studying him intently. "Why are you selling this so strongly? Clearly, you don't care what happens to me."

"This is for both of our benefits." Andrew was nothing if not convincing.

"How does helping me benefit you? You're successful and rich, right?" She met his eyes again, but his expression turned standoffish. Though she sensed he wouldn't give her anything, she still asked, "What's in this for you?"

"Let's just say I have my reasons and leave it at that."

His answer was lacking, to say the least. Here she'd laid everything bare, and Andrew was keeping things from her. Cassandra didn't like it one bit, but did she have time to further interrogate him?

No. Time was running out.

"What exactly would be expected of me, if I were to agree to your outrageous proposal?" She stood, meeting him face-to-face.

"We would appear to date, and we would appear to be in love. The more convincing we are, the more successful we'll be. You won't be the jilted wedding planner bride and my business will probably get a bump from positive exposure."

His business would probably get a bump. "I thought your business was booming. Doesn't scandal sell?" Cassandra didn't know why she was testing him, but she needed to hear more.

Shrugging, Andrew exhaled deeply. "Let's just say that looks can be deceiving. Remember when I said that you can craft your own narrative? I'm proof."

The strong breeze whipped Cassandra's hair into her face. "If you wanted to help your business, why not use this encounter of ours to write a story about me, or ten? You could have helped your business without the bother of a phony relationship."

"That would be a short-term solution. Besides, I'm nothing if not loyal."

"Loyal?" Cassandra suppressed a laugh. Was he serious?

Andrew pushed a lock of her hair away from her eyes, his fingers brushing against her cheek ever so gently. It caused her skin to tingle beneath his warm touch. This was becoming a thing between them, and she wondered if he recognized the intimacy this one motion insinuated.

"You may not be my girlfriend anymore, but you were once. Roth had no right to treat you the way he did." His fingers twitched. Though it was a slight motion, she felt it nonetheless.

"I'm still everything you couldn't stand when you dumped me and more. A lot more now." She stepped out of his reach as another wave lapped against the shore, washing away her footprints in the sand.

He shoved his hands in his pants pockets. "Then your moving in with me will be fun for both of us." His statement dripped with sarcasm.

"I haven't agreed to move in with you." Though she argued against it, Cassandra had long lost her battle of wills with Andrew, and she knew it.

Andrew clucked his tongue. "No, but you will. Because that's the key to our successful narrative. No one would think that you'd give up your freedom and live with a guy you weren't really committed to. You didn't even live with Roth, and he was the man you were about to marry."

His honesty caused Cassandra to wince. He sure seemed to know a lot about her. "Andrew, have you been keeping tabs on me?"

Though his face was tanned by the sun, Cassandra could swear that Andrew was blushing. She studied him hard, the pink tinge growing more noticeable. Until—

She was yanked backward by Bailey, who lunged at a seagull, barking and baying with all his might.

"Woah!" Cassandra struggled to remain upright and keep up with her canine bestie, who refused to listen to her pleas for him to "Bailey, stop!"

Bailey glanced at her with his wide black eyes and ceased barking, though only for a moment. He was nothing if not persistent. And he was stubborn. His repeated barks proved that and then some.

Another seagull swooped into the fray, joining the first gull, causing Bailey's barks to grow louder. He pulled against the tie-leash, stretching it to the breaking point, while Cassandra held on so tight that her hands hurt.

Bailey jerked forward, tripping Cassandra. As she groaned, she hit the wet sand hard while the tie slid from her tight grasp just as Bailey broke into a run. "Bailey!"

Andrew ran after the dog and scooped him up as a current flowed between his paws. He held the squirming beagle, speaking to the dog in low tones. Cassandra couldn't make out what Andrew was saying, but somehow, as if magically, he made Bailey calm down.

With a great deal of effort, Cassandra managed to sit up despite her tangled gown with its heavy, wet fabric. As she struggled to stand, the sand beneath kept shifting.

Andrew jogged over to her and gave her a hand up.

"Thank you," she said breathlessly, as she shook out the damp skirt of her dress. Sand was sticking to her everywhere. Even in places she never thought possible. "I must look like a hot mess."

He regarded her with a hooded look in his eyes. "You could never look like a mess. Not even if you tried." His voice was a deep, raspy whisper.

She stared into those dark, fathomless eyes, wondering what was hidden in their depths. Then the squawking gulls made Bailey growl, and the moment was gone.

"Calm down, Bailey," Andrew commanded the dog, who stopped growling at the seagulls in an instant.

He handed her the drenched dog with sand matted in his recently groomed fur. "So, this is your best man?"

With a grin, Cassandra nodded. "Bailey was my bridesman."

"You were destined for that wedding to go sideways." Andrew brushed sand from his now wet pant legs. "You realize that, don't you?"

"Were you keeping tabs on me?" She wouldn't let her previous question go. Why would Andrew know so much about her, her wedding, and her relationship with Jeremy?

"Did you keep up with me?" he countered.

"Who doesn't? You're the man to watch when it comes to celebrity news and pop culture binges." She imitated the announcer's voice on his YouTube channel. "Besides, everything you say becomes a headline and goes viral. It's hard to ignore you."

"I see. So, you're just following the latest trends?" He always did challenge her.

She smiled. "I'm in the business of catering to the needs and whims of many celebrities. I've got to keep up, right?"

"Yeah, right," he said, his voice sounding noncommittal.

"Okay, enough with the Mr. Mystery act. You still haven't answered my question. Have you been keeping tabs on me?"

"Let's just say that given your line of work, it's only natural that I would follow your life, so to speak."

Cassandra rolled her eyes. She seemed to be doing that a lot around Andrew. "Okay, fine. I get it. You like being a man of mystery. That's your specialty now."

It stung that he was being evasive.

"You're beautiful—" His eyes widened in terror. As if he'd admitted something he shouldn't have. He looked away from her before adding, "For someone going with the disheveled jilted bride look." His baritone was smooth, in direct contrast to his callous words.

She cringed, and so did he.

Rightly so.

"Wow. That's charming of you." She'd take his ensuing silence as an admission of guilt, or at the very least, a modicum of shame, as she contemplated his arrangement.

Would she really move in with Andrew?

The man got on her nerves like no other, and that was on a good day when she only saw his social media posts and stories. Now, while talking to him, it had become obvious that he lacked a filter and was downright insensitive.

"I'm sorry. When I'm with you, I seem to say all the wrong things." Gone was his ego, and his overconfidence. Instead, his eyes emanated a softness that she'd never before seen. "I don't quite know what to say around you, if that makes sense. And I get tongue-tied around you. A lot, it seems."

"Why do you think that is?" She petted Bailey in an attempt to calm her nerves, which were humming from Andrew's nearness to her.

"I have no idea. I just do." He offered her a grin. "So, what's it going to be? If you want to partner up, we'd better get started now, before it's too late."

Based upon what she gleaned from his online presence, Andrew could be shrewd, competitive, and downright calculating. He thrived in a setting that she abhorred, and his chosen lifestyle was that of exposing the rich and famous.

Regardless of her Westhampton Beach wedding, Cassandra had stepped away from that society lifestyle a long time ago. Then there was the fact that Andrew employed his own paparazzi—the very people who had used Cassandra for monetary gain during one of the most difficult moments of her life.

"Do I really want to partner up with someone who would hatch a 'mutually beneficial fake relationship' on the side of the road, only to insult me when I am clearly down?" Her use of air quotes wasn't lost on Andrew.

"Yes, I did. Though, technically, we're no longer on the side of the road. Call it a change of venue." It was his turn to roll his eyes, as the lines etched in his forehead deepened. "Have you made your decision?"

"Let's see… Do I light the small remnant of my pride ablaze and accept your help or keep walking?" She shrugged. "I don't like being kicked when I'm down."

"I don't like the way you disarm me, if I'm being honest. That's difficult for me to admit. Look, I'm sure Lauren would give you a ride. But I hope you take me up on my offer. We could be a formidable team." Andrew winked at her. She didn't remember Andrew ever doing such a thing when they were dating.

Andrew was winking up a storm as part of his charm offensive.

Maybe he didn't even realize he was doing it. Or maybe he did it so frequently now that he didn't even think about it. That was probably it. Cassandra wasn't special, he probably just winked at women now.

"Where's all of your stuff by the way? At Jeremy's place?" Andrew threaded his fingers through his thick, wavy hair.

Only after swallowing hard did Cassandra finally make her admission. "No. I hadn't moved in yet. Not until after the honeymoon. All my stuff is still in a moving truck heading to a storage facility. I packed what I needed for the honeymoon and planned to move my things in slowly once we returned."

"Your fiancé wanted you to live out of a storage unit?" Andrew's face contorted, his disbelief evident.

He was right.

That *was* strange.

Looking back on it now, that decision was beyond odd. Did she suspect on a subconscious level that the relationship wouldn't last? Perhaps, in the deepest crevices of her mind, she'd had a sliver of a doubt?

Though the silence between them was strong, the breeze was warm, and the seagulls' squawks were enough to entertain Bailey, who barked, bayed, and hopped.

"Does your dog always bellow like that?"

Cassandra grinned. "He bays. It's a beagle thing. Does it annoy you?"

"Nope." Andrew stiffened, and just like that, Cassandra knew how to annoy him—with her dog's relentless "bellow," as Andrew called it.

"Just wait until he's in your apartment. His bark resonates through the interiors of buildings."

Andrew narrowed his eyes. "Really? You don't say."

A horn, the second of today, caught Cassandra's attention and Bailey howled as Lauren parked her car next to Andrew's. "You remember my friend Lauren Quinn, right?"

"I wondered if she was the same Lauren." Andrew kept pace with Cassandra as she met her friend halfway.

Cassandra hugged Lauren while the latter issued an expletive-laced diatribe to voice just what she thought of Jeremy. It was a very colorful commentary, and quite creative.

"Him?" Lauren stopped midsentence when she saw Andrew for the first time. "What is he doing here?"

"We hatched a plan." Cassandra smiled at her friend. "It was Andrew's idea."

"Oh, that won't bode well. Trust me." Lauren turned to Andrew.

Andrew frowned. "Say what you must, but I made a compelling argument."

"And it's mutually beneficial," Cassandra assured her friend, as Andrew took her carry-on out of Lauren's trunk.

"Cassandra, think for a moment." Lauren placed her hands on her friend's shoulders. "This is Andrew Steele we're talking about. The same Andrew Steele who dumped you. Since when does he ever do anything for anyone else's benefit but his own?"

Though her friend had a point, Cassandra didn't need someone *good* right now, she needed someone strong. Someone with the clout to defuse the damage Jeremy had caused.

And that someone was Andrew.

"I know what I'm doing, Lauren. I promise." Cassandra managed to smile.

Lauren shot Andrew a skeptical look as he stowed Cassandra's suitcase in his trunk. In turn, he flashed Lauren his charming, crooked grin, as he took Bailey from Cassandra's arms and gently deposited him in the dog carrier in the back seat. Right beside his bridesman tutu. "Oh! Did Jeremy say anything after she ran out of there?"

"No. He just stormed off without a word." Lauren shook her head.

"I knew it!" Andrew made eye contact with Cassandra, wearing a rather smug smirk. "See? What did I tell you? It'll work. I'm never wrong."

While he might never be wrong, Cassandra was certain that Andrew was never humble, either. At least not anymore.

"Are you sure about this?" Lauren asked her friend.

"I'm sure. I've considered it long and hard." It was the only way. Cassandra had resigned herself to that fact.

"You can always stay at my place. You have the keys." Lauren moaned. "I wish I wasn't traveling. Do you want me to postpone?"

"No. Go and make some deals in the Golden State like you planned. There's no reason both of our lives should be upended by what Jeremy did today." On this Cassandra was adamant.

"I love you. Remember that. Know that you can stay at my place at any time, and call me or text me later with more info." Lauren wrapped Cassandra in a tight hug.

In turn, Cassandra held on to Lauren a little longer than usual. "I will. I love you, too."

"Don't get caught up in him. Andrew is still the same guy he always was. A leopard can't change its spots."

"True, but they do know how to hunt their prey and protect

themselves from predators. I think I could use a little bit of that right now." Cassandra spoke the truth on that front.

Lauren squeezed her friend's arm. "Just make sure you aren't the prey, okay?"

With a firm nod, Cassandra plopped into the passenger seat, then grabbed the hem of her gown and shoved it in the car. Lauren stepped back as Andrew closed the passenger door and proceeded to the driver's side. Once he placed his car in drive and pulled out of the parking lot, Cassandra waved to her friend, hoping to calm Lauren as much as herself.

This is going to work. It must.

The objective of this arrangement was to salvage Cassandra's life, her wounded pride, and her business. Nothing would detract her from her goals: protect her company, and her brand. If Jeremy ended up regretting dumping her, well, that would be the icing on the proverbial wedding cake.

And if Andrew were to also regret his own decision to dump her all those years ago, well, all the better. Cassandra could use all the wins she could tally right about now.

Chapter 3

ANDREW STEELE HAD GROWN UP WITNESSING FIRSTHAND THE disparity between the haves and have-nots. As a child living in the Hamptons, and as the third-generation son of a hardworking restaurant/bar owner, he'd witnessed many rich jerks act like their money was more important than character or hard work.

His dad had character in abundance and worked harder than anyone Andrew had ever met, but Stephen Steele hadn't garnered much respect while Andrew was growing up. Neither had Andrew back then.

For years, he watched his father hustle to keep their family business alive, while those with an abundance of wealth skipped out on tips or shortchanged his dad over their meals to where his dad had to cover the difference. It seemed effortless for some of them to screw over others in search of the almighty dollar.

Andrew had observed from the sidelines, all but invisible to those with any real power and influence. It fueled his anger, but it also taught him many valuable lessons about life. In a strange way, he learned most of what he knew from them.

As a child, Andrew was known as *the kid with the mom who died*. He was also the shy kid, and the nerd. Being a nerd, he soaked up all the knowledge he could. From books, from people—he absorbed everything like a sponge and used it to his advantage.

Coming from nothing, Andrew tried harder to succeed than anyone else he knew. He worked relentlessly, strove higher, and possessed an insatiable thirst for knowledge. As he got older, Andrew had the good sense to realize that his compulsion for knowledge might come in handy one day. So, he waited and watched with one goal in mind: to save his father from debt and create a future for himself. A future where he'd never have to worry about money again.

And Andrew had done just that.

To Andrew, knowledge equated to power and success, but perhaps his greatest driving force was never forgetting that feeling of being invisible.

He had been invisible for years while his dad scrimped and saved, and Andrew hustled to earn a buck by starting his own lawn mowing company at the age of eleven. Andrew had brought in a modest income to help his dad and studied hard to earn scholarships. When he was old enough, he worked as a busboy in his dad's restaurant, then as a waiter. He even did odd jobs for his dad; in other words, Andrew had done everything he could to help.

Andrew and his father were a team and Andrew convinced himself that they were invincible. He'd needed no one other than his dad and grew up a loner without many friends. That choice was really a no -brainer. What other kid would choose to be friends with him over those popular rich kids he grew up with?

Dressed in thrift store jeans and Walmart T-shirts, he was often bullied by the rich kids who wore designer everything while living in their fancy homes on the other side of town.

Invisibility had been a great motivator.

And Andrew had been more than motivated as he watched and learned.

In truth, Andrew never minded the lack of respect for himself. It was the lack of respect his father received that fueled him more than anything. So, Andrew studied harder and worked harder than anyone in any of his classes. He earned a full scholarship to NYU. All the while, he remained invisible, until he met Cassie in college.

She had been the first person to notice him and the first person to like him for who he really was, nerdiness and all. She also understood what it was like to lose a parent, though the loss of her father had happened when she'd been in high school, and the wounds were much fresher for her. She hated talking about it, and Andrew respected that. He didn't like talking about his mother much, either. He had been too young when she died to truly remember her, and thinking about it, or trying to, was more triggering than not. Cassie got that. She got *him*.

A breath of fresh air, Cassie was sweet and easy to talk to. She was also funny and quirky. Very quirky. Andrew could relate. Cassie was the girl with an old soul who loved vinyl records and classic rock and pop music, as opposed to classical music. Her favorite musical artists were from the seventies and eighties. She also loved wearing statement rings with crystals, and chose the stones based upon their meanings and healing qualities. Most people didn't get Cassie. He did. He always had, right from the start.

What started out as friendship slowly, eventually, grew into something more because dating her had seemed natural. Then again, Cassie wasn't your average socialite. She shied away from all the trappings of her family's wealth and from other society kids, other children of celebrities. She flew under the radar and, unless Cassie confided in them, one would never have guessed that she was the daughter of famous actress Julia West. Cassie usually did nothing to help them put that connection together. She confided in Andrew, and he kept her secret.

During those four years of college, Andrew cultivated both knowledge and confidence—one could never know enough or stop learning, stop growing, as far as he was concerned. His confidence stemmed from growing into his own, and from his roommate and friend Noah Carr.

Everything seemed to change when Andrew met Noah, his roommate in his junior year. Noah was young, ambitious, and eager to prove himself. Though Noah came from money, he was just as hungry to make a name for himself as Andrew had been. Noah was a friend, and eventually became a business partner. He introduced Andrew to many of his influential contacts, who would be crucial as they built their business and their financial portfolios.

It was Noah who guided Andrew's physical transformation during their senior year. With his guidance, Andrew worked out, cultivated his own style, and made sure to avoid the easy pitfalls of excessive alcohol that often accompanied college parties. Andrew worked on his body as much as improving his brain, recognizing that both would be essential for his plan to succeed.

His constant drive, and his ever-expanding confidence, began to take a toll on his relationship with Cassie, who didn't seem to understand why he was so determined and single-minded in his purpose. Then again, she'd come from a privileged background. Even if she shunned her privilege, she still didn't know what it was like to be poor.

Cassie had spent her life running away from her mother's fame and diva persona on screen and off. That's what initially drew Andrew to her—that and the fact that Cassie had always been closer to her dad than to her mom, even more so after her parents divorced. Cassie's dad grounded her, and his death when she was in high school had a profound effect on her. She never would go into detail, but she did say that her relationship with her mother had always been rocky. After Cassie's father's death, it became strained to the point that they never spoke, and Cassie had essentially moved out when she graduated from high school.

Maybe that's why, despite her affluent upbringing and her natural, effortless beauty, Cassie wasn't interested in being popular. She also never cared about fitting in. Neither did Andrew, because he never wanted to fit in; what he wanted—what he had always wanted—was to stand out.

He soon made sure that he did.

His wasn't an overnight transformation. But it was noticeable to Cassie, and they drifted further away from each other. She never approved of his chosen business profession and never gave him a reason why. In the end, Andrew grew tired of the arguments, and he figured she just wasn't into him anymore.

By the time Andrew graduated from NYU at the top of his class, with majors in both journalism and business, along with a vast knowledge of computer science, he and Cassie were arguing more often than not. It was always about the same thing: his business. His plan had been in the works for a while. With the popularity of reality television featuring the rich and eventually infamous, and social media's explosion, it made perfect sense to him that he needed to create something that would feed fans' cravings for all things celebrity and pop culture.

Shortly after graduation, Andrew launched his celebrity society gossip website, The Steele Dailies. With Noah's financing, it sparked a rabid fan base desperate for everything pop culture. Whether it was celebrity news, gossip, or, heaven forbid, fashion, Andrew made sure his site delivered. Who knew reporting on salacious scandals would make for a successful business model?

Andrew did.

He had recognized that there was an inherent need, a desire, to peek into the lives of the rich and famous and expose their underbelly. He'd bet everything he owned on it.

And it had paid off big-time.

As the face of The Steele Dailies, he adopted a lifestyle befitting a successful pop culture influencer, and it was a world that Cassie never wanted to be a part of. In the end, the launch of his business brought too much tension to their relationship. Cassie pulled away even more, and Andrew thought they were over. That made it easier to break things off with her.

Andrew was the one who broke things off, but he thought she wanted their relationship to end. As far as he was concerned, his feelings were proven correct when she picked things up quickly with Jeremy Roth. They started dating right after the breakup, which had been all the proof Andrew needed that he'd been right.

He watched from afar as she launched her own business and saw her own social media influence rise. Cassie was a relatable social media darling, filming tutorials on flower arrangements, choosing venues, and making a house a home. She quickly became the go-to person for romantic proposal ideas, wedding planning, and life after the big day. He'd followed her career online, and she seemed happy. That was enough.

Why, then, had he come to her rescue today?

Because he wanted to support her. No, it was more than that. It was a burning desire to be there for her. That same burning desire now simmered within his chest like molten lava as he unlocked the door to his penthouse.

Andrew's nerves prickled at the back of his neck and down his spine. Those same spindly pricks wound their way into his gut, coiling into a tight knot of apprehension.

Would she like it, his home? Would she like him—no, not *like*. Would she *approve* of him? Be impressed by him? Be impressed by this multimillion-dollar investment—by his home?

His penthouse served as his home and his business, all rolled into one. It was hard earned. He'd hustled for it. He was proud of it.

So why was it so important that Cassie like it? Why did he even care? This was his dream. This was his life, and no one could take it away from him, nor would he allow anyone to diminish it. So, given all that, why had he given Cassie all the power?

Because here he was, inviting her into his home, his life.

"Come on in." He motioned for her to enter as he held the door for her, then dragged her luggage inside. Bailey's bag was larger than Cassie's, he realized, and heavier.

"Wow. Look at this view." Cassie rushed over to the bank of windows overlooking the Manhattan skyline past New York Harbor. Bailey trotted close behind her. "You didn't oversell it, that's for sure."

Andrew took a deep breath. Until then, he hadn't realized that he had been holding it. "Wait until sunset, when you'll see the skyline light up."

Though the sun was still shining, it would set soon enough. Along with the brilliant colors that would ignite the sky, the skyscraper lights would slowly illuminate the twilight.

That was his favorite view and his favorite time of day.

She smiled at him. "You did all right for yourself. Selling people out does pay, I'll give you that."

"The ones I expose deserve what they get. The scandals wouldn't be an issue unless they committed wrongdoings, would they? Besides, I do some good. Like what I'm about to do for you." He dropped his keys in a bowl crafted of blown crystal in white and gray swirls on his island countertop. Andrew hadn't expected an argument so soon.

As if ignoring his obvious irritation with her statement, Cassie glanced at her cell. After a few seconds, she said, "Nice. Very classy."

"What?"

"Jeremy must have transferred my plane ticket. The confirmation email was just sent to me." She held out her cell, pointing to the time stamp with her manicured fingernail, painted a delicate nude color.

"He wasted no time." Andrew's own phone rang. "Sorry, I've got to take this. It's my partner. Hi, Noah."

"Tell me you got the scoop on the wedding." Noah sliced through pleasantries faster than Andrew, and that was saying something.

Andrew's Spidey senses began to tingle. "What have you heard?"

"I haven't heard anything from you because you haven't published anything yet. As for me, I've been working overtime and learned from a business associate of mine that the would-be groom transferred an airline ticket to his girlfriend. They're going on the honeymoon together. My friend saw them at the airport."

Another woman?

"Who are we talking about?" Andrew's chest constricted. How would he tell Cassie?

"My source was checking in at the same time as the groom and the mystery woman. He recognized the groom as that Roth guy. Unfortunately, he couldn't get a name on the woman Roth's bringing on the honeymoon. Why haven't you published something about the non-wedding yet?"

"I just got back home. I'm on it."

"You had better beat everyone to the scoop, Andrew. Tell me you got it." Noah's impatience was strong. "I don't like waiting. Besides, I've got a feeling that this story is going to be huge."

"About that. There's something you should know…" Andrew strode into his office. The afternoon sun was shining through the bank of tall windows. He loved this place, his work hub.

Painted and furnished in monochromatic tones with dark wood and metal accents, it was much like his living room, or great room, as it was called. Andrew's trappings and décor represented everything he'd become: most notably powerful and efficient. That same theme was duplicated throughout his penthouse.

"I'm listening. Bracing myself, but listening." Noah sighed. "What did you do now?"

Andrew tapped his fingers on his desk. "I got myself mixed up in the narrative. Cassie is here, at home, with me. We dated in college, remember?"

"How could I forget? Cassie hated what you had chosen to do for a

living. That woman absolutely despised the business we were creating."
Noah wasn't wrong.

Cassie didn't like the whole gossip thing. Not at all. She never would
tell Andrew why. It never made sense to him, while Noah chalked it up
to Cassie being a snob. That didn't make sense to Andrew either. While
Andrew had known her, Cassie was anything but a snob. Andrew would
know. He grew up with snobs and could recognize one a mile away.

"Why would you get involved in this failed wedding fiasco short of
writing an article and publishing it?" Noah asked.

"That's a long story, involving a jilted bride hiking down Dune Road
with a broken heel and a dog in a tutu." Andrew waited for it…

"A dog in a tutu? Are you serious? Andrew, what the—"

"Look, she needed help, and I was there. It doesn't matter why I
involved myself. I just did, and now I've got the fake relationship angle.
It's an exclusive. It's the exclusive you wanted, remember?"

Noah expelled a jagged breath into the phone. "You're pretending
to date Cassandra Benedict? Wasn't she just publicly dumped at the
altar?"

"Like I said, I'm changing the narrative." Andrew powered up his
computer and keyed in his password, logging in to his site.

"By making yourself the narrative? Andrew, if you get caught, it will
ruin us. You're not in the PR business, you're in the celebrity news and
pop culture business." Noah was right, of course.

Still, it didn't matter.

Andrew had committed to helping Cassie.

"I know, but this will work, and Cassie's reputation won't suffer.
What Roth did was mean and hurtful. I couldn't watch her suffer, Noah."
Andrew was adamant. He did the right thing. It was the only thing he
could do.

"Get the story up, and remember, I warned you against this."

"I got it. I'll let you know when it's up." Andrew disconnected the call as Cassie padded into his office in her bare feet.

"Nice office." She whistled, admiring his view, while Bailey followed close behind her. They were quite the pair. One couldn't go anywhere without the other, and the canine was making himself more than comfortable in Andrew's home.

As for Cassie, she still wore her wedding gown, which was much the worse for wear. It was dirty, and more beige than white from the fall she took in the sand. Her hair was a tangle of curls and frizz, yet she was breathtaking.

Somehow, she'd always managed to take his breath away.

Andrew returned his attention to the dual monitors in front of him. It was time to present their sham relationship to the public and beat everyone to the punch.

Bailey howled.

"Holy—" Andrew jumped. "You weren't kidding about how that dog's bellow resonates."

"He bays." Cassandra petted Bailey's head, and the dog did an excited butt wiggle thing, as his tail wagged nonstop. Andrew had a retriever when he was a kid, and that dog did the same thing when she was excited.

"Bay, bellow…Call it what you will, it's loud." No matter what Cassie told him, there was no mistaking a howl. Of that, Andrew was certain. Just like he was certain that the beagle holding out his paw to Cassie wasn't a purebred.

The dog stood on his hind legs and got more pets from Cassie until a seagull swooped down and the dog howled again, mixing it with some ferocious barks.

"Does he have an off switch?" With that bit of sarcasm, Andrew returned his attention to the task at hand.

Cassie knelt beside her dog, holding his paw. "What else should we tell Andrew? Oh. I know. You should probably know that Bailey also suffers from separation anxiety. He can get loud when he's not around me."

"Louder than that?" Andrew stopped typing.

How could the dog be louder than that?

Cassie smiled at him. "Bailey is very loving."

"He's a pain in the—"

"Is this more than you bargained for, Andrew? You can back out now if you want."

"It's too late for that. Stuff is happening, so I need to publish ASAP." His cell pinged, and he read the text. "My assistant is on his way up. With your assistant, apparently."

"What do you mean 'stuff is happening'?" Her tone hardened as she stood, then walked over to him.

He didn't answer, instead choosing to type. Cassie swung his chair around until he faced her. She bent over him, placing her hands on the armrests.

"What stuff?" Her voice was cold as ice, as was her glare.

Andrew took a deep breath. "Roth is on a plane with someone else. He's...How do I say this tactfully?"

There was no way to not hurt Cassie's feelings with the news. So, Andrew just came out with it. "He's with another woman."

Cassie straightened. "That was your way of saying it tactfully?" Despite Cassie's attempt at sarcasm, her green eyes filled with unshed tears. Those mesmerizing green eyes, the color of soft spring moss, were truly the mirror to her soul. They'd now lost their luster. Because Andrew had been too direct. But that's the way Andrew was—direct to a fault.

Since seeing her that afternoon, Andrew realized that he tended to say the wrong things when he was with Cassie. He'd always been comfortable with her, but now he felt nervous. This was new for him and he didn't like it. Not at all. She affected him more than he thought possible.

Ever since he saw her enter that oceanfront great room and walk down the aisle holding her beagle, Andrew had been a wreck. Because Cassie was moving on without him.

He'd carried a torch for her for way too long, and he thought that seeing her marry another man would help him get over her. Instead, it made him feel worse. As much as he hated to admit it, when Cassie ran back down that aisle, unmarried and with her dog in hand, a sense of relief had overpowered him. Of course he chased after her. He'd had no choice in the matter.

Because Andrew still cared about Cassie.

Even though he dumped her years ago, and even though he hadn't seen or spoken to her since, he still cared about her. Which went against everything he was. Andrew Steele was not sentimental. He was logical, pragmatic, and currently thinking of himself in the third person, which was also against type for him.

What has Cassie done to me?

She'd reminded him how much he still cared about her.

For years, he'd tried to ignore it, tried to move past it and leave her to her life with Roth, but he still thought of her. He couldn't help it. He was incapable of letting her go.

That's why, when he saw her limping along the side of the road earlier with one shoe and struggling with her squirming dog, she'd taken his breath away. Even with her matted golden mane blowing in the breeze and that white lace gown that had been through the wringer, he thought Cassandra was the most beautiful woman he'd ever seen. He had always thought that, but in her present state, it had never been truer. He'd told her, of course—told her she was beautiful right there and then. He blurted the words like a lovestruck kid, and an intense embarrassment immediately overwhelmed him. That was the real Andrew. The person he'd always be beneath the designer clothes and successes that he now wore like a badge of honor.

Always somewhat awkward.

Always a sucker for Cassie.

"Are we going ahead with our plan or not? If you're having second thoughts, now's the time to tell me." He studied her, from her pink pout to her porcelain skin.

Her face remained stoic. But for her eyes, he wouldn't have a clue that his admission hurt her. Those mesmerizing green eyes, the color of lush spring lawns, were truly the mirror to her soul.

Cassie blinked, held her head high, and swung his chair back around. Only then did she say, "Start typing and make it good. Just don't mention the other woman. Not yet. Agreed?"

He glanced over his shoulder, and in that moment, reflected in her beautiful green eyes, he saw a challenge. A silent dare to refuse her. "Yeah, okay. But—but why not mention her?"

"I won't let Jeremy win, nor will I promote his new relationship like he's some catch. He's not. Anyone who would dump me at the altar is a CREEP in all caps." She leaned her hip against his desk. "We're stuck with each other—you and me. At least for a little while. So, we will make ours the most convincing fake relationship ever, in the history of the world. Because fool me once, shame on you, but fool me twice? It's not going to happen. I won't let it."

A knot coiled within his abdomen. "Why do I think that you're not just referring to Roth?"

She arched her brow and Andrew knew—she meant *him* too. That was before she added, "Did I say that men suck?"

"No. You left that part out. But I get it. I'm one of those men who suck." He did break up with her, after all. Though it was a long time ago, it did happen.

For the first time, Cassie truly smiled. "You were always the smartest person in the room. Or so you thought."

His doorbell chimed, and Bailey howled in immediate response. That dog was loud, with a bellow—bark—bay that sliced through Andrew's nerves like nails on a chalkboard.

"I'll get that. Keep typing. I'll send your assistant in and take mine to my room. I'll find it myself. Bailey needs a bath, and we have our own bathroom, or so I gathered from your Realtor pitch." Bailey trotted behind her as she sauntered out of the room and Andrew returned his attention to his keyboard.

Now to make everyone believe that he and Cassie were a couple. Again. After all this time. Before word got out that Roth was taking someone else on the honeymoon.

Andrew had never shied away from a challenge. Perhaps this time he had bitten off more than he could chew. Odds that Cassie would ever trust another man, let alone one who had broken her heart once before, were slim to none. And yet, despite the odds, Andrew wanted her to trust him.

Even more, he needed her to trust him.

Cassie had always been the one who got away—the one he'd sent away. Never, ever had he regretted it more than at this very moment.

"Keep going. You've got work to do." Her edict was issued over her shoulder as she strode back down the hallway past his open office door with her assistant and Bailey following close behind.

"What do you need me to do, sir?" Andrew's assistant popped his head through the doorway.

"Help them get settled and keep all of this to yourself, okay? I'll find you when I'm done." Andrew typed at a frenzied pace, knowing full well that regardless of how much he wanted to help Cassie, he would be the one to pay for Roth's mistake and callous treatment of Cassie.

Was it fair? *No!* But Andrew would pay, nonetheless.

The very least he could do was make this announcement good.

Chapter 4

ANDREW WAS SEATED ON THE SOFA IN HIS GREAT ROOM, UNDER THE dim recessed lighting with his laptop open on his lap. The sun had set, and the Manhattan skyline was now illuminated through the tall bank of windows. He was monitoring comments posted on his Cassie announcement, as well as watching his tip line. A new show was premiering in the popular *Househusbands* franchise, and there was some chatter about a scandal brewing behind the scenes. He'd gotten in touch with some reliable sources and was waiting to hear back.

Bailey leaped up on the sofa beside him and Andrew jumped. "Holy cow, you scared me. For a loud, obnoxious guy, you can be stealthy when you want to be."

"I'm sorry about that. I just couldn't sleep." Cassie padded into the room wearing her hair in some messy bun thing atop her head, and pajamas with beagles on them that looked a lot like Bailey, and socks.

"You look good." He couldn't help but stare.

For a woman whose world had imploded that afternoon, Cassie looked comfy, fresh faced, and like a nice long shower had done her good.

"I feel human again." She offered him a grin. "That shower is incredible. Talk about water pressure."

Andrew laughed.

"I mean it. After the day I had, I appreciated that water pressure. So did Bailey." She walked over to his wall-to-wall bookshelves and browsed his vinyl records. "Oh, this one is my favorite."

Andrew didn't need to see which album Cassie referred to. It was

The Stranger. He'd had it forever. She turned to him. "The sleeve is empty."

And Andrew knew precisely why—because that record was his go-to, on nights like this when he couldn't get Cassie off his mind. It didn't happen that much anymore, but it happened far more often than he would have liked. "It's on the turntable. The remote's on the shelf beside it."

No sooner had Cassie reached for the remote than the music began to play. "Moving Out" began to play. "I love this song." She sang along with some of the words, then squealed. "You've got Queen. Wow! Your taste in music has evolved."

"If I didn't know better, I'd say you were impressed," Andrew teased her. Though he'd never admit to it, it was all thanks to Cassie's influence. He'd hated classic rock, disco, and all things pop before meeting her.

"Not impressed, just surprised. Don't get ahead of yourself." She slid the album sleeve back where it belonged. "I need a drink. I can't sleep for anything. Can I borrow a corkscrew?"

"Sure. Do you want a bottle of wine to go with that?" He grabbed his electric corkscrew from his kitchen cabinet.

Cassie shook her head. "My assistant placed an order for me at your local grocery store. She ordered me the absolute necessities—lots of wine and doggie pâté."

"What?" Andrew halted, watching her reach into his built-in wine chiller and pull out a bottle of Moscato that didn't belong to him. "What's doggie pâté?"

She grabbed the electric wine opener. "It's Bailey's favorite dog food, and it's refrigerated. Oh, it's in your fridge, by the way. I hope you don't mind."

"Great." Now he had dog food in his fridge.

Seriously, Andrew was sacrificing a lot for Cassie. Dog food being in his top-of-the-line stainless steel refrigerator wasn't something he ever expected to deal with when he offered to help Cassie craft her narrative. He opened his fridge and saw that the food was in a large Ziploc bag. Andrew exhaled a sigh of relief. Okay, that was something he could live with.

After placing two wineglasses in front of Cassie, Andrew sat beside her at his island. "How are you doing?"

It was a silly question. Really. How did he think she'd be doing?

"I'm…I don't know." She held up her glass in a toast. "Here's to figuring out how I'm doing so I can have a coherent answer the next time you ask."

"I'll drink to that." Though Andrew wasn't a fan of white wine, he took a swig. It was the least he could do.

"So, Noah, huh?" Cassie prompted him.

Andrew narrowed his eyes. "Noah, what?"

"I take it your business partner named Noah is the same Noah Carr from college. That's who called you earlier?" She took a sip of her wine.

This was awkward. "Yes, he's the same Noah from college."

"I'm glad things worked out between the two of you." She sounded convincing. "What? You look surprised."

Andrew raised his hands in the air. "No, I just…Well, I guess I am somewhat surprised. You didn't like him much when you and I were dating."

"That's because he seemed to parrot everything you said. And he was kind of spoiled." Cassie grimaced. "I'm sorry. He's your friend. I don't mean to be critical."

"That's okay. Especially since he thought you were a snob." Andrew was nothing if not brutally honest most of the time.

"Ouch." Cassie took another sip of wine. "Well, maybe I was. Or maybe I came off that way. I don't know. It feels like forever ago."

"That's true. But you look great. It's as if no time has passed." He meant it as a compliment, of course.

Cassie set her wineglass on the Italian marble island countertop. "Then why do I feel like such a mess?"

Her eyes held his for a long moment, one in which they both stared at each other while Billy Joel played from his living room speakers. The song was "Vienna" and it set a mood, one in which Andrew remembered his relationship with Cassie in every word.

It was a carpe diem song to Andrew, one that reminded him of where he was at in his life when they dated. He was going a million miles an hour back then, and theirs was a relationship that burned bright and imploded too quickly.

If he'd realized that it would be over before he'd wanted it to be, Andrew would've taken it slower, and he would have enjoyed his time with her so much more than he had.

"You're staring at me." Cassie was right.

He was staring and moving closer to her. It was as if there was a driving force propelling him toward her. It had been there today at the beach, and now at his penthouse. They'd always shared a sizzling chemistry, though now there was a magnetic pull between them, one he couldn't ignore, one he wouldn't ignore.

She drew closer to him, then closer still.

Until…

"I was going to marry someone else today," Cassie admitted in a whisper, halting when her lips were close to his, so close that Andrew could have kissed her.

Cassie's reminder made Andrew feel as if he'd been doused by an icy rain. He needed no such reminder that she had been in love with someone else, had been committed to Roth. As a matter of fact, they'd be married now and on their honeymoon, had Roth not called it off.

"Yeah, you were going to marry Roth. You would have, had he not left you at the altar." His tone sounded judging and biting, not how he'd intended. So, he tried to course correct. "Though I guess you left him, which technically works to our advantage with the narrative."

"Wow. You keep reminding me that I sure know how to pick them, don't you?" Cassie exhaled, her smile fixed in place. "I mean, first you, then him. Just think, you had unfettered access to both of my break-ups—my biggest breakups, the ones that hurt me the most."

Oh boy.

He'd stuck his foot in his mouth this time.

"That's not what I—"

"What, not what you intended? Why not? It's true. As is the fact that I was foolish enough to believe that you and I had a future, just like I thought that Jeremy and I did. I really am a fool."

Cassie's cell pinged and she removed it from the pocket of her paja-mas. She frowned as she read her screen. "God, I am such a fool." Cassie turned away from him and headed down his hall to her room, calling over her shoulder to Bailey, who followed her close behind.

If Andrew didn't know better, he would have thought she was crying.

But he couldn't see her eyes. Instead, he stood in his kitchen until he heard her bedroom door close. What had just happened? They'd been having a good conversation, right up until Andrew said something insen-sitive and their moment of peace was gone, replaced by an animosity that sent her out of the room as quickly as possible.

Andrew downed the rest of his wine, then washed both glasses in the sink before turning the lights off, along with his turntable. He had no choice but to get his jealousy of Roth under control. That's what his comment about Roth stemmed from, right? Jealousy that Cassie had fallen for a guy who could hurt her like that.

The last thing Andrew should feel was jealousy. He had no right to feel anything, let alone that. He'd given up all rights when he broke things off with Cassie.

Had he known that Cassie being within such close proximity would stir up these memories and these feelings, Andrew would have...what? Never helped her? No, he would have done it anyway.

But he must get his feelings under control.

Cassie wasn't a lover, and she wasn't a friend.

She was his past.

Andrew would do well to remember that before he got hurt.

Chapter 5

Approximately sixteen hours had passed since Andrew published his announcement, and it had been reposted, repeated, and featured in countless social media stories and news reports. It had gone viral in ways Andrew had never anticipated. He had hoped to change the narrative about Cassie being dumped at the altar, and he had.

Unfortunately, now, when he googled Cassandra Benedict, which he last did just a half hour ago, the first things to pop up were articles titled "Wedding Planner Dumps Fiancé in Quest for Love," "The Runaway Wedding Planner," and "What She Did for Love: The Rise and Potential Fall of a Successful Celebrity Wedding Planner."

While changing the narrative was great, none of those headlines had been on Andrew's wish list. He'd wanted Cassie to be received in a favorable light, and painting her as a callous runaway bride wasn't the way to do that.

The adage that no publicity was bad publicity was wrong. Terribly wrong. There *was* such a thing as bad publicity, and unless Andrew took control of this story, Cassie would feel the repercussions. And she would hate him for ruining her reputation and her livelihood.

Andrew tapped his fingers on his large mahogany desk with its minimalist lines and chrome legs. His desk was where he usually crafted all his celebrity stories that out-scooped every other entertainment news site. Sure, he posted the occasional emergency update from his cell or laptop, but he liked working in his office. It was where he'd come up with the best stories of his career.

For the most part, he was usually satisfied with the results of his efforts, but not today. Because Andrew knew what he must do, but at the same time, he dreaded it. Cassie would no doubt despise him for not consulting her. That was part of their agreement, and he'd be going against her specific instructions. He didn't have a choice, though. She wasn't here, wasn't picking up her cell, and they were losing the PR battle. Andrew couldn't—no, he wouldn't—allow Roth to be seen as a victim in this mess.

A high-pitched howl echoed throughout his office.

"Again, Bailey?" He turned toward the dog, just in time to see the mutt flop against the love seat cushions and whimper.

Andrew crossed the room and picked up the dog's stuffed toy giraffe before tossing it on the cushion. "Mom will be home soon. Just stop dropping your toy, and you'll be fine."

The dog gave him side-eye. Andrew would swear to it in a court of law. Bailey then bit his toy and flung it onto the floor. Again—along with another high-pitched howl that resonated throughout the room, followed by the dog's usual flop against the plush cushions.

"You really are a drama king." Andrew bent down again. "For the last time, keep it together. Your mom will be home soon."

His *mom*. Andrew was now referring to Cassie as the dog's mom and referring to his penthouse as Cassie and the canine's place of residence. This was quickly becoming all too real. He sucked in another deep breath and stood over his monitor, reading the article he had just written.

Using a terrible picture of Roth, because why give the guy who broke Cassie's heart a good angle, Andrew had reported that Jeremy had slithered off on what was supposed to be his honeymoon with another woman. It was the truth. Andrew had fact-checked it and heard from numerous sources about Roth and his fling, including the one who took a picture of the couple holding hands in Las Vegas. There was no mistaking a cheater, and a picture was indeed worth a thousand words. In it, Roth was showing an intimacy with the woman that couldn't be confused with brotherly love or friendship.

Of course, Andrew wouldn't publish *that* photo without the woman's consent. But he did use an image of Roth at a polo match, looking sweaty and somewhat shady.

Bailey jumped down from the sofa, barking, and Andrew hit *publish*. Did he have Cassie's approval to run this? Nope. The last thing she told him was not to announce the story about the other woman, but he did it anyway because her reputation needed protecting. It's what he signed up for, and he was going to deliver. Besides, there was no way that Jeremy would appear to be some catch in any way, shape, or form. Not with the picture Andrew just published.

Following the dog into his open kitchen and great room area, Andrew found Cassie placing a couple of shopping bags on one of his living room chairs. She kneeled and scooped up her dog.

"Hi, bud! How are you?"

"He's one hundred percent drama. He kept tossing his toy, then crying about it. It was pitiful." Andrew shoved his hands in his pants pockets.

"Oh, someone wanted attention." Cassie smiled at her dog as she put him back on the floor.

"He's been walked, and fed, and got lots of attention while I was supposed to be working. How was your day?" Andrew was deliberately making small talk, prolonging his inevitable confession. He'd need to tell Cassie about the article eventually, but wanted to give her a chance to decompress first.

Yeah, it was all about Cassie.

No chance that Andrew was doing this for himself, right?

Cassie saved him from answering by pulling a red dress out of one of the bags. "This is what's known as a revenge dress. I'm wearing it on our first outing tonight. What do you think?"

With a plunging neckline and what Andrew imagined was a tight skirt, he couldn't think much except… "I can't wait to see it on you."

Smooth…not.

It was enough to make Cassie laugh. "I've got a fresh mani-pedi, and black nail polish to match my charred heart and bad attitude. I'm ready for war."

"Just don't shoot the messenger, okay?"

Cassie's smile turned into a grimace. "What did you do?"

"I didn't do anything except report the truth." He raised his hands in surrender.

"You wrote a follow-up article? Without running it by me first?"

"My answer would be 'yes' to both questions, but hear me out." Andrew crossed the room and motioned for her to join him on his leather sofa. "The tide was turning against you. I've been monitoring the news cycle since my announcement last night, and people were starting to paint you with the bad girl brush. So, I had to make a move, and you weren't answering."

She sat beside him with a grace he'd forgotten about. Cassie could always command a room, but she did so with a certain vulnerability and a degree of poise that no one else possessed—at least no one he'd ever met. "What did you report?"

"I reported that Roth is on your honeymoon with another woman. I know we agreed not to publish that yet, but it was necessary." Andrew dropped his confession like a bomb and waited for the fallout.

One second passed, then two, and still no response from Cassie. Not a word, not a twitch, not a tear.

"Did you hear—"

"Yes. I heard you. And I can't say I'm surprised. It had to come out eventually, right? I mean, he isn't exactly being discreet, is he?"

Had he heard her correctly?

Andrew leaned forward. "Based on our conversation yesterday, I thought you'd be upset."

"I booked our honeymoon hotel in my name, on my credit card. I received a text last night that the first nightly charge went through." Cassie shoved her hair behind her ear.

"Wait!" Andrew rose with force. "He's charging his tryst on your credit card?"

With a grimace, Cassie nodded. "He tried. I saw the text right away, when we were having wine in your kitchen, and immediately called both the credit card company and the hotel. I reported the fraud and made sure that my credit card number was changed. I'm being credited, and the hotel promised that they will make sure they get Jeremy's card on file. The credit card company is mailing my new card to me via my assistant. Long story short, I spent hours last night changing my mailing address on all my credit cards."

"That son of a—"

"Jeremy's not the man I thought he was, that's for sure." Cassie petted her dog, who rolled onto his back and was clearly enjoying the belly rubs.

Though he hated to admit it, even to himself, Andrew was somewhat relieved that he hadn't made Cassie as angry as he'd thought the night before. She didn't seem to notice.

"I just keep thinking that he must have been seeing her for some time. It's the only explanation I've got. I just wish I knew who she is." Cassie stared at her nails, which were black with what looked like some glitter. Then there was her statement ring with an onyx stone to match her black nails.

Ring...wait.

"Did he pay for your ring?" Andrew asked.

"Talk about a sudden change of subject." She did a double take. "Yes, Jeremy paid for my engagement ring. Why?"

"No reason. I was just curious." Andrew unlocked his cell screen, pulled up the photo texted to his tip line, and showed Cassie. "This was Jeremy last night. With that woman."

"Wow." Cassie stared at the photo, her eyes wide. "He traded up."

"No, he didn't." On this, Andrew was adamant.

"She's rich, Andrew. Her family is one of the wealthiest in Manhattan." She tilted her head to the side, and her blond curls fell into her face. Andrew longed to smooth them away from her eyes. "You don't recognize her? You? Gossip and society sleuth extraordinaire?"

Sadly, Andrew didn't. He studied the photo.

"Picture her with brown hair," Cassie prompted.

Just like that, the pieces clicked into place.

"She's the daughter of Neil Phillips." Andrew snapped his fingers. "I didn't recognize her with the change in hair color."

"Yep. Her dad's a tycoon, and Jeremy is nothing if not attracted to wealth and status. Or so it would seem." Cassie's tone was laced with regret.

"You didn't see it, but you wish you had?"

Cassie nodded. "I wish I'd done a lot of things differently."

Meeting his gaze, Cassie managed to grin. "I can't do this or I'll fall apart, so let's change the subject. I've booked a Bailey-sitter, and—"

"A Bailey-sitter?" Andrew remembered, again, just how quirky Cassie was. It was good to see that hadn't changed. It had been one of her most endearing qualities, in his opinion.

"Yes, Bailey suffers from separation anxiety, remember?" Cassie tipped her head to the side as if waiting for Andrew to acknowledge that fact.

"I remember. It's just…" He paused, trying to choose his words with care. "Between Bailey being a bridesman, and having a Bailey-sitter, he's one lucky dog."

Andrew smiled. He'd navigated that mine field like a champ and he was proud of himself.

"And here I thought you'd mock me again." Cassie stood and grabbed her pastel-colored shopping bags. "I've got to get ready for tonight. Let's make this convincing, okay?"

Without hesitation, Andrew agreed. Once Cassie was out of the room and headed to her primary, Andrew shoved his fingers through his hair. Roth had joined forces with a powerful family—one who had unlimited PR resources.

"Frack," he muttered. They were going to have a fight on their hands. Andrew sensed it, his muscles now taut with tension. Phillips would no doubt support his daughter, and if that meant taking Andrew's site down to keep Roth's name out of the mud, so be it. But Andrew was a warrior, if not a scrapper. He would fight for Cassie and his own business.

Nothing would take him down. Nothing, and no one.

Striding back to his office, Andrew dialed his partner. It was time to bring Noah Carr up to speed. They'd need to fight Phillips together. It was their only shot at getting in front of this nightmare.

Andrew wasn't going to let Cassie down, but he also wouldn't sacrifice his own business. It was time to walk the tightrope known as elite society.

Noah picked up on the second ring.

"Hey, what do you know about Neil Phillips? He's probably going to come after me, and I need all the info I can get."

His friend sighed. "What did you do to piss him off?"

Andrew checked his Rolex. "How much time do you have?"

Chapter 6

Did it surprise Cassandra that Jeremy brought a side piece on what was supposed to be their honeymoon? Not really. Not when Cassandra truly considered it. Why else would he decide to dump her on their wedding day?

What hurt Cassandra the most, what caused the ache in her heart to fracture into a million painful pieces, was that Jeremy so callously threw her aside and didn't care what his public rejection of her would do to her or everything she'd worked so hard to build.

Humiliation: Check.

Heartbreak: Check.

Disillusionment: Triple check.

Cassandra studied her reflection in her compact and reapplied her lipstick. It was a nude tone to balance her ruby-red dress.

"You look great. Don't worry." Andrew was studying her. Like he had been doing incessantly since finding her on the side of the road. She'd felt like a science experiment.

"This is going to be a piece of cake," he added for good measure.

"Cake…What a poor choice of words." She snapped her compact closed and placed it in her gold clutch. She then laughed at the lines of confusion etched in Andrew's forehead. "Cake. You know…as in the wedding cake I meticulously chose, that went—where, exactly? With Jeremy and his side piece?"

He offered her a wry smile. "Point taken. It was a poor choice of words. But this will be easy. You're in my element now."

"I never fit into your element, remember?" If he didn't, that would be okay. Cassandra remembered enough for them both. Andrew's element was the same box she had clawed her way out of and fought so hard to escape. "Your element isn't where I was ever comfortable."

"Why is that?" Andrew shifted in his seat. They sat in the back seat of his Escalade, on their way into Manhattan for a bar opening.

Andrew had made it a point to mention that his usual driver was chauffeuring them, and that Andrew trusted him completely. That's why she answered honestly.

"That element, your element, is more my mother's scene, and she's a prima donna. I wanted to be as unlike her as I could possibly get. Besides, I never needed any more drama." She crossed her legs. "And look where I am…mired in drama. My ex-fiancé is the epitome of drama, my mother is the very definition of a drama queen—"

"Your dog is a drama king," Andrew added.

"Hey now. Keep Bailey out of this. He's loving and faithful. The world needs more Baileys, as far as I'm concerned." Cassandra smiled.

"Keep smiling like that and I'll lay off Bailey. It's good to see you smile." Andrew paused, then opened his mouth to speak, only to close it.

"Go on. Say it…" Cassandra waited for him to speak up, bracing herself for what he'd say next.

"Bailey isn't a purebred beagle, is he?"

She feigned outrage. "How could you suggest such a thing?"

Throwing his hands in the air, Andrew apologized for offending her.

"Actually, you're right. He's fifty percent beagle on his mom's side. His dad was supposed to be half soft-coated wheaten terrier and half Pomeranian. It tuns out Mommy stepped out on Daddy and Bailey is twelve breeds instead of three."

"I knew he was a mutt." Andrew laughed, clearly impressed with himself.

"Well, I knew what I was getting into, but I loved him and paid the breeder's fee anyway." Cassandra looked at her black fingernail polish with glitter that shone more in the dimming daylight. Maybe her heart wasn't as charred as she thought. She certainly loved her canine bestie.

"Why would you pay the breeder's fee anyway?"

"Bailey needed a home, and I would have adopted the entire litter if I could. The shelters had nothing but large dogs at the time, about a year ago, so when I found Bailey, I knew he was for me." She shrugged. "Long story short, I loved him right from the start."

"Remember when you said you wanted to be as unlike your mother as possible." Andrew gave her a wry grin.

She nodded.

"Well, you succeeded there. Your mother would never adopt anything but a purebred. Never." There was no love lost between Andrew and Cassandra's mother.

To say Julia Benedict didn't approve of Andrew Steele would be an understatement. He had the audacity to stand up to her, even when he was still in college, and that Julia could never abide.

"I miss your mother. She was fun to torment." Andrew winked at her.

"What is it with the winking?" Cassandra pointed at him. While she didn't mean to blurt it out, Andrew was perplexing her with his winking, and her eagerness to find an answer won out. "Do you wink at all the girls now? Is it cool? Is it some celebrity thing?"

Andrew's shoulders stiffened and his eyes narrowed. "Am I winking at you?"

"Yes. And I can't figure out why." Her tone was deliberately teasing. This was her attempt at charming him after she so callously drew attention to what she now wondered was an eye tic of some kind.

"I…" Andrew studied her, his brown eyes growing darker, with more intensity. "I don't know how to act around you. I mean, I'm trying to cheer you up, and I'm trying not to be a jerk and say something insulting without meaning to, which I tend to do now. You may have noticed."

"Oh, I noticed." How could she not?

So, Andrew winked at her because he was self-conscious around her. Now she understood. It was the tongue-tied thing Andrew admitted to the day prior. Cassandra clearly made him uncomfortable. His winks were his tells. "I'm sorry. You're being kind, and now I'm the one who's being insensitive."

"No, you're being honest. That's who you are, and it's pretty special if you ask me."

"Thanks." Cassandra shoved her hair behind her ear. It was a nervous habit, it always had been.

Andrew freed her hair from behind her ear. "Stop. Don't keep messing with your hair. You're a knockout. Besides, you're going to be fine."

"Why are you being so kind to me?" Cassandra studied Andrew's shocked expression. She had surprised even herself with that question, but since they were being honest, why not go full tilt? "Don't say that this is mutually beneficial, because I've heard that before. I'm asking seriously: Why are you being so nice to me?"

"Would you rather I be cruel?" he asked, his baritone a husky murmur.

Cassandra swallowed hard against the lump of emotion forming in her throat, threatening to choke her. How honest did she want to get?

"Given everything that's happened to me since yesterday, I'd trust your cruelty more than your kindness right now." Yep, she went there.

Talk about a truth bomb.

Linking his fingers through hers, Andrew squeezed hard, as if holding on for dear life. "Don't let Roth do that to you. Don't let him take away your ability to see goodness in people, or to expect kindness in return. You're still the sweetest person I know. You don't deserve what Roth did to you."

And she still had no idea why Jeremy did it to begin with, let alone so publicly. If she had known, would it have made a difference? Probably not. But the fact remained that Andrew, who she hadn't spoken to in years, was being far nicer to her than the man Cassandra had agreed to marry. That was messed up on too many levels.

Blinking rapidly, Cassandra turned to the window. Only once she was staring blankly at the tall buildings, crowded sidewalks, and streets, did she extract her hand from his. Honesty, Andrew's unadulterated honesty, was too much for her to endure, so she chose to hide from it.

Their connection was broken as she studied the streaks of pastel accentuating the sky between buildings, though Cassandra wasn't engrossed. Instead, she replayed her admission to Andrew. And wondered why she seemed to trust him now when she knew better.

Not now, not then, not ever.

It was safer not to trust him. Yet she was opening her heart to him and speaking honestly. In spite of his infuriating dig the night before.

As the sun sank behind the many skyscrapers that comprised the Manhattan skyline and the lights illuminated around them, they both remained silent. Cassandra concentrated on the sounds of car horns, whistles for cabs, and the bustling noises that together created Manhattan's famed soundtrack.

She tried to ignore her rapid heartbeat and her every nerve humming in tune with Andrew's close proximity. Sure, he seemed sincere, but who was she to judge? She'd believed that Jeremy was deeply and unabashedly in love with her until he broke her heart. If one thing was for certain, it was that Cassandra was a poor judge of character.

Stop thinking about Jeremy—you've got bigger things to worry about.

That was true, Cassandra thought as she inhaled a deep, calming breath. She must concentrate on charming the elite who would be in attendance tonight. After the articles that Andrew had published, there was sure to be a crowd of people clamoring for gossip, for the scoop that Andrew so readily dished on a daily basis. How was Cassandra going to convince them that she and Andrew were in a real relationship when she couldn't be near the man without second-guessing herself?

"Okay, we're about to pull up. Are you ready?"

"You're joking, right?" Upon studying his features, Cassandra noted that Andrew was most certainly serious.

No, she wasn't ready! She was anything but ready.

However, since the driver had stopped the car in front of the bar where a long red carpet stretched from the sidewalk to the entranceway, Cassandra didn't have much choice in the matter.

Her eyes were drawn to a woman strutting down the red carpet with teased strawberry-blond hair and garbed in a violet-colored, sequined cocktail dress. The matching satin Manolo Blahniks were a dead give-away. Cassandra would have recognized that woman—with her signature purple wardrobe choices—from a mile away. Like a neon sign, she was calling attention to herself, and only one woman did that better than anyone else in the world…

"Mother." Anyone else within earshot might have thought Cassandra was muttering the beginning of a curse word, but Andrew knew better.

"She's here?" He turned and peered out the tinted Escalade window as his jaw clenched so tightly that a vein pulsated in his neck. "Mother—"

The sound of chatter drowned out Andrew's statement as their driver opened the door, and Andrew turned to Cassie, smiling wide. "Fake it. And ignore your mother if you must, but let's make this believable."

She followed his lead and smiled at the cameras, whose flashes were going off as reporters called out questions to her. The hows and whys of her canceled wedding were among the many questions Cassandra dodged, while Andrew was peppered with questions pertaining to his Jeremy posts and questions about Andrew's own relationship with Cassandra.

All the while, Andrew held Cassandra's hand possessively and smiled for the cameras, while her frantic pulse hammered against her temples. Above the high-pitched ringing in her ears, Cassandra could make out a female reporter asking, "Is this relationship real?"

"Excellent question, darling. That's precisely what I'd like to know." That raspy, Bette Davis–inspired voice, the same one that Cassandra grew up with, caused Cassandra's heart to lurch in her chest. She turned to face the woman, who was now scowling at her, ever the center of attention.

"Hello, Mother." Cassandra's grin was plastered in place.

"Are you going to answer me, darling? Or must I ask again?" Julia Benedict was nothing if not a pain in her daughter's derriere.

For the first time in Cassandra's life, she threw caution to the wind, grabbed Andrew by his lapel, and tugged him closer to her. His eyes locked with hers, burning in intensity, as Cassandra parted her lips and drew him closer, then closer still.

Until she crushed her mouth against his.

Their kiss was slow and seductive, as her tongue tenderly probed his mouth for entrance. He parted his lips. The moment her tongue stroked his, a jolt, much like that of an electrical surge, pulsated through her.

Had he felt it, too?

Andrew's breath caught in his throat, and that one reaction sent a rush of excitement through her. He felt it, too. He must have, because he pulled Cassandra even closer with a moan, then held one of his hands in front of them, as if to shield them from the cameras. It was as if he wanted to make sure the photographers got good shots and hide anything that might not photograph well. Though she suspected that cynicism from Andrew, he didn't pull away.

To the contrary.

Theirs was a full-fledged, passionate kiss, for all to see and analyze.

It left her weak, breathless, and yearning for more as Andrew's free hand slid to the nape of her neck. He was warm, strong, and he felt oh so right.

Yes, he was making this fake kiss look and feel very realistic.

He was also proving that their sizzling chemistry had grown exponentially since their breakup. Perhaps that's why, for the first time in a very long time, Cassandra wasn't self-conscious when it came to public displays of affection. As a matter of fact, she was currently a strong proponent of PDA, because she couldn't trust her voice to be steady.

No, her mother's demands for answers had left Cassandra feeling weak and shaky. Or those feelings might have been caused by Andrew's ravenous lips. At this precise moment, she couldn't tell the difference. All she knew was that Andrew's kisses were addictive and all-consuming.

She wanted more.

Thankfully, Andrew had the foresight to pull away from her. When their lips parted, he grinned at her, his eyes emanating a spark of surprise and…dare she say it, pleasure?

"Hello there." His baritone was more husky than usual, and the look of approval on his face said it all.

Andrew Steele was proud of her.

"Hi." It was all she could manage, though she was now smiling, too.

"I suppose I have my answer." Her mother gave Andrew a pretentious kiss on each cheek, then wrapped Cassandra in a stiff hug. "You owe me an explanation later."

And what an explanation it would be.

Cassandra's mother dared to question the legitimacy of her daughter's fake relationship in front of reporters, after all. What was a girl to do other than make it look convincing by throwing in some good old-fashioned media-friendly public displays of affection?

Judging by the varied looks of surprise and glee on the reporters' faces, she and Andrew had done just that. And given those filming their kiss headlines for days.

"I think you just scooped me," Andrew whispered, as they proceeded to walk down the red carpet and into the bar.

"Didn't you have a photographer here?" She'd never known Andrew to be unprepared.

"Of course I did. Who do you think asked if our relationship was real?"

This man was good. And she wasn't even referring to his red-hot kisses from moments before.

Chapter 7

"WHAT A SURPRISE TO SEE YOUR MOTHER HERE." ANDREW'S WORDS dripped with sarcasm.

Cassandra grinned, well aware that all eyes were on them since their red-carpet kiss. "Isn't it, though?" It was all she could manage as she realized that her mother wouldn't return home in time for her canceled wedding, but she would fly in for a bar opening. It was all about priorities for Julia, and this was yet another example of precisely how misplaced the woman's priorities truly were.

After escorting her to the bar, Andrew ordered a vodka soda for himself while Cassandra ordered a lemon drop martini with the bartender's choice of top-shelf vodka. Andrew's hand remained firmly on her waist, Cassandra noted as she leaned into him.

For all intents and purposes, he was the epitome of an attentive boyfriend. Was it for the crowd, or was Andrew putting extra care into his role because Julia was present? Cassandra didn't know and wouldn't dare ask for fear that someone would overhear.

"What do you think would irritate your mother the most?" he whispered in her ear as his warm breath fanned her cheek. "Us kissing again, or me discussing something mundane like the weather forecast or the economy with her?"

She laughed, and it came out raspy and rather flirty even to her own ears. "If you want to irritate her the most, talk about your successes. She loathes gossip sites and paparazzi now."

Yes, her mother despised them now. Unfortunately, she hadn't felt the same when Cassie's dad died. Julia West had used them to her advantage back then, even if it meant that her daughter would be collateral damage.

"Your mother loathes the paparazzi until she has something to promote, I'm sure." Andrew paused long enough to toast to Cassandra before adding, "When they want publicity, celebrities will do anything to get the paparazzi's attention."

"While that's true, my mother has held a personal grudge ever since her affair during marriage number four was divulged by a reporter working for one of your competitors." Cassie remembered that well. Her mother's marriage to husband number four, also known as Luc Larson, almost didn't survive.

"That's interesting." His tone was teasing as he traced lazy circles on her shoulder, causing her pulse to race.

Between his low, husky whispers and the mischievous glint in his eyes, Cassandra was drawn to him more and more. It was as if an invisible magnet was pulling her closer to him, then closer still until she was close enough to kiss him again.

Small talk aside, she did consider kissing him again, if only to relieve the tension. Sure, Andrew's flirtations were fun, but they were also exhausting, as was being under everyone's intense and never-ending scrutiny. Cassandra couldn't help but be aware of the inquisitive eyes watching them, following their every move. She kept catching sight of people studying her long enough to be caught, then looking away. If ever Cassandra felt like a hamster on a wheel, being watched through its cage, this was the time.

Without a doubt, kissing Andrew had been the easiest part of tonight and the most enjoyable. Their kiss made her forget the humiliation she had endured, the heartache she'd experienced at the hands of Jeremy. She'd also forgotten all of the trust that had been shattered. For a moment.

For one brief moment.

Then it flooded back.

It was as if a dam had broken, and strong rapids were drowning her. The pain of Jeremy's callous disregard caused the walls around her heart to harden just in time for more memories to assault her.

Not only was she battered by Jeremy's betrayal, but by Andrew's, because the latter dumped her first and that past hurt had resurfaced. Yes, Andrew was the first to break her heart.

She'd loved him once, and he discarded her, shut her out, choosing glitzy parties like this one over her. The fact that Andrew made his choice privately didn't make it sting any less. It had broken Cassandra's heart to know that Andrew chose vapid social climbers over a woman who loved him and who would have always put him first.

Blame it on the fact that Jeremy had reopened her wounds, or that Cassandra might not have been completely over Andrew like she once thought, but she refused to let Andrew into her heart again. So, no more kisses, or at the very least, no more *enjoying* their kisses. They were just a means to an end and nothing more. If she had to kiss him in public for the sake of this charade, she would, of course. But not in private.

Never in private.

Andrew was still the same *man* who chose money, power, and fame over her. She never would have cast him aside as he had done to her. Turning away from him, Cassandra took a large gulp of her lemon drop martini. The alcohol burned her throat, and she swallowed hard. Her determination not to fall under Andrew's sensual spell was forged under the fire of ninety-proof vodka and a scorned woman's sheer force of will.

I will not fall for Andrew Steele again.

It was her silent mantra as she scanned the guests in attendance, the same people who were watching her intently. Movie stars mingled with reality television celebrities and social media influencers. All taking selfies with each other, all pretending to get along for this one splashy public event. Most of this scene was an act. For instance, Cassandra knew for a fact that her mother despised the director she was currently laughing and chatting with.

"Look at you, watching Julia intently," Andrew whispered in her ear. "Should we save her?"

It was obvious that he remembered the casting-couch story that Julia had written about in her tell-all memoir published six years prior. As Julia had explained in vivid detail, a certain movie executive would only allow the filmmakers to cast her if she slept with said movie executive, which Julia refused to do. The director in question, the one she was currently engaged in a discussion with, didn't fight for her. Instead, he cast someone else. Someone who was willing to sleep with the movie executive, or so her mother had implied in her memoir.

"Come on, follow me." Against her best judgment, Cassandra grabbed her drink and joined what, despite appearances to the contrary, was a rather heated discussion. "I'm sorry to interrupt, but I haven't seen my mother in ages. Do you mind?"

Andrew, who'd been a step behind her, shot the director a challenging look and the director excused himself with very little fanfare.

"How are you, Mother?" Cassandra asked with a kiss on the woman's cheek.

Julia's lips upturned in a grin. "Grateful for the save, though it was unnecessary. I can handle myself."

"I know. It was Andrew's idea," Cassandra countered, knowing full well that this would annoy her mother. Call it a small slice of Cassandra's revenge for her mother not returning in time for her wedding day fiasco.

If Julia had been there, maybe she would have saved Cassandra. Maybe she would have taken her home, instead of Andrew. Oh, who was Cassandra kidding? Her mother would have never come to her rescue.

Not in a million years.

"Thank you, Andrew. Imagine my surprise at seeing *you* accompany my daughter here this evening. I know I never could have predicted this turn of events." Julia offered her cheek to her daughter's date, her expression cool.

"I can only imagine. I'm sure that you thought you were rid of me." Andrew kissed the woman's cheek as bid.

"Well, I'd hoped so, yes, but here you are...popping up like a bad penny." Julia laughed again.

Why hadn't this woman won a Daytime Emmy? She'd been nominated eleven times during her soap tenure. And she'd never been nominated for an Oscar for her indie movies, though this performance was proof that she should have been.

At least once.

Andrew offered her his famous wry grin. "Let's cut the crap, shall we?"

"Gladly. That was terribly tedious. So, what brings you back into my daughter's life? Really?" Julia gave his silk tie a firm tug. "The crap has been cut, remember."

"Cassie and I reconnected, and I won her heart." Andrew flattened his palm against Cassie's back and slid it possessively around her waist. He turned to give Cassandra a hooded look brimming with sensuality. "She realized we belong together. Didn't you, love?"

Love?

Andrew was laying it on thick. But Cassandra played along with him and his over-the-top term of endearment, aware that his use of her nickname was a shot off the bow.

Cassandra knew it, and she was certain that her mother did as well.

And Julia was most likely prepared to pounce on Andrew at any moment.

It was a truth universally acknowledged by those who were well acquainted with Julia West that her designer cocktail dresses and matching Manolos were the actress's armor, and she was perpetually prepared for war.

Cassandra straightened her shoulders under her mother's scrutiny, then casually sipped her delicious yet potent lemon drop martini, savoring its sweetness. "Yes, I succumbed to Andrew's charms. Who wouldn't?"

Now it was she who was playing up their connection. *Big-time.* It was easier to act the part of his smitten girlfriend when in front of her mother than admit to their secret. Perhaps because it so vexed Julia or perhaps because Julia couldn't be entrusted with the truth. She'd sell her daughter out in a New York minute if it meant that Julia would once again be in the spotlight.

"I didn't believe it when I'd read that you left poor Jeremy at the altar. Now I see I was wrong." Julia's words were enunciated with a bite that wounded Cassandra to her core. "Oh, and Cassandra, dear. Didn't I ever teach you that blonds can't wear red? It clashes with your hair, darling."

Lovely.

This was Cassandra's mother. The woman she knew all too well.

An overwhelming sadness threatened to overtake Cassandra, but she silently pushed it to the side. Instead, she concentrated on her anger. Rage was a powerful motivator, and Cassandra was determined to have her say as far as her mother was concerned.

"And here I thought you might not have heard about my non-wedding." Cassandra placed her empty martini glass on a passing waiter's tray before meeting her mother's stare. "You didn't call me. Did you wonder, even once, if I was all right?"

"Clearly you didn't need me to. You were with *him*." Her mother tossed a nod in Andrew's direction.

Julia was right. Cassandra didn't need her mother. She might have *wanted* her mother, though there was a huge difference between need and want. One that Cassandra hadn't allowed herself to feel until that very moment.

While she'd once been in denial when it came to her mother's priorities, Cassandra could say with certainty that she'd outgrown that stage and had learned at a very young age not to count on her mother for anything. Sadly, Cassandra had been proven correct when her father had died. That's when she'd learned that Julia didn't have a maternal bone in her body. It was easy for Julia to make her daughter feel small, and comments like the one Julia had just made about the color red came as no surprise for Cassandra.

All it took was auditioning in a grade school musical for Cassandra to understand that her mother wasn't and never would be supportive or encouraging. It was her mother, after all, who told Cassandra not to audition because, in the actress's expert opinion, Cassandra wasn't good enough to get the part.

Of course, her mother had been right and when Cassandra didn't get it, she had been met with an "I told you so" from Julia. Though it hurt at the time, it taught Cassandra what to expect from her mother.

Not a thing.

Which served Cassandra well. She lived with her dad full-time by the time she turned ten, and she had loved living with him. Because Julia was such an absentee parent, it hadn't upended Cassandra's life at all, because Julia was never around.

When Cassandra's father died in her sophomore year of high school, Julia didn't help her daughter grieve or cope with her loss. Instead, when Julia showed up for the funeral, she only did so to use it to her advantage and sell out her daughter.

If Cassandra could survive that tragic part of her life without her mother, she would survive the end of her relationship with Jeremy. There was no question about it, though, Cassandra had had one weak moment the night before. She'd actually checked her voicemail in between calls to her credit card companies and honeymoon hotel to see if her mother had tried to reach her. But Julia hadn't tried to communicate with her daughter.

Not even once.

That was all Cassandra needed to know to snap herself out of thinking, or hoping as the case might have been, that her mother was capable of caring about her only child.

"It was lovely seeing you, Mother. And thanks for the advice, but I like wearing red." Cassandra's mother barely acknowledged her.

She turned to leave, and Andrew added, "Let's have dinner soon. Is your husband in town?"

Anger rose to a crescendo within Cassandra, and she shot Andrew a warning glance. He ignored her, returning his attention to Julia.

"Soon. Luc returns to Manhattan next week. I suppose we can do dinner. He loves going head-to-head with you. It's good sport for him."

Do dinner.

Julia was the quintessential Hollywood snob. What would she say next?

"I'll have my assistant call you, Cassandra."

Plastering a sarcastic smile on her face, Cassandra countered with, "I suppose that's better than 'I'll have my people call your people.'"

"You're too funny, darling." Julia excused herself after one final bout of laughter.

Good to know that Cassandra amused her mother. *Not.*

In hindsight, Cassandra should have left her mother to fend for herself, she thought as she watched Julia work the room. It was a thing of wonder, second only to watching Andrew do so. He ruled the room and commanded everyone's attention. Sexy, confident, and wittier than Cassandra remembered, Andrew made it look effortless.

The man Cassandra once knew was gone and in his place was someone self-assured, who was the envy of almost every man in the room and the desire of many a female. Andrew seemed to play off that desire by stoking it every time he possessively held Cassie's hand or casually stroked her arm.

What was his endgame? More attention for The Steele Dailies? A boost in followers? Offering subscription-based content? Her mind raced with the possibilities, none of which had been confirmed by Andrew.

He had confided that their fake relationship would be mutually beneficial, but never explained how, despite her all but interrogating him. Based upon how well his suitor act was playing out, and from the reaction of those in the room watching them, Cassandra was beginning to make assumptions.

Their fake relationship would have to end eventually. Was Andrew hoping that this stunt would propel him into prime bachelor status? If that was his motive, and based upon the interest in him tonight, it looked like Andrew's plan was working.

This isn't the same man I once knew.

No, this Andrew wasn't an outcast or an outsider. This Andrew didn't fit in, either. Instead, he led the way. He was prominent and revered, from the looks of the enthralled celebrities hooked on his every word. Andrew had accomplished what he always wanted to. He had accumulated wealth, power, and even his own celebrity status by flipping the tables on those who once thought him beneath them.

It came at Cassandra's expense.

She sure knew how to pick them. First Andrew, then Jeremy. Now Andrew again, even if their relationship was fake. Each of her exes rejected her for wealth and influence. So why did Cassandra resent Andrew so much more than Jeremy at this very moment?

Why am I more upset by Andrew's betrayal than Jeremy's?

Because she still wanted Andrew. Darn her, she knew it to be true. With his sensual whispers and charismatic personality, Andrew ignited her desire like no other man ever had. He also got on her nerves like no other, and that included her ex-fiancé.

She and Andrew could have been good together. Scratch that—she and Andrew would have been incredible together. But they'd never know just how much so because he chose *this* life over a life with her.

Andrew had robbed them both of infinite possibilities and Cassandra would never forgive him for it. Nor would she forgive herself for falling for his humble act that he wore when they were alone. No, this wasn't the same Andrew she once knew.

She must remind herself of that.

And she must never fall for his act again.

Chapter 8

ANDREW USED THE DOG AS AN EXCUSE TO ESCAPE HIS PENTHOUSE. IT would have been comical if it weren't true, but there he was, walking the beagle. Or was the beagle walking him?

Andrew glanced at the dog leading him by the leash. Yeah. The dog was definitely walking him. But at least he'd gotten out of his penthouse. Cassie had a tendency to talk loudly on the phone, sing when she fed her dog lunch, and was an all-around pain in his—

Honk!

It wasn't a car horn. It sounded like a goose. But it wasn't. He searched his surroundings to see where the noise was coming from.

Honk. Honk!

There it was again. Andrew looked down at Bailey, whose neck was outstretched and who let out the earth-shattering honking sound again. Andrew ran to him, thinking maybe the canine had tugged on his leash too hard, or that his collar was too tight. But loosening the dog's collar didn't help. The poor thing just kept honking.

Andrew looked around, but couldn't see anyone to help, nor could he see a sign for a vet close by. And there was no cab in sight. When the dog honked yet again, he scooped Bailey up and began to sprint the five blocks back to his penthouse.

The whole jog there, all he could think about was that he had just broken Cassie's dog. Her beloved Bailey.

Honk.

"It's okay, Bailey." Even he wasn't convinced by the sound of his own voice.

I broke her dog.

Oh my God. I killed her dog.

Andrew ran faster, aware that he'd already broken into a sweat. Today of all days, he took his walk in his suit and tie, while wearing his new leather oxfords. Now, with the honking, he was lugging a twenty-plus-pound beagle-non-beagle. If he'd been wearing his sneakers, this run would have gone much faster, not to mention easier. He tripped, scuffing his shoe.

What did that matter in the grand scheme of things?

He broke Cassie's dog.

She'd never forgive him.

He'd never forgive himself.

By the time he'd reached his building, Andrew was soaking wet, out of breath, and so frantic that he ignored his doorman completely. At the dog's honk, the doorman backed away with eyes wide and a look of horror on his face.

The elevator took forever, but he couldn't run up twenty flights of stairs. Sure, he was fit and worked out, but that last block all but killed him, probably because the dog was solid and getting heavier and hotter with each passing minute. Seriously, his run had made him feel like he'd been carrying a furry, dog-shaped pile of cement blocks that had been baking in the hot sun for hours.

Honk.

"It's okay, Bailey. I'm taking you to Mom." Andrew rocked the canine, trying to comfort him, but the honking was only getting worse. Somehow the dog seemed to be getting heavier still.

Would this torture ever end?

By the time the elevator dinged, sweat was pouring down Andrew's face. He got into the elevator and pressed his floor's button in time to see another resident of the building step inside. The older, gray-haired woman took one look at Andrew and retreated to the safety of the lobby.

He must have looked terrible to garner such a reaction, but he didn't care. All that mattered was getting Bailey to Cassie. At least she'd be able to say goodbye. At least she'd have closure. Andrew could and would give her that much.

He began to pant. Or maybe he'd only just noticed he was doing it. *Oh dear Lord, no.* He was hyperventilating. There wasn't enough air in this elevator, in this small cube thousands of feet in the air—

This must be what a panic attack is like.

Honk. Honk. Cough. Honk.

It was getting worse… Bailey was getting worse.

"It's all right. We're almost there, Bailey." By the time the bell dinged announcing his floor, Andrew breathed a jagged sigh of relief.

The doors opened and he ran inside his penthouse. "Cassie! Come quick!"

Honk. Honk.

Shit! "Cassie, I've broken Bailey. He needs you." Andrew rounded the kitchen and hurried down the hall, only to bump into Cassie.

"What's wrong? You look awful." Her eyes were wide.

He didn't even have a sarcastic or witty comeback. "I broke him. He keeps honking."

"It's okay." She bent down to gently stroke Bailey's neck and chin. "Relax, Bailey. You'll be fine."

The dog didn't honk. Andrew counted the seconds, while the dog breathed normally, with no annoying honking sound whatsoever.

"What the…" What sort of sorcery had Andrew just witnessed?

The duration of his run back to his apartment had seemed to take forever, and Bailey honked through the whole entire thing. Yet here he was, ceasing the terrifying honking in record time.

Andrew stared at the dog that he hadn't broken after all. Waiting for a sign, a thank-you, something…but none came, much to his disappointment.

Wordlessly, Cassie took Bailey from Andrew and walked into the kitchen. "Let me get you some water."

"Thanks," Andrew managed, though his voice was raspy, and he was still panting as he followed her to his kitchen island.

"I meant Bailey," Cassie shot back as she poured water into Bailey's bowl and placed it on the kitchen floor. Once the dog was lapping up water, only then did Cassie look at Andrew. "You really do look awful. Did you do laps with my dog?"

Rage, unfiltered rage, coursed through his veins. "I ran what felt like ten blocks in these shoes, which are ruined by the way, to get your dog back to you because I thought I had broken him. I thought he was going to die."

Andrew shrugged out of his jacket and tossed it onto his countertop, then untucked his button-down linen shirt, which was so wet that it was sticking to him. "What the hell was all that honking? Why aren't you worried? Did Bailey prank me?"

While Andrew knew dogs were incapable of pranking grown adults, he wouldn't put anything past that pain in the—

With her pointer finger in the air in one of those *hold that thought* motions, Cassie said, "Let me get you some ice water."

"How about getting me an explanation while you're at it." Though he was talking back and acting irrationally, at this moment in time, Andrew couldn't stop himself. Somewhere between the dog's first honk and its last, Andrew's limit had been reached and he was ready to blow.

By the time Cassie presented Andrew with a glass of flat water with ice cubes, his breathing had returned to normal. He was hot, sticky, and needed a shower STAT. "I need answers. Better yet, I deserve answers."

Cassie nodded. "Yes, you do. What happened wasn't a prank. It's called a reverse sneeze—"

"A what now?" He did a double take.

"A reverse sneeze." Cassie spoke slowly, as if she were talking to a child.

Andrew scoffed. "Now *you're* pranking me."

"Nope. I'm not pranking you either, I swear. Google it if you'd like, but I'm telling you the truth. It's a real thing." She sat at a bar stool at his kitchen island. "It's caused by allergens, among other things. It occurs when a dog has a long snout, like Bailey does. I was terrified the first time I heard it, too, and rushed him to the vet."

"You've got to be kidding me." Andrew slumped onto the stool beside hers. "He was sneezing?"

"His throat was contracting, but long story short, yes—kind of." Cassie slid his glass of water closer to him, the condensation leaving a watery streak on the beige veins of the ivory Italian marble countertop. "Did you really run to get him here?"

"Look at me. What do you think?" He ran his fingers through his wet hair, then gulped down about half of his glass of ice water.

Cassie reached out and smoothed his brow, seeming to do it unconsciously, which, strangely enough, made him feel better.

"I think it was very sweet of you to get Bailey home like that. How about I buy you a new suit, or replace the shoes, or both? You deserve both and then some for your heroics today." She offered him a reassuring grin.

Andrew shook his head. "That's not why I did it. I just wanted you to see him one last time. I seriously—I thought—I thought I killed him." His eyes got misty.

Was he about to cry? Andrew never cried. What was happening to him?

"Oh, Andrew." Cassie placed her hand on his shoulder. "I'm sorry."

Was Andrew truly attached to this beagle with a long snout who didn't even belong to him? Or was he attached to Cassie, who was a pain in his—

Bailey barked, and Andrew looked down to see the dog sitting beside his barstool staring at him. "Hey. What's up?"

The canine raised his paw and scratched Andrew's pant leg.

"He wants you to hold him." Cassie stood, scooped up her dog, and handed him to Andrew.

In turn, Bailey licked Andrew's chin and cheek.

"Well, that's a 'thank you' if I ever saw one." Cassie's tone was sweet. "Thank you, Andrew. If Bailey were ever in trouble, I'd want you by his side if I couldn't be."

High praise, Andrew supposed, from a woman who didn't seem to like him very much.

He handed the pup back to Cassie. "I need a shower. I have a video meeting soon."

"Give me your clothes. I'll send them to the cleaners." She stopped midstep. "And your shoes. I insist on buying you a new pair."

Andrew nodded.

"Hey." Cassie came up behind him and tapped him on the shoulder. When he turned, she kissed him on the cheek. Andrew's hand immediately touched the spot on his cheek where her lips had made contact, his eyes wide.

"Thanks again." She walked down the hall and into her suite, shutting the door behind her while Andrew stood in place, his palm still resting on his cheek, where Cassandra kissed him.

What was this he was feeling? And why? Cassie couldn't stand him, and the feeling was mutual, as far as he was concerned.

Cassandra. Benedict. Drove. Him. Mad.

As did her little dog.

Woah! Who was Andrew turning into? The villain in *The Wizard of Oz*? Besides, Andrew really couldn't fault the dog. It wasn't Bailey's fault that he was born with a large snout. Or that he suffers from…from what now?

A reverse sneeze?

He'd have to google that. But first, Andrew hopped in the shower with one goal in mind: to wash off the effect that Cassie had on him.

Though it might sound easy, it was anything but.

Chapter 9

Just when a newfound sense of *I've got Andrew's number* had swept over Cassandra, Andrew ended up running countless blocks, ruining his expensive leather shoes, and enhancing his designer suit with sweat stains for the sole purpose of saving her dog from what he thought was a case of *Andrew Steele Broke Me* disorder.

And with that, she'd returned to square one. Or worse, because how could she be angry at a man who ran who knows how many blocks to save the life of her precious dog? Worse yet, how could she *not* trust such a man?

Of all the times to be battered with guilt and enraged that Andrew had inadvertently made her feel guilty, today wasn't ideal. Cassandra was currently weathering the onslaught of back-to-back events while being seated beside Andrew in his Escalade, on their way to Mallard's Landing Vineyards in Water Mill.

They were about to attend yet another swanky celebrity function this afternoon, complete with live music, dancing, a wine tasting, and selfie stations, because what respectable celebrity-slash-influencer function *wouldn't* include selfie stations? Not this one. Andrew made certain that Cassandra knew what to expect prior to burying himself in his cell.

To say that he was a workaholic would be an understatement. But then again, so was Cassandra. Usually. She'd taken some time off after her failed wedding, but that was because she'd already blocked that time on her calendar and didn't want to inconvenience anyone. Also, that time off allowed her to lick her wounds and perfect this act with Andrew. Little did she know at the time they hatched this agreement that the pretense of their fake relationship would be difficult to pull off.

Blame it on his ability to annoy her like no other and the fact that he always seemed to be in close proximity to her. Whether it be via video meetings, talking to sources, not to mention his business partner, and recording his YouTube updates for his fans, the man talked incessantly. She could hear him even when she was in her room with the door closed. Cassandra suspected that Andrew was louder than Bailey, which was a feat in and of itself.

Then there was the fact that living with him, and faux dating him, was dredging up feelings she'd long since thought were dormant. Their relationship ended when he broke up with her. It was a fact, and she'd moved on quickly. Another fact.

So, why then was she now incapable of *not* thinking about Andrew, about the way he used to be versus now, and about their relationship… the good, the bad, and the ugly? Looking at it through the lens of a jilted bride, their breakup—Andrew and Cassie's—now seemed more difficult to understand and more heartbreaking than she had ever thought possible.

Revisiting past heartache only made her present heartache worse. Which is why she had instructed her assistant to begin booking appointments again. It was past time she returned to work with a new life, and a brand-new (if not completely positive) attitude about said new life. If she envisioned it, the rest would come. Or so Cassandra had hoped.

Today, she was wearing another of her new acquisitions from her post-breakup shopping spree: a fuchsia halter dress with cream and white lilies of the valley imprinted on the soft silk charmeuse fabric. It was sexy yet classy and, when paired with her strappy heels, the ankle-length flowing maxi dress would look quite romantic against the winery backdrop and any influencer stations that she would undoubtedly come across.

At some point during her shopping excursion, Cassandra decided to step out of her comfort zone and buy dresses that she loved and that made her feel confident. Prior to her wedding-non-wedding fiasco, Cassandra had chosen looks in neutral colors. As a wedding planner, she never wanted to outshine her bride-to-be or look more glamorous than the bride. Especially when she was meeting with them for the first time or during the rehearsal. And certainly, never on the wedding day. That's why when it came to fashion, her motto had always been *tasteful but muted.*

But something had shifted within her since what she would forever refer to as her non-wedding fiasco. Cassandra had realized that she no longer wanted to set her personality on mute, especially while being illuminated under the glaring pop culture spotlight with Andrew. No, she wanted to express herself. And if that meant wearing outfits that helped her stand out, then so be it. It was the price she was more than willing to pay to be herself.

It had taken most of her adult life, but Cassandra had finally come to the realization that she would never please everyone and didn't really want to try anymore. Hence, her new clothes and black dip nail polish. It was called Cityscape and featured a glittery effect that made it prismatic in the sun. In other words, it looked different in various lights.

There was some irony there that Cassandra could silently chuckle at while being dissected by the influential New Yorkers that she and Andrew were supposed to be convincing. After all, Cassandra herself was more than what met the eye, why shouldn't her nail polish be representative of that?

As for Andrew, he didn't seem to notice her dress, or her hair for that matter. He'd been glued to his phone during their entire chauffeured trip to the Hamptons. It hadn't fazed her because she was too busy dreading their route. They'd taken the Long Island Expressway to Exit 70, then traveled east to Sunrise Highway. After that, they passed

Exit 63—Westhampton Beach. The scene of her wedding massacre. *Game of Thrones'* Red Wedding had nothing on the heartbreak that occurred at the Roth estate in Westhampton Beach, though the fictional Starks might beg to differ.

By the time they arrived at the vineyard, Cassandra was a bundle of nerves. It didn't help that all eyes were indeed on them, and that since the photos of their kiss went viral, their fake relationship had shot to infamy status overnight.

Andrew, exuding his usual confidence, stepped out of the car first, then offered her his hand. His stance was proud and strong, and his hand was warm and possessive. *Same new Andrew, different day.* He was nothing if not consistent now.

At least she could count on that.

Waiting at the end of the red carpet were photographers and a backdrop with fresh flowers. Embedded in the floral wall were a plethora of cream- and white-colored roses and greenery, along with a pink neon sign in a fancy font with the winery's name illuminated. It was here that she and Andrew stopped and posed for photos.

This was their routine, and what their fans had come to expect. Based upon the *#AndCass* that had been trending in the comments on both her social media feeds and Andrew's since their kiss was first published, this was what everyone short of a few anonymous internet trolls wanted. Lather, rinse, and repeat. It was what Cassandra signed up for and if it saved her business, that's all she cared about.

His hand slid to the curve of her back as a photographer asked them for another kiss.

"What would you like to do?" Andrew whispered in her ear.

So, he wanted to kiss her again. It must be good for business, she thought, and immediately wondered if the question had once again come from one of Andrew's photographers.

"Sure," she grinned, trying to look as seductive as she could for the prying eyes.

Something happened when Andrew leaned into her, something that made her forget about everything but kissing him. His eyes deepened with an intensity that was undeniable. Then slowly but deliberately, his lips claimed hers. His tongue probed for entrance, coaxing them to part. She obliged, making a concerted effort to ignore the rush of longing surging through her veins as his tongue stroked hers.

Achingly slow and tender, his kiss offered her a promise of more.

That promise became more pronounced with every caress of his tongue, and with the warmth of his hand, which was flattened against her back. A breathless moan escaped him that was audible only to her. With that one reaction, Cassandra was certain that he was feeling the same strong connection that she was.

She was so certain that she returned his passion tenfold.

Andrew's grip tightened around her waist, and he bent her backward, his lips still touching hers in what she was certain was one hell of a rom-com-esque photo. It was a classic wedding pose she'd seen many a time from her couples. Heck, she'd directed her couples to pose just this way.

She was certain that the flowing fabric of her ankle-length maxi dress would complement this pose to perfection. Andrew must have sensed the same thing. With that realization, her heart sank like an anchor, weighted down with the cold, hard truth: Andrew set this kiss, this pose, up…for his photographer, who was undoubtedly in attendance. This was every bit a staged photo op and Cassandra had willingly walked into his setup.

Willingly and eagerly.

Andrew pulled back and whispered, "You did amazing. Great choice with the dress. I have a feeling we're going to go viral again."

How could she have been so gullible? Again?

Andrew was so convincing that Cassandra believed him to be sincere. With that knowledge came another realization: he wasn't interested in her, just another story that would lead to increased traffic to his site and an increase in his social media followers. That traffic, in turn, would provide him with even more clout. It was obvious to her now. Just as it was crystal clear that she had fallen for it again, despite her avowals to the contrary.

What was the saying?

Fool me once, shame on you. Fool me twice, shame on me.

Shame burned hot on her cheeks. Cassandra was certain they were a brilliant shade of crimson as she extracted herself from Andrew's warm embrace. This man had been quite convincing.

*Fool her once…*He'd done just that.

*Fool her twice…*Yep, she'd let him do that, too.

"Well played," she spoke succinctly, then turned on her heel and led them to the patio where live music was already playing. She hadn't noticed the music before while she was enthralled by Andrew's all-consuming kiss.

"What's going on?" Confusion clouded his features. It wasn't a good look for him, and she didn't buy it for one second.

A waiter offered her a glass of chardonnay from his tray, and she gladly accepted it. She was more than eager to lose herself in a dry chardonnay or two while Andrew studied her intently. Averting her eyes, she plastered a grin on her face and watched as the other couples in attendance danced to a cover band singing "Just the Way You Are." It was one of her favorite songs.

"Dance with me." Andrew placed her glass of wine on the table behind them. "You love this song."

How did he remember? And why did she care that he remembered? Because this had been their song…the song that was playing when he first kissed her, and Cassandra couldn't help but wonder if Andrew remembered that fact in particular.

Probably not.

This was all for show, after all. She must remember. And she did. Of course she did. Just like she remembered that Andrew hated to dance. Yet here he was, with his hand around her waist, holding his own on the dance floor.

"What happened earlier?" he asked in a husky whisper.

It was her turn to play dumb. After plastering on a smile, she shrugged. "Nothing happened. It was all an act, as it should be, right?"

Her question lingered along the warm breeze as he pulled her closer against his length. "Was it?"

His intense, unswerving stare unnerved her, causing her to stumble, but Andrew held her tight, keeping her from falling. "That's right. I'm asking you if that's all it was—an act?"

"What else would it be?" Her voice quivered, as did her hand within his.

This man was unnerving her, which irritated her to no end.

"Something more," he countered as the singer, who was not Billy Joel, sang Billy's lyrics: "You always have my unspoken passion, though I might not seem to care."

Fitting, since Andrew didn't seem to care about Cassie. What he truly cared about was how they appeared to the outside world.

"Whenever I hear this song, I can't help but think about us," he murmured in her ear as they swayed to the live sax.

"You are such a liar. You always hated Billy Joel." Andrew hummed with the music, as she added, "I remember that fact just like I remember that you hated to dance. In fact, you flat out refused to dance with me back when we were dating."

Andrew shook his head. "You're wrong on both counts. I loved Billy's music, though some of it hit a little too close to home. And I didn't dance because I didn't know how."

"Well, you certainly know how to dance now—"

"I learned. For you." Andrew sucked in his breath and held it. Like he'd just imparted some big secret to her.

"You what?" Had she heard him correctly?

"Let's just dance—"

"Nope. You're not changing the subject. I won't let you this time." Though he spun her around, she ended up right in front of him, leaning against him as they swayed in sync to the saxophone player's solo. "When did you learn to dance? And why?"

"After we broke up. I figured if I ever saw you again, I could finally give you that dance you always nagged me about." Andrew shrugged, like what he'd said wasn't a big deal. Like he hadn't just made a mockery of what she thought was an actual moment between them on the dance floor.

His sarcasm sliced through her, because she once would have been desperate to hear such an admission from him. And because this had been *their* song once upon a time. Even though he'd claimed to hate Billy Joel's music, they shared their first kiss to *this* song. And it was now obvious that he didn't remember that. No, she'd meant nothing to him then, and even less to him now.

Was this man even capable of a sincere thought, let alone an actual moment of real substance? Or was he just not capable of it with *her*? Cassandra's conscience told her it was the latter, which caused even more inner turmoil to coil within her abdomen.

"You are such a jerk, for lack of a better word." She stopped in the middle of the dance floor and pulled out of his reach. Studying his eyes, she noted shock—he was probably dumbstruck that she'd called him out.

Good!

"Your answer to my question was sarcastic and insensitive. And cruel. For once you could have answered me honestly. But you didn't. Per usual." Though she turned to leave, she caught herself and swung back around to face him once more. "I'm taking the car back to the penthouse. Get your own ride home."

She strutted off the dance floor, aware that she was making a scene. The news flash for the day was that the Cassandra portion of *#AndCass* no longer cared.

Andrew deserved it. Besides, knowing him, he'd spin an even better narrative in his own favor. She proceeded to their Escalade and climbed inside, startling the driver. "Back to the penthouse, please."

He studied her with wide eyes. "Where is Mr. Steele?"

"He isn't here. I am. Please drive." The man looked uncomfortable until Andrew climbed into the back seat with her.

"Going somewhere?" More sarcasm.

What a surprise.

Apparently, the man couldn't function without exhibiting some form of sarcasm.

Cassandra turned away from him, choosing instead to study the lush vineyards outside her window.

"Hi. Hey, Cassie. Quick question," Andrew turned her face toward him, his thumb resting against her chin. "Why am I the only person trying to make this work?"

"*You?* You are *the only person* trying to make this work? Is that really what you think?" Cassie leaned back against her seat, returning her attention to him while meeting his anger with her own unfiltered rage. "What I think, what I see is that every time I give you a chance, every time I fall for your nice guy act, I'm reminded that you're a selfish, self-centered egotist."

"I'm not an egotist. I'll have you know that confidence is very important to success." Andrew was animated, using his hands to express himself.

At least she'd finally gotten him to drop his smooth operator facade.

Cassandra pulled her cell from her clutch and googled *egotist*. "And I quote: 'An egotist is self-centered and excessively conceited or absorbed in oneself. He's selfish, egotistical, and arrogant.' That sounds about right. How about lacking in empathy?" She typed a few different traits. "There's got to be another word for it. Wait…narcissist? No, that's not right. You're not a narcissist."

"I'm not a narcissist—"

"I just said you're not a narcissist. Are you even listening to me?" She turned to him, noting that he was tapping his fingers against his leg. She was clearly annoying him.

Serves him right.

"Well, that was disappointing. I thought I might be on to something there with that search." She sighed, realizing she watched too much reality television.

"I'm sorry to disappoint you." Andrew rolled his eyes.

"Don't you dare roll your eyes at me. We were dancing to our song, after all, and you shrugged off my very personal question." Cassandra wouldn't relent, no matter how much he seemed to want her to.

"Okay, I get it. I'm insensitive. Really, truly insensitive." This time he typed in the word *narcissist*. Cassie could read his phone screen. He then held up two fingers. "If it makes you feel any better, by my count, I might possess two of the traits you described, but not all nine of them. I'm in no way a narcissist. Sorry to disappoint you."

"That's what you gleaned from our conversation? That I want you to be a narcissist?" She inhaled, then exhaled, trying to control her rage.

"Let's go to the restaurant, Kyle," Andrew instructed their driver, then settled into the back seat.

"Restaurant? What restaurant?" Cassie glared at Andrew, waiting for his big reveal.

"My dad's restaurant in Sag Harbor. I can't come to Water Mill and not head just a little farther east to see my dad." He glanced at his phone, but Cassie blocked his screen with her hand.

"You front-loaded me with information about selfie stations and failed to tell me that I'm about to meet your father?"

The only response she received was a curt nod.

This. Man. Is. Insufferable.

Only after a long, heady silence as they were driving east on Montauk Highway did Andrew turn to Cassie at last. "Just to set the record straight, I knew that 'Just the Way You Are' was our song. I just didn't think you'd remember. You were the only one of us who got serious with someone else not long after we broke up, you know."

Was he trying to shame her?

"What did you think would happen when you broke up with me? Did you think that I wouldn't move on? Or maybe you thought I'd pine for you." Cassie studied his profile and noted that his jaw was clenched so tightly that a vein was pulsating in his neck. "You left me, remember?"

"Yeah, I do remember, but I thought that's what you wanted. You had made it quite clear that you didn't approve of my decision to go into business with Noah. That you loathed my profession and my business decisions."

"I—I didn't approve of your business because I thought that you were better than that." Why was she forever lobbing these truth bombs at him when they never seemed to hit their mark?

Andrew met her stare with his own. Dark and brooding, his intense glare scrutinized her, as if he was searching into the depths of her soul. "We have a lot of issues to work through." He turned to look out his window, rubbing his chin as though he was deep in thought. "Can a fake couple go to therapy? Because I really think we might need it."

Cassie scoffed. "Another joke?"

He turned to face her once again. "Nope, I'm quite serious. Cassie, we have issues." His scowl left deep lines indented in his features.

"What we have is baggage. A lot of baggage." She leaned against the leather seat and stared at the scenery through her window again, though the sunny landscape and greenery passed in a blur.

What had she gotten herself into? This fake relationship was becoming more complicated than any real relationship she'd ever been in. With one exception: her relationship with her mother. And that was saying a heck of a lot. The only difference was that Andrew infuriated her far more than her mother ever did.

Why is that?

Because she still cared about him? Possibly. Or was it that she still thought Andrew was capable of more?

The painful ache in Cassandra's chest confirmed that was indeed the case. Despite her anger, she still believed in Andrew; therefore, he possessed the power to let her down. Repeatedly, it seemed.

Perhaps they did need counseling. Or perhaps she never should have agreed to this arrangement. Cassandra never thought her feelings for Andrew would be unearthed after so much time had passed, let alone be so volatile. Where did that volatility come from?

It came from the fact that the paparazzi were relentless and not always the most ethical people Cassandra had ever encountered. And Andrew was now firmly entrenched in that world.

For the sake of her peace of mind, her career, and her future, she was left with no other option but to see this farce through knowing full well that's what it was—an act.

Seriously, though, why would Andrew bring her to meet his father? She'd never met his dad, not even when they were actually dating.

Cassandra's pulse pounded against her temples, as her cell pinged with an alert.

"Are you reading what I am?" One of Andrew's competitors had published a picture of them kissing in the bride/groom pose at the winery. It was an epic photo—*the money shot* as they call it in the wedding business.

"'Fiery passion: a kiss and an argument. The tale of the Wedding Planner and the bad boy Mogul gets hotter.'" Andrew quoted the same headline Cassandra was reading. "They ate that stunt up. We should argue in public more often."

And with one headline, her very real feelings—their very real argument—were likened to a publicity *stunt* by the one man who should have known better. Rage boiled beneath the surface, stewing during their ride to his father's place. Silent, but aggravatingly stubborn, it festered throughout their ride, even when Cassandra insisted they stop at a farm stand for a gift for his father.

By the time they got back into the Escalade and headed toward Andrew's family business, Cassandra had made a decision. After today, she was done playing Andrew's game. If the public loved that winery tantrum of hers, then they'd get more of them.

Plural.

So would Andrew.

Being real had gotten her nowhere. It was time to beat Andrew, Jeremy, and the rest of them at their own game. Cassandra had learned the art of being a diva by one the biggest divas who ever lived—her mother. She'd use that to her advantage.

Why conform, when one can stand out instead?

The quote came from page one hundred and forty-two of Julia West's autobiography. Little did Julia know that her daughter had been paying attention. And was about to practice all she had learned.

For once in her life, Cassandra had found herself in the spotlight.

It was about time she enjoyed it.

Chapter 10

ANDREW HADN'T SEEN HIS FATHER IN A FEW MONTHS. HE WAS supposed to head home after Cassie's wedding ceremony, but things didn't turn out as planned and he wound up taking her and Bailey to his place instead.

Since Cassie insisted on stopping at a local farm stand first, they arrived bearing gifts: assorted jams and a blueberry pie. In record time, she'd arranged their offerings in a basket and made it look like a presentation befitting Martha Stewart herself, with fresh-cut sunflowers and something called raffia.

Andrew hadn't a clue what raffia was prior to their farm stand jaunt, but Cassie had made him a believer in its decorative powers in record time. She was truly a force to be reckoned with, and he'd bet that her lifestyle blog would take off to the moon if she devoted more time to marketing it. It was a topic he'd broach later. Not now.

Their Escalade pulled up during the afternoon rush and their driver, Kyle, temporarily parked at the steps leading to the restaurant's deck to let them out.

After handing Andrew the basket, which was surprisingly heavy, Cassie leaned forward and tapped Kyle on the shoulder. "Please, park and have dinner here, on us."

"That's okay, ma'am." Kyle was formal. Andrew wondered if Cassie made him nervous, too.

"I insist. I snapped at you earlier. It's the least I can do as an apology."

With one of her smiles that makes the world seem brighter, Cassie managed to convince Kyle to have dinner at Steele Harbor.

Upon exiting the vehicle, Andrew stood in front of his family's restaurant, viewing it with weary eyes. Every imperfection was glaring. Like the logo, once emblazoned with bright colors on a sign that was now faded, with chipped paint that his dad refused to update because Andrew's grandfather had crafted it himself. Then there were its lopsided shutters from each storm that battered the building. And its creaky entrance door. All these flaws were on full display for Cassie to witness.

He felt vulnerable.

Too vulnerable.

"This is it, huh?" Cassie took the basket from him and peered around the structure, setting her sights on the bay view. "It's gorgeous."

The structure itself was anything but. The bay view, however, was breathtaking.

Nestled near a dock, with bayfront views, the Steele family restaurant was under third-generation ownership. Andrew's great-grandfather had owned it, followed by his grandfather, and now his own dad. Someday, it would pass to Andrew, just not yet. He didn't want it to. Truth be told, Andrew didn't want to run the place, but he wouldn't let it go, either.

It had been Andrew's home away from home for most of his life. He'd done his homework here, he'd bussed tables here, and he'd even waited tables here. He also did most of his people watching at Steele Harbor. It's where he first witnessed the discrepancies between the haves and have-nots.

Unlike the restaurant at the yacht club, Steele Harbor was a far cry from fine dining. Even with Andrew's infusion of cash, his dad wanted to keep what made the place unique—its ability to make the real people, the little guys and gals, feel comfortable. Which meant keeping the rustic, weathered look, the old, peeling sign, and the lopsided shutters.

What Steele Harbor was, what it always would be, was a hole in the wall where you could get great-tasting burgers, thick-cut fries, drinks, and most importantly, draft beer. It was cheap, which helped keep its customers—like the fishermen who caught the locals' catches—coming back for more.

It had been a money pit when Andrew was growing up. Yeah, he learned the value of a dollar at the joint. He also learned what he wanted—more specifically, he learned *who* he wanted to be, and it was *more*. He'd always wanted to do more, be more, than the family business would allow. And he'd wanted to ensure that his father had more, too. The only way had been to make more. Fortunately, Andrew created his own business, which earned more than enough for him to make good on his promise to help his dad.

The moment when Andrew was finally able to cover the restaurant repairs and interior upgrades on his own was one of the proudest moments of his life. His dad was proud, too. So proud of his son that he made Andrew a partner.

Andrew had written his dad a blank check. The place was his, regardless of whether or not Andrew was a partner. So, his dad bought state-of-the-art kitchen equipment, and with the man's approval, Andrew bought a brand-new jukebox. They splurged on new tables, booths, and chairs. And they splurged on a cleaning company because Andrew insisted his dad have help. He also made sure to keep more staff on their payroll so his dad could take it easy and hang with his friends and customers. It was good for the man's health. As it turns out, it was also good for business, which had increased by forty percent. The rest of the restaurant, and its natural, down-to-earth aesthetic, was left the same per his dad's request.

The place was on pilings, because Long Island, especially the Hamptons, got a lot of hurricanes, nor'easters, and other storms. It helped to have a joint that was above flood level. Andrew helped guide

Cassie up the ramp and a flight of stairs, then opened the restaurant door for her.

"Andrew. My man!" his dad called from the bar. "You're early! Look, everybody. It's my son."

Stephen Steele couldn't have sounded prouder if he tried.

"Hey, Dad." Andrew weaved between the crowded tables to give his dad a hug. "I've missed you."

"Me too, son. Who's this?" His dad smiled at Cassie.

"Dad, this is Cassandra Benedict—"

"You can call me Cassie." She handed Stephen the basket with a warm smile and an ease that immediately calmed Andrew's frayed nerves. "It's nice to meet you, Mr. Steele."

His father carried the basket over to an empty table. "This is heavy. Thanks for this. I only wish we'd met sooner. Andrew never introduced us when you were dating in college."

The realization cut Andrew through to his core. Why hadn't he introduced Cassie to his dad? Was he ashamed of where he'd come from? Or did he think Cassie would have judged him based on the dump his family owned?

At the time, it was probably a bit of both. It had been pre-renovations, after all. Although, knowing the kind of person Cassie was, both then and now, she wouldn't have judged him. The realization caused his pulse to hammer against Andrew's temples. Three generations of Steeles had worked tirelessly for this place, to keep it afloat. That was nothing for him to be ashamed of.

"The introductions were a long time coming. I'm sorry about that." It was all he could offer as his voice cracked. He cleared his throat, hoping Cassie wouldn't notice the surge of emotion emanating from his every pore.

"Better late than never. You've got a great place here, Mr. Steele."

The classic jukebox began booming "Scenes from an Italian Restaurant."
"Wow. You've got some great taste in music, too."

"Andrew insisted Billy Joel be part of the playlist when we revamped the place a few years back. Andrew's my partner, you know."

Seriously?

His own father had just inadvertently revealed that Andrew had been carrying a torch for Cassie. And right in front of her.

For the love of all things.

Cassie turned to Andrew, who tried his best to look unaffected and innocent. "Is that so? Congrats."

There was something behind her smile, something to the extent of *I don't buy your shrug.* Something like *I can see right through you and your nonchalance.* Yeah, he was certain she could.

"Hey. Do you want to have dinner? Andy and I were going to have burgers and beer. You know, catch up a bit. It's been a while and I've got the bar covered." His dad liked Cassie—that was evident in how hard he was trying to please her, to make her feel welcome. He'd even used Andrew's childhood nickname of Andy. Andrew hadn't been called that in a long time, but he didn't mind. His dad could call Andrew anything he wanted. He'd earned that right and so much more. Plus, it kept Andrew grounded and reminded him that despite their financial struggles, he really did have some good memories with his dad from his childhood. That was all because of his dad.

"Burgers sound great." Cassie nodded. "But only if you have cheese."

"American or cheddar? This place doesn't serve any of those fancy gourmet cheeses—"

"Please, no gourmet cheese on my cheeseburger. That defeats the whole purpose." Cassie's tone was sweet, and kind. She had a special way of putting Stephen at ease.

Andrew watched as his father relaxed, transforming back into the funny and unaffected man he was. The same man who could make a stranger feel like a friend, the same man that made customers feel like family.

Stephen led them to a back booth he'd reserved for them. On their walk over, several customers shook Andrew's hand or waved, and he stopped to say "hi" to every single one. Old, young, it didn't matter. These were the folks who'd accepted him long before he had money or influence. These were real friends, his real family, if not by blood, then by choice.

They had been good to his dad. That's what mattered.

Aware that Cassie was watching, Andrew offered her a grin, then returned his attention to a table with a group of guys he'd gone to high school with. They were jocks, and he'd never fit in with them. After high school graduation, they'd flunked out of an upstate university where they partied too hard. All three of them wound up going to a local college back home.

One had become a fisherman like his father, and two others were partners in a landscaping company. Though their lives weren't what Andrew had chosen for himself, they were respectable, hardworking guys. Andrew was no better than them or anyone in this room. What was Andrew? Lucky. Plain and simple. He succeeded at what he wanted to do and got out. Despite that, every single time he returned home, his initial trepidation was soon replaced with appreciation.

If not for his dad, and the man's hard work, Andrew wouldn't possess everything he did today. If not for Andrew's loner outcast invisibility in high school, he wouldn't be who he was. Yeah, invisibility *was* a powerful motivator. So too was seeing all these people here on a Saturday afternoon, spending their time and money in his father's bar—Andrew's bar, because no matter how much he ignored it, it was his bar, too. He was a partner, after all.

When he finally made his way to their table, he found Cassie in a deep huddle with his father, discussing what kind of child Andrew was. She was holding his dad's wallet, looking at a photo. "Dad, you keep pictures of me from when I was eight in your wallet?"

To Andrew's dismay, Cassie turned the wallet to face him. It contained a wallet-sized photo of a very young, very geeky Andrew wielding a makeshift light saber made from what must have been an entire box of tin foil.

"Okay, this is embarrassing." Andrew groaned as he plopped in the booth seat next to Cassie.

"No, it's not. I think it's cute." She winked at him this time.

Did she have any idea how awkward he'd been as a child? Or how awkward he still was? He was still that geeky kid, except he'd traded thrift store clothes for designer labels and a fancy car.

That was the Andrew that most people saw. It was a superficial exterior, flashy and distracting. Most people usually didn't see beyond the surface shine, but Cassie might. If anyone would, she'd be the one.

"So, what else have you been discussing? My first kiss or something even more humiliating?" Andrew shot his father a knowing grin.

"Something even better. Remember how you used to reenact those light saber scenes on the bar when we were closed?" His dad's eyes were bright. "You were always a handful. And brilliant."

Cassie smiled. "Imagine that. Brilliant even at a young age. It must be because Andrew had such a great dad."

Stephen beamed with pride.

"Yeah, I learned from the best." Andrew's voice was raspy.

Why was he constantly getting choked up today?

"You sure did." Cassie's gaze held his, warm and brimming with sincerity; she was being honest, not simply trying to make Andrew feel less self-conscious.

He could tell the difference.

By the time their cheeseburgers came, they were each on their second beer and Stephen was telling the story of a hurricane that had passed through and the damage the restaurant had taken on. It was a few years after Andrew and Cassie ended things, when the Dailies had truly taken off. "My boy left everything behind and spent weeks with me putting this place back together. We had no power, but he brought a battery-operated CD player and some CDs. We listened to Long Island's son, Billy Joel, and sweated our asses off. Sorry—I cursed."

"Billy Joel again?" she asked, shooting Andrew a wry grin.

"Hey, Stephen. Come over here. You've gotta hear this," one of the customers shouted from the dartboard.

His father excused himself, and Cassie's intense gaze held Andrew's as "Just the Way You Are" began playing.

Cassie held her index finger in the air. "This song. Your dad said that you insisted on having this song be on the new jukebox you bought for him."

"Wow. You covered a lot of topics while I was gone, huh?" He cleared his throat.

He couldn't for the life of him escape that song, *their* song, or her.

Even when Cassie had been with someone else.

"Tell me you don't care." Cassie's green eyes searched his with an intensity that he'd never seen before. Andrew could swear that she'd been searching straight into his soul. "Tell me that you don't care, and I won't believe you because everything I'm learning about you tells me otherwise."

Andrew's hand twitched under her intense scrutiny. He felt like she could see right through him, and it was irritating to no end. He didn't want to be this easy to read.

What difference did it make anyway? She'd moved on.

"Why are you making a big deal of this? It's a song. Just a song." He shrugged it off, shoving his plate aside.

"It was more than just a song to me. That song was my favorite song. It still is, yet I didn't put it on the playlist for my reception. Would you like to know why? Because it was—"

"Our song." The realization slammed into Andrew harder than a gut punch.

"Precisely. So, I'm asking you again: tell me you don't care about me." She repeated it, her eyes growing greener and more intense as she silently dared Andrew to lie to her.

And he couldn't.

Or wouldn't.

He wasn't sure which. Thankfully, he wouldn't have to, because his dad returned just in time to save Andrew from answering that dreaded question. No. Andrew planned to never answer that question.

Doing so would open old wounds for both of them. It would also help neither of them. No, Andrew didn't want to relive their breakup.

Even though it had been a long time coming, that breakup had all but killed him at the time. Because of Cassie's reaction. It haunted him. Even now, years later, he could still remember the pain reflected in her beautiful eyes when he told her they were over.

He'd always remember it.

It was seared into his soul, in the very fabric of who he was. Even though she'd been unhappy, and they'd been arguing about his chosen career path, and it'd been a long time coming, she'd still been hurt.

That's why he'd been tempted to take it back.

No one knew it, but he'd even had second thoughts, though they'd been brief.

In the end, Andrew played the role of the bad guy so Cassie would finally be free. She had known what she wanted, and it wasn't Andrew.

It was never Andrew, which was proven when she began to date Roth so quickly, mere months after their breakup.

Despite their fake relationship charade, despite pretending that they were a real couple and kissing in public, Cassie would remember all of it eventually. Sure, they'd been convincing, to the point where even he questioned if their recent kisses had been real.

Andrew couldn't deny that their chemistry was still there, and more intense than ever. It was almost enough to make him forget...*almost*. Until he remembered that all of it was an act, and eventually they'd have to stop pretending.

This thing with Cassie would come to an end at some point and when it did, she'd remember that she didn't like who Andrew was. Then there was the fact that she despised what he did for a living.

Andrew would never forget it.

Neither would she. He would bet his life on it.

Chapter 11

THEIR EVENTS HAD BEEN ENORMOUS SUCCESSES, JUST AS ANDREW
had hoped. In turn, the photos of their impromptu kisses, and a surprise argument, went viral and generated nothing but positive buzz.
The gossips loved that *#AndCass* were a normal couple, as if any
couple could be *normal*. Regardless, it made Andrew and Cassie's fake
relationship more appealing. It even spawned many a social media
influencer to discuss how healthy it was not to bottle up one's feelings.
Real emotion—that's what it was about. Even Andrew was surprised
at that unexpected twist.

The tide had turned in Cassie's favor. She should have been ecstatic.
So why did Andrew feel like she'd been angry at him ever since?

Because she had been.

Sure, the press got great pictures of them kissing, and the subsequent
articles were generating nothing but positive buzz, however, Cassie didn't
seem to like all the talk about their very real argument on the dance floor.
Then there was their very uncomfortable and much too silent car ride
home after their dinner with his dad. Talk about a disaster. Cassie didn't
like his response when she questioned him about the jukebox and their
song—that same song he couldn't escape. Even though he'd managed to
avoid answering Cassie's question, it still loomed large, because he knew
the answer all too well.

Did he care about Cassie? Of course he did. Too much. That was
the problem. Andrew was still hung up on someone who wanted nothing to do with him in the real world. While their chemistry sizzled

when it came to their fake relationship, there was no future for them when she couldn't stand what he did professionally. That was the bottom line.

But that was his real world, the world he resided in.

Instead of wallowing in the mess he'd made by brushing off her questions, Andrew went ahead with his plan of crafting their narrative. Just like he told Cassie he would do on her non-wedding day. So he went with popular opinion just as his competitors had done, chalking their argument at the winery up to their fiery passion. His subscribers ate that up. Everyone did.

Everyone except Cassie.

In public, at their events, she continued to flirt with him, and even kissed him. She also teased him in her fun, vivacious way. But without fail, once they retreated from public view, she would become aloof if not downright hostile.

At first, Andrew had thought that being vulnerable with her about how she made him feel was helping Cassie get to know him again, but he was reminded that Cassie just didn't like who he was now. It was a constant reminder and kept him in his place.

He was here to craft a narrative and nothing more.

So, the act continued at yet another event. Then another. And yet another.

It had become their routine. They were currently at an indoor venue for the red carpet premiere of the newest Househusbands franchise, and Cassie was pretending to hang on his every word, seated close beside him. So close that each time Andrew inhaled, he was assailed with her sultry signature scent. This perfume was a knockout and sent his senses reeling each time he was with her. It was a mix of floral, musk, and champagne, Cassie had explained. If you asked Andrew, it was a sensual mix, and he would swear she wore it for the sole purpose of driving him wild. If she was trying to turn him on, it was working. Especially now when Cassie rested her palm against his thigh.

As the room went dark and the stage illuminated with an enormous flat-screen TV, Cassie slid her hand up his thigh beneath the table where drinks and appetizers had been served. By the time the introductions for each male cast member had aired, Cassie's hand had inched higher still, sending his every nerve and sinew into overdrive. He suppressed a groan and shifted in his seat.

Did Cassie know she was torturing him?

Slowly and surely, it was indeed torture, as Cassie's hand inched higher still. Andrew gritted his teeth, trying to maintain control as the audience around him chuckled at the antics of the Househusbands attempting to do chores while the franchise's jaunty music played in the background.

It was killing him.

Not the show, although it was corny even by unscripted reality television standards, but her hand, because it had inched even higher up his thigh, and higher still, until Andrew was glad the table hid his erection.

Andrew snatched her hand, then placed it on top of her lap before excusing himself. He needed to walk off the intense physical response his body had to her touch, because it was more than evident that Cassie didn't feel the same for him. Not by a mile.

How could Cassie not realize the effect she was having on him?

Upon rushing into the all-gender restroom, Andrew ran his hands under the cold water before splashing it onto his face. He turned off the tap, and dried his face with a paper towel, staring at his reflection in the mirror.

What are you doing?

He hadn't a clue. What was he doing? Did he really think that Cassie needed him to rescue her? He was no Knight in Shining Dior, that was for sure. Nope, he was just plain Andrew Steele, businessman and all around *no one special*. He'd be the first to admit that. But when she cried that day on her non-wedding day, it had been enough for him to step up.

The problem was that without fail, every time he got real with Cassandra, he seemed to plant his foot firmly in his mouth and Cassandra either became angry with him or indifferent.

Andrew didn't know which was worse.

The door squeaked on its hinges, and he was relieved that his arousal was no longer obvious as he discarded the paper towel.

"Are you all right?" Cassie called to him from the lounge area.

"What are you doing in here? They'll talk." His exasperated tone was new. It had arrived with Cassie. She was both infuriating and exciting— she was everything, all at once.

"That's a good thing, right? We want them to talk." Cassie crossed the lounge area. "Besides, would it really be so bad for people to think that I'm hot for you? It would make them want you more, wouldn't it?"

"What?" Now she'd lost him.

"It became obvious during our dinner with your father, and every event we've shared since. You want me to act like I care about you, while you refuse to admit to anything personal to me. The more I thought about it, the more I realized that over the course of our outings, *you* became more desirable with your followers and with the elites. As if you needed any help in the popularity department."

She talked with her hands.

A lot.

"I mean, look at you. You're attractive, rich, and influential. You've got it all. That makes you the cherry on top of the crème de la crème of Manhattan's movers and shakers."

"I'm beyond confused here. Are you accusing me of something?" He really was lost.

Cassie rested her hand on his chest, beneath his jacket, where her warmth seared his skin through the fabric of his button-down shirt. "I figured out what benefits you the most—their attention and desire. With every kiss you and I share, traffic flocks to your site in droves. Your social media platforms are exploding and many articles on the celebrity sites I read are zeroing in on *you*. It's safe to say that you've blasted through that fifteen-minutes-of-fame barrier that most *people* can only dream of. You're the man of the hour."

His mind was racing. He was trying his hardest to keep up with her.

"Imagine what will happen if someone catches us in here." Her voice was low, and downright sexy. "You'll be seen as being so powerful, so virile, so irresistible that no one can touch you. Of course, the implication would be that I was doing you in a bathroom, but you can spin that to your benefit, right? You can spin anything."

Crass was never in Cassie's nature.

"Stop." He grabbed her hand as it inched downward. "I don't know what you think I'm getting out of our arrangement, but it's not this. I don't want *this*."

On second thought, he did want *her*, just not in this way.

Pulling away from her, Andrew checked the stalls in the next room, then locked the door connecting the unisex bathroom to the outside hallway. "What are you doing? We could have gotten caught with this stunt of yours. We still can. What happens if they learn the truth about our relationship?"

"Perhaps that's better. You can spin it that I'm so desperate for you that I would go along with this silly arrangement. It would help your site, and—"

"Stop." Andrew held her hands in his, leaning into her, until her lips were mere inches from his. "Just tell me what you're really feeling. Tell me what you think is happening. Please. Because I don't get what's happening here, and I'm really trying to understand. You want honesty from me, and that's the honest-to-God truth. So, what's your truth? What's really going on with you?"

Cassie backed away from him and leaned against the wall behind her. "You want my truth? Try this. You were the one eating up the attention that first night at the bar. Even with my mother, to the point where you invited her to dinner. Then at every event since, *you've* been soaking in the praise, the attention, the accolades, and staging our kisses. Isn't it obvious?"

Nothing was obvious. At least not to him.

"Is this about your mother? Or is it about our kisses? The PR has been positive from those kisses, hasn't it?"

"Yes, it has. And no, it's not about my mother. This is about you and me." She expelled her breath, her green eyes achingly familiar to the point where he could feel her pain…raw and uncensored. "I've *begged* you to be honest with me. And you refuse. Even when I can't ignore the fact that our song is everywhere—even in your dad's bar. And you put it there long after we broke up. Why would you do that?"

She leaned into him, her tone pleading. "Honestly, why would you do that? After you chose this glamorous life with these strangers who fawn all over you instead of choosing a future with me."

Was that what she thought he'd done? The idea that this was how Cassie felt nauseated Andrew.

Cassie skimmed her cool fingertips against his jawline. "This is no longer about protecting my business, or my pride. It's not about our fake relationship being mutually beneficial, either. It's about you, needing more from them. Like that dinner with my mother. You want to use me to stick it to her. And on top of it, you traded me for this life, yet here I am making this life more successful for you. At the expense of my pride and everything I believe in."

"No, Cassie, you've got it all wrong." He placed his left hand atop hers to infuse warmth, while he slid his free palm to the slender curve of her hip. "I didn't trade you for this life. It was you who didn't want to be a part of this with me. You made that quite clear."

"I can't compete with any of this. I never could." She leaned forward, so close that her sensual scent assailed his nostrils. "I have never been enough. Not for my mother, not for Jeremy, and certainly not for you."

He planted a soft kiss on her forehead, and she shuddered beneath his lips. It was a slight tremor, but enough for him to notice. "Why would you think that?" He drew her closer to him.

"My mother traded me in for yet another husband, Jeremy traded me in for a much richer blond, and you...You traded me in for fake, swanky parties, Italian marble, and a view of New York Harbor."

"Is that really what you believe?" Andrew asked, his heart aching at the knowledge that he, in some way, had made Cassie feel like she wasn't enough for him. In truth, she was more than enough, but she wasn't interested in the career and, in turn, the life that he had committed to, that he'd invested in.

He slid his arms around her back and held her close against his chest, where his heartbeat was thumping erratically. He hoped she would hear it, or feel it, because then she'd know that what he was about to admit was true.

"You are enough, Cassie. You always have been. I just knew you didn't want to be a part of the life I had made for myself and saw no other way through. I had to take care of my dad, to help him with his debts. I owed him. And let's be honest. You don't respect what I do for a living, the company I built. That hasn't changed. Has it?" He searched her eyes for any signs that her opinion had changed on the matter.

"I despise what you do, but I'm not a hypocrite. I accept it. How can I not when you're using it to my own personal and professional advantage?" She exhaled. "I don't know. Maybe that does make me a hypocrite."

Were they turning a corner on his profession, about his business? It sounded like it. "You're not a hypocrite. You're just annoying and so am I. Join the club."

At his weak attempt at a joke, Cassie melded against him, wrapped in his embrace, like they were one. He didn't know where she ended and he began.

She was his perfect fit.

It was all he needed from her to continue.

"I promised myself long before I met you that I would help my dad. I chose to keep that promise, but not over you. Never over you. If I had thought for one moment that you'd be interested in a future with me, I'd have fought for both him and you. I'd have made it work, Cassie, and that's the truth."

It's the first time he'd ever articulated aloud what made him launch The Steele Dailies and why he'd pushed himself so hard to become a financial success. Perhaps if he'd confided the truth to Cassie all those years ago, things might have turned out differently.

At the time, he wasn't strong enough or mature enough. He'd also been too hungry and too eager to prove himself. Money was addictive, and the more he earned, the more he wanted to invest and turn an even bigger profit.

His most successful investments had been in real estate, and in a social media company that he made a killing on. Those investments, along with his own company, had been windfalls for him.

Being this vulnerable wasn't an option for him then. And now? It still wasn't easy. Though holding Cassie in his arms made his confession easier, it was still difficult. He was still a loner after all, and still terrified of her rejection. So much so that the very thought robbed him of breath.

Caressing her shoulder, he reveled in her soft flesh beneath his fingertips. She wore a strapless dress tonight, and her skin felt like sin. Pure, unadulterated sin.

It was enough for him to continue.

"When you moved on with Roth so quickly, I assumed I made the right decision for the both of us. He was reputable and in finance, a business far more respectable than mine, for the most part." Roth was from old money and a well-respected family.

In other words, Roth had been the complete opposite of Andrew.

"You assumed that you made the right decision for us?" Her voice was flat, devoid of emotion, as her body stiffened. "*You* assumed."

Why did Andrew's admissions, without fail, make Cassie so angry?

"It should have been *our* decision, not yours."

Ah, yes, well…She had him there.

Before he could admit defeat, Cassie pulled away from him. "You are such a—"

"A jerk. I know." Right now, he wholeheartedly agreed with her. "You're right. But I'm trying to be less of a jerk. Doesn't that count for something?"

Cassie studied him. "A leopard can't change his spots. Lauren told me that."

"With respect to your friend, she doesn't know me, at least not the me I am today. And I beg to differ with her." He trailed his fingertips up her neck, until he heard her breath catch in her throat.

That raspy moan was all the encouragement Andrew needed to kiss her, for real this time. The air between them was charged, it had been since he'd found her on Dune Road. However, when his lips claimed hers, that electric charge between them became more forceful.

Cassie melded to his body, and quickly granted him entrance. She kissed him with a ravenous hunger as her tongue sought his, heightening his own desire as it brushed against his with an urgency that caught him off guard.

With each kiss, each sensual stroke of her tongue against his own, his unquenchable thirst for her intensified, until his erection had reached an excruciatingly painful state.

As if sensing his yearning, Cassie arched her back, deepening her kisses even more. It was almost his undoing as he welcomed her and released a deep, jagged breath.

He raked his hands through her thick curls, wanting more from her. *So much more.* But not here. Not in a bathroom of all places. When he tore his mouth from hers, Cassie's chest was rising and falling, as was his. Andrew then trailed kisses down her neck and throat.

Inhaling deeply, her scent intoxicated him, just as her kisses had.

Andrew held her in his tight embrace, until their breathing slowed to normal. Then and only then did he suggest, "Let's do something together tomorrow night. Just us. No cameras, no crowds, nothing to fake. You can see the real me for once. If you're brave enough."

He suppressed a grin, knowing full well that she would never turn down a challenge.

"You have yourself a deal. Although…" Her voice was sultry. "That kiss we just shared is a tough act to follow."

How right she was. The pressure was on. And Andrew had to find something to do that was private-ish and that would help him win over Cassie, or at least help her see him in a new light.

Only after he'd unlocked the door and poked his head out, making sure the coast was clear, did he take Cassie's hand and lead her back to the screening. His mind raced as they proceeded through their evening with the Househusbands. Andrew just hoped he'd be able to keep his feet planted firmly on the ground, and not in his mouth.

For one night only. For one real date with Cassie.

Was that too much to ask for?

Chapter 12

"HOW LONG HAS IT BEEN SINCE YOUR LAST KISS?" NOAH SAT IN THE chair across from Andrew's desk, with his laptop open, reviewing the proposed changes to The Steele Dailies website layout.

With the huge success of its social media feeds, especially Insta, it made sense to revamp the main website and present a more streamlined way to view the articles, especially for mobile devices.

Andrew's computer science background came in handy at times like this, and he was always looking for ways to improve the process of delivering celebrity news and hot takes.

There was no way he'd confess to his off the charts sweltering kiss with Cassie the night before. Instead, he avoided the topic altogether by comparing the content on his dual monitors, which rested side by side in the center of his desk. "Let's finish this first. Are we good to go on these changes?"

Noah shut his laptop. "I like it. I say publish it along with—"

"The article announcing our new layout? That's ready and waiting for publication on all of our sites, including social media feeds and stories." Andrew glanced at his partner over his monitors, offering him a reassuring grin. "Your approval was more of a formality. I knew you would agree to the improvements."

As Noah narrowed his eyes, the lines around them became more pronounced. "I'd love to throw you a curveball one of these days. But today is not one of those days. You did well."

"Thanks. I always do." Andrew hit publish on his posts and just like that, their new format was live and in living color.

"So, let us get back to it. Your kisses were popular and attracted people to us in droves. So did your fight." Noah sat back in his leather chair, studying Andrew intently. "I want to see more of it."

Andrew arched his brow. "I'm not kissing Cassie again, on camera, to increase traffic to our site. Nor will I argue with her in public for the same reason."

"Why not? Now would be the perfect time to do it. We can make it an exclusive." A hint of desperation was behind Noah's statements.

"But why, Noah? The Dailies are doing great. We don't need additional exposure." It was true. Regardless of how Andrew tried to sell Cassie on this mutually beneficial narrative, it was just that—a narrative he'd created to help her and her career.

Yep, Andrew had stretched the truth to save Cassie's pride. In doing so, he risked injuring his own pride and ruining her good opinion of him. Because it was the only thing that he could think of to help her, and Andrew had been beyond desperate to help her.

Of course he wanted Cassie to see just how successful he was. He wanted to shout it from the rooftops and perhaps he would one day. Just not while she was down. With Jeremy sacrificing her on the altar at their non-wedding, Andrew knew that Cassie needed him, even if she would never have admitted it at the time. She didn't need to admit to it.

He just knew it.

It was always about Cassie for him. Then and now, even after he'd called their relationship quits. Their breakup was his biggest regret, especially now.

Cassie's voice boomed through the walls as she belted Queen's "We Are the Champions" from the kitchen. As usual, Bailey joined in, howling with her at the top of his lungs.

"What the hell is that?" Noah stiffened. "I swear someone is being tortured."

"Yeah. *Me!*" Andrew stood and crossed to the front of the desk. He raised his voice so he could be heard above the chaos. "This happens daily, like clockwork. Cassie and Bailey get home from their walk, and she and the dog have at it. Usually while she's plating the dog's favorite refrigerated organic doggie pâté, or so she calls it. I swear, that canine eats better than I do."

"We are the champions, my friends…" Cassie belted out.

"Does she know I'm here?" Noah shouted, while grabbing his laptop.

Andrew shrugged, then followed Noah out of the room. They entered the kitchen, then stood still, watching as Cassie sang into a spoon while Bailey howled, jumping up and down, trying to lick her.

Fresh faced, with minimal makeup and her hair pulled back in a high ponytail, Cassie was dressed in yoga pants, a sweatshirt, and sneakers. Even without her glam makeup, she was effervescent, filling Andrew's home with light and with noise.

A lot of noise.

She also made her casual workout clothes look like haute couture. With her height and curves in all the right places, this woman was a knockout, even when she wasn't trying. The thing about Cassie was that she rarely tried. Beauty, her beauty, was effortless. So was her love for the canine.

She bent down to pet Bailey, and he jumped, headbutting her.

"Ouch." Cassie tried to calm her hyper dog down by petting him, but Bailey was too excited and knocked her over, assaulting her with licks. If Andrew had been concerned for her, Cassie's laughter and smiles would have assuaged his fears.

He cleared his throat, and Bailey barked.

"Hey. It's me. This is my home, remember?" Andrew reached for the dog's bowl and placed it on the floor in front of him.

Bailey trotted to his bowl and began eating while Cassie muttered,

"Traitor." It was her very own special brand of sarcasm that Andrew had grown familiar with. Cassie was very competitive when it came to her dog's attention, or so she made it seem.

They went through the same routine every day with one exception: the song would change. Yesterday's song of choice was "Bohemian Rhapsody" while the day before it was "Under Pressure." Apparently, Cassie and Bailey were fans of Freddie Mercury.

After offering Cassie a hand, Andrew yanked her to her feet.

"You're a fan of Adam Lambert?" Noah asked, in what Andrew was certain was his partner's attempt at small talk.

"That's blasphemy." Cassie widened her eyes in mock indignation.

Andrew laughed. "About that… Freddie Mercury is the only Queen front man who ever mattered. I say that with respect to Mr. Lambert."

The smile on Cassie's face was all the approval Andrew needed.

"Sorry. I didn't mean to offend." Noah's tone was light. He was on his usual charm offensive and seemed to understand Cassie's sense of humor.

With a nod, Cassie raised her hands in the air. "No offense taken. Sorry about the noise. I wasn't aware we had a guest."

"I'm his partner."

Andrew was certain that Cassie didn't need the reminder. Not only had Noah been a part of Andrew's college life, but he'd been a part of Andrew's business from the very beginning. That same business that had caused such a strain on their relationship back then, and a little now as well.

If Cassie still harbored any hard feelings about Noah in particular, she didn't show any signs of it today in front of him. Her face remained serene as Andrew said, "Cassie, you must remember Noah Carr. We were roommates in our junior year. As he said, he's my business partner."

Cassie shook Noah's hand. "Right. I recognized you. It's nice to see you. And again, I'm sorry about the noise. Bailey gets a little hyper."

Her obvious attempts to put Noah at ease seemed to be working.

"He's a beagle," Andrew added for good measure. He'd done a lot of research on beagles since Cassie and Bailey had moved in. The breed was notorious for noise, chaos, drama, and love.

They were also extremely protective, and Bailey did indeed protect Cassie. That's why whenever they got lost in song and Andrew walked in on their duets, Bailey barked at him. The dog was all bark and no bite as far as Andrew was concerned. At least so far, but he was also enjoying torturing Andrew. This daily chaos was proof.

Noah glanced from Cassie to Andrew, then back to Cassie. "So where are you going tonight? Do you have any plans?"

She pointed to Andrew. "He's surprising me."

Yep, Andrew was surprising her. It was time he did something outside of the public eye for Cassie. "I'm not giving any hints, either. Oh, before you ask, cameras won't be there." Andrew stressed this point again to his partner.

"Got it. No cameras. I promise." Noah backed away. "I've got to get going. See you soon."

Andrew walked him to the elevator.

"You're in deep," Noah muttered.

Andrew shook his head. "I don't want to hear it."

"I'm trying to warn you—"

"Nope. No warnings." On this Andrew was adamant. "No interference either. Whatever happens, happens."

Noah stepped into the elevator, tapping his fingers against his laptop. "I can't promise anything when it comes to interference. We made a deal that the site comes first, that our business comes first. Remember? You're no exception."

"Understood."

Andrew did indeed understand and after the elevator door slid shut, he walked back into his penthouse, fighting against the feeling of dread that had settled in his chest. He had enough to contend with without adding his business partner to the mix. But he wouldn't be deterred. Not today.

Because tonight was about making up for lost time, and making Cassie see that he was in this arrangement for her, and that they had more than red-hot chemistry while in front of the cameras. There was also red-hot chemistry away from the cameras—that fact was indisputable—but there was a lot more to them than that, and he'd make her see just how special she was to him at one of the most romantic places in Brooklyn.

It was time for a moonlight carousel ride.

If that didn't tip the scales in his favor, nothing would.

Chapter 13

ANDREW INSISTED THEY DRESS CASUAL FOR WHAT HE CALLED THEIR "first date." Even though they'd dated before, Cassandra herself would be forced to admit to herself that this time did feel different. They were different now. Of course, they were full-fledged adults with businesses now, not college kids, after all. But even more so, they'd grown into much different people than they used to be.

Garbed in a casual dress, denim jacket, and her favorite ankle boots, Cassie was the epitome of boho chic. She also wore a large statement ring of lace agate, one of her favorite stones. She had a tendency to choose gemstones for their meanings, the one exception being the engagement diamond that Jeremy had picked out for her.

Gone were her black nails. Instead, her nails were blue, with one nail painted gold. She'd evolved from the heartbreaking black, a sure sign that her blue lace agate stone was working and helping her heal emotionally from her heartbreak.

Perhaps it wasn't just the stone, though. Cassandra had a strong suspicion that Andrew was a cause for her healing too, at least in part.

Cassandra surveyed him as they walked from their car to their destination.

Despite what she suspected were designer labels, he wore a Henley top and slacks. No suit jacket, and certainly no tie. While he still wasn't the Andrew she'd once dated, this was a more intimate side of Andrew than what he presented to the rest of the world. This was also who Andrew was today, and she really wouldn't have him any other way.

She'd grown to like Andrew, just as he was.

They arrived at the carousel as the sun was setting. Though she'd never been there before, she knew of the carousel that overlooked both the Brooklyn and Manhattan Bridges in what's known as Brooklyn Bridge Park. It was originally housed in Ohio, but was lovingly restored and repainted before being relocated to Brooklyn, where a glass pavilion allowed it to function year-round. The sound of waves lapping against the bluff that buffered it from the East River could be heard as they approached, along with Billy Joel music coming from the carousel's sound system.

Illuminated in all its glory and surrounded by the bridges and Manhattan skyline, the colorful carousel was breathtaking.

"This is more gorgeous in person," she said, studying the rectangular glass structure and the many painted horses going round inside.

"And it's all ours. For the next two hours."

Cassandra turned to Andrew, who was studying her intently. "Ours? As in…" She smiled. "You rented the carousel?"

He threaded his fingers through the hair at the nape of her neck, nodding while a boyish grin swept across his features. "How else could I ensure that no photos were taken, or that our own personal soundtrack was playing for us?"

"Andrew, you're making this very difficult." She wrapped her arms around his neck and spoke with mock severity. "I promised myself that I wouldn't fall for you again, yet here I am, in this romantic setting with you saying all the right things. You're making me rethink my promise."

He shot her one of his wry grins. "I had hoped that our kiss last night might have been enough to convince you. Dare I ask why I haven't been able to convince you yet?"

"Our kiss last night was spectacular, and it was most certainly enough to make me rethink my stance. But..." But there was more to it than a kiss, or several kisses, as the case may be.

Was she really about to confide in Andrew her deepest fear? Swallowing hard gave her a reprieve. Though not a long one, it was long enough for Cassandra to decide that she must be honest with Andrew. "I'm terrified that you'll hurt me worse this time around."

Yes, she went there.

Cassandra studied Andrew's reaction. His lips pursed, and his expression had become marred with worry lines. His voice was equally somber as he leaned into her, then pressed his lips against her forehead in a kiss. "I can see why you're hesitant. I mean, my track record with you hasn't exactly been stellar. But that's why I did all this. To prove that you're special to me. To show you how sorry I am that I hurt you."

His sincerity struck her like a bolt of lightning, drawing her closer to him. "There you go, breaking down the walls I've erected around my heart with your honesty."

"I'd be lying if I said that's not what I was hoping for." He held her close. "Now, listen. Full transparency. There's a staff manager and a carousel operator present who have been instructed to ignore us and not take any pictures. Is that good enough or do you have any other conditions you'd like—"

"That's perfect." She kissed his cheek. "This whole setting is perfection."

Cassandra meant every word. Andrew had certainly surprised her tonight. Not simply with the carousel, but with his willingness to be honest with her, and apologize to her.

His honesty was a total turn-on.

"Here's an idea: how about we have some fun? I think you deserve that. We both do." He led her by the hand to the carousel, where he helped her onto her first choice of horse: white with silver armor, flanked in gold, yellow, blue, and red paint.

After a span of countless songs spent laughing, singing, and riding different horses, they moved on to a chariot where they sat and looked at the night sky through the glass ceiling. "The last time I was on a carousel was with my dad. He used to take me on them all the time when I was a kid."

Andrew caressed her cheek. "I remember. That's what gave me this idea in the first place."

He remembered?

Cassandra sat upright. "How did you remember that? I don't recall mentioning it to you when we were dating."

Leaning into her, until their lips were mere inches apart, Andrew answered in a raspy whisper. "I remember a lot more than you think I do."

Cassandra thought he was going to kiss her. She even parted her lips and drew closer to him, as her eyes locked with his hooded gaze.

"I missed you." Andrew kissed the top of her head, smoothing her hair. "I missed you more than I ever realized."

He missed her. The revelation caused Cassandra's insides to flutter. That's why she captured his mouth with hers, and that's the reason she kissed him with all the passion in her heart.

After arguing with Andrew for what seemed like forever, Cassandra felt free with his one simple admission. Was that what she needed? To hear that Andrew missed her? Why? She hadn't missed him, had she?

No, she didn't think so. Or had she been fooling herself?

It was probably the latter, which would explain why he had the ability to hurt her, albeit unintentionally.

Cassandra leaned against him and kissed him passionately, stroking his tongue with hers, even nibbling at his lower lip until he moaned and raked his fingers through her hair, tugging her closer to his warmth, then closer still.

By the time Andrew slowed their kisses, both were breathless. "I think we've been going about this whole fake relationship thing wrong. Look at what we've been denying each other."

With a chuckle, she nestled in his embrace, watching the stars through the glass above, as Billy Joel's "Just the Way You Are" began to play. "From your use of the term 'first date,' it seems like we've moved past the fake dating stage. Unless you're having second thoughts?"

"Nope. No second thoughts. Except that I wish we'd done this sooner. I was too busy being a jerk, as you so rightly pointed out." His voice had taken on a husky quality with his admission. "There's a reason for that."

She snuggled closer, not wanting to break their connection. "What is it?"

"Isn't that obvious? With all of this?" He whispered it. Like it was a secret. "You're the one who got away. The one woman I pushed away, and I've been trying so hard to impress you with everything I have and everything I've become that I forgot why you fell for me in the first place: because I was unlike any of the guys you knew before me."

That was the truth. And it hung in the air between them, hidden in the lyrics playing over the sound system. "I wouldn't leave you in times of trouble... I'll take you just the way you are."

Their song.

"You always have my unspoken passion, though I might not seem to care." Andrew's raspy baritone sliced straight through to her soul. He wasn't simply reciting the lyrics; he was making a promise to her.

And she wholeheartedly believed him.

That's why she kissed him again. Because this kiss was the promise from *her* heart. Made to him, *this Andrew*, who she was falling hard for. When their tongues brushed against each other, it fused their souls as one. And that connection grew with each subsequent kiss.

These kisses were *real* kisses, not meant for anyone else but them.

Romantic, and sensual, they left her breathless and yearning for more. When their two hours were up, Andrew asked if she wanted more time.

That's when she handed him her cell and they posed for a picture. "Just for us. No one else. Because I want to remember this night."

Only after Andrew had snapped photos with her cell, and his, did she whisper in his ear that she wanted to go home.

"Bailey must miss us." He kissed her hair while they were still seated in their chariot.

Cassandra turned to him, holding his gaze with hers. "Bailey isn't why I want to go home." She leaned into him and nipped his earlobe with her teeth.

Judging by the way Andrew's breath hitched in his throat, and how his voice cracked when he said he'd text their driver, he knew precisely what Cassandra wanted to do with him once they reached his place.

And she was one hundred percent ready to give herself completely to him. To *this* Andrew. Because he had proven that he was everything she had once thought and more.

So much more.

Hopefully, she wouldn't regret letting her guard down with him.

Chapter 14

ANDREW EMBRACED CASSANDRA IN THE ESCALADE RIDE HOME AND then kissed her during their elevator ride to his penthouse. His kisses, just like his embrace, were sensual and rich with meaning. Cassandra sensed that he was trying to make up for lost time and trying to make her feel that he cared.

Wasn't that what she'd asked of him?

Yes, though she hadn't expected that their date would have been so romantic, let alone so achingly honest. But with his admissions of how he felt about her, the walls Cassandra had erected around her heart had been demolished. Of that Cassandra was certain as they petted Bailey, who'd met them with a yawn as they entered Andrew's penthouse before he trotted off to his doggie bed, which was near the vast bank of windows in the great room. His babysitter, or Bailey-sitter as Cassandra liked to call her, had taken care of his walks, food, and water, so there was nothing to worry about on that front.

Cassandra followed Andrew into his bedroom suite, where he took great care to close the door with as little noise possible. "Why do I feel like a teenager sneaking around in my dad's place?" His statement was a mere whisper.

"I can't believe what I'm about to say." She smothered a laugh behind her hand. "Bailey, a beagle of all things, has rattled you—the bad boy mogul of Manhattan. Who would have thought that was even possible?"

Linking his fingers with hers, Andrew tugged Cassandra closer until she was in his arms. He wore a wide grin, visible in the warm, dim lighting of his bedroom, which was decorated in the same monochromatic colors as the rest of his place.

"Yes, your dog has me rattled, which is why I'm whispering. Why are *you* whispering?" Andrew arched his brow.

"Touché." She leaned into him, her tone full-on flirty. "I'm whispering because I'm thinking about doing things with you that Bailey has never seen and probably never should see."

"Oh really?" Warmth radiated from Andrew as he kissed her neck, trailing a path up to her earlobe, which he nipped with his teeth. Her flesh twitched beneath his breath and beneath his dexterous caresses as she yearned to lose herself in him.

Cassandra inhaled deeply, reveling in Andrew's musky scent. Warm and spicy, it ignited her senses as she welcomed his onslaught of kisses by exploring his mouth with her tongue. A jolt of...what, exactly? Energy, hunger, thirst, desire...or perhaps a combination of all four, pulsated within her. Cassandra's every nerve was on fire and in tune with his nearness, with his unadulterated passion.

Andrew splayed his palms on her waist, then trailed his hands up her back. Higher, then higher still, until she shrugged out of her jacket. As it fell to the floor, Andrew's hands trailed higher, then higher still to the nape of her neck, then to her curls, where he combed his fingers through her hair.

Cassandra's breath hitched in her throat as her eyes locked with his. That smoky gaze tethered her to him as Andrew's hands traced a path across her chest to the buttons of her dress. As he unbuttoned the first button, then the second, Cassandra's heart began to race.

Had he sensed a change in her?

Yes, he must have. Because Andrew spread the fabric open before kissing her harder, with a moan of appreciation. The fabric dropped to her ankles as he ran his fingers through her hair, yanking her head backward. He then kissed her lips with his ravenous hunger.

When he tore his lips from hers, Cassie heard her breath catch in her throat. Breathless, her chest heaved up and down as his lips trailed a fiery path lower, to her neck, then lower still.

Through the lace fabric of her bra, Andrew captured one of her nipples with his teeth, and a guttural moan escaped her lips. Andrew suckled harder as his fingertips trailed to her bra closure, where he freed her breasts from their confines. That's when she noted the shift in tone. Gone were his moans. Instead, she was met with a heady silence.

Upon opening her eyes, Cassie realized that Andrew had ceased his exploration of her. Instead, he was studying her breasts with a look of pure reverence.

"You are so damned beautiful." His rich baritone dripped with adoration. "God, you are perfection."

Cassandra hadn't been called attractive in a very long time, and never with the passion that Andrew's gaze and voice exuded. His thumb grazed her taut nipple, causing her to tremble beneath his touch.

"I thought I remembered everything about you, yet I am completely blown away by how sexy you are. And how supple your skin is." Andrew kissed her again. It was a slow, sensual kiss and she arched her back, drawing closer to him, eliminating the distance between them until…

She was met with his erection. All his talk was making him hard, or maybe it was her body, or their kisses, or all of the above. Regardless, Cassandra could feel his erection poking her through the fabric of his slacks.

Well aware that she was all but naked, with her breasts exposed, Cassie wasn't self-conscious.

On the contrary, she felt liberated.

"Take your shirt off." It was a command; her voice was low and determined.

She wanted this man more than she'd ever wanted her ex-fiancé. Her body had never responded to her ex the way she did to Andrew. No, not at all. Because Cassandra was never his. And while she and Andrew had a satisfying sex life and strong sexual chemistry back then, that was nothing in comparison to what it was now. It was off the charts now. Perhaps because they'd both grown, or because they were both different now. Either way, it didn't matter. The bottom line, what Cassandra had realized at last, is that Andrew had always been the man of her heart, only she hadn't allowed herself to see that.

Not until now, until this very moment.

It had been Andrew all along.

With a sly smile, Andrew took several steps back, then lifted his Henley over his head. Cassandra had no idea where he tossed his shirt because all she could see were his abs. *This* Andrew was ripped. He'd started working out while they were together, but his physique then was nothing like it was now.

Andrew laughed. "Am I that different?"

Cassandra blinked before realizing that her lips had parted. "Let's just say you're hotter than I remembered."

"Very diplomatic." He bridged the distance between them, then coaxed her lips to part once again. This kiss was passionate, hungry, and all-consuming. She reveled in his kisses. In truth, she couldn't get enough of them as a surge of urgency began to pulsate within her as he deepened the kiss, his lips and tongue probing, his kisses becoming more demanding.

Her fingertips traced the contours of his chest, then abdomen, then lower still, until she reached his belt. His muscles twitched beneath her fingertips and his erection hardened even more, she noted, suppressing a grin.

His body responded to her with force, which meant one thing.

Andrew wanted her just as much as she wanted him.

Why wait any longer? Cassandra unbuckled his belt, then fumbled with the hook and zipper of his pants. By the time Andrew stepped out of his slacks, she was throbbing for him. And he seemed to sense this, because he scooped her up in his arms and carried her to his bed, where he placed her down on his soft mattress with ease.

Yeah, this Andrew worked out.

A lot.

And she couldn't complain.

He removed his watch and placed it on his bedside table. Then and only then did he join her on the bed. Cupping her breasts in his hands, he moaned and captured her mouth with his.

Their kisses were quickly becoming more intimate than any act of sex she'd ever experienced. Andrew's heart, his very soul, was fused in each and every kiss, in each of his caresses. In the way he teased her and tempted her. In his soft yet possessive touch that she'd never tire of.

His mouth descended lower, to the hollow between her breasts, where he licked her, then nibbled. Then he licked a fiery path to her nipple, which he seized with his mouth. He blew on one nipple before nipping it with his teeth, then did the same to the other.

With his every teasing flick, with his every kiss, he stoked the flames of desire that had long remained dormant. No, she never felt any of this with her ex-fiancé. And now that Cassandra had this taste, she was hungry for more.

It was an insatiable hunger.

Reaching for his boxers, she tugged them free from his erection. It was at this precise moment that Andrew released her nipple and looked at her, meeting her gaze with his. Dark and brimming with adoration, his eyes mirrored her own feelings for him.

She belonged to him now. In this moment.

And he was hers.

It was an unspoken promise. She could see it in his eyes as they remained locked with hers. Seconds passed, until his fingers skimmed the lace at her waist and Andrew tore his eyes from hers.

"Did you wear this for me?" There was an element of surprise in his tone.

Perhaps subconsciously, she might have worn the sexiest thong she owned tonight in the hopes that something like this might happen, but she'd never admit it to Andrew.

"This is the new me. Don't you like it?" she teased, her tone deliberately seductive.

"Oh, I love the new you. Then again, I liked the old you, too." Andrew tugged her thong down, then planted his lips gently between her legs. It was his turn to tease Cassandra. And he did. With his sensual lips, and with his dexterous tongue.

When her spasms subsided, then and only then did Andrew make love to her. Fully, completely, Andrew gave himself to Cassandra, and she recognized the significance.

They were one.

When their raptures had subsided, Cassandra remained in Andrew's embrace until Bailey scratched at his bedroom door. Without hesitation, Andrew let the dog in, then carried him to the bed.

The beagle nestled between them on top of the comforter, while she and Andrew lay beneath it.

While petting Bailey, Cassandra imparted a secret. "I'll have you know that Bailey didn't exactly approve of Jeremy. He'd bark incessantly at him whenever Jeremy kissed me. He also had a tendency of blocking Jeremy from kissing me."

"That dog has excellent taste and I admire his tenacity." Andrew caressed her neck idly with his thumb. It ignited her sense of yearning for him again tenfold. Then, Andrew tipped her chin up. "Do you think he'd let *me* kiss you?"

Cassandra smiled. "There's only one way to find out." She captured his lips with hers in a soul-fusing kiss.

There was no bark, no growl, not even a snort from Bailey.

Instead, the canine snored.

"I think we bored him," Andrew muttered.

"Well, I think you passed the Bailey test." Cassandra laughed, as Andrew cupped her breast in his hand beneath the covers.

He felt sinful, but oh so right.

This felt right.

Her phone, which was on the other side of the room, pinged. A text must have come in. Then another ping. And another. "I've got to mute that. It's in the pocket of my jacket."

"I'll get it." Andrew rose, and she watched his naked silhouette walk across his bedroom and back. To say he was sexy would be an understatement. Another ping jolted her from such thoughts.

"You're not going to like this." Andrew joined her in bed, handing her the cell. "I only saw it because your screen lit up with another message. Just know that the choice to read your texts is just that—a choice. You can wait until morning."

"Okay. Now I've got to check. You've made me nervous." Her screen had gone dark again. She unlocked it and saw that five texts had come in. All from Jeremy. She read the last one aloud. "'You're not going to get away with humiliating me. The truth will come out.'"

Her eyes met Andrew's. "You were right. I should have waited until morning."

"Did Jeremy threaten you?" Andrew grabbed her phone and scrolled through the texts as Bailey awakened with a bark.

After giving Andrew a moment to catch up with the texts, Cassandra said, "Jeremy wants the truth about who dumped who to come out. Apparently, humiliating me is fine. He only has an issue when he's the one being humiliated. That's some Jeremy logic right there."

Bailey barked twice, followed by a growl.

"Jeremy." Cassandra tested a theory. "Jeremy."

Sure enough, every time Cassandra spoke her ex-fiancé's name, Bailey barked, followed by a low growl.

"Does he always respond to Jeremy's name like that?" Andrew asked, as Bailey barked again, then growled.

Cassandra shook her head. "Not until now. This is new."

With a pat on the dog's head, Andrew laughed. "He really does have excellent taste. Now put your phone on mute, or better yet, block Roth and let's show Bailey a thing or two."

"Andrew Steele, are you trying to corrupt my dog?" Cassandra played coy like no other. Who said she couldn't act? Oh, that's right...Her mother had when she wanted to try out for a grade school play, but what did that woman know?

Only after Andrew nipped her earlobe with his teeth did he trail a path of fiery kisses down her neck. Her flesh quivered beneath him. Andrew kissed her again, then nipped her with his teeth, sending a tingling sensation straight to her core.

"I'm trying to corrupt *you*. Is it working?"

Cassandra melted when he teased her, and he was getting very proficient at doing so. "Yes, Andrew. Everything you're doing is working perfectly."

"Good." He kissed her neck again, then licked and kissed lower, then lower still until he'd reached her breast. Andrew's warm breath fanned her nipple, sending shock waves through her system.

Cassandra shoved Andrew onto his back, then straddled him and splayed her palms against his chest. "I think it's time for me to corrupt you."

The fact that he got hard beneath her was a perk, as was the fact that his muscles twitched beneath her fingers, and beneath her tongue. It was her turn to tease and tempt him. By the time they reached their climaxes, the sky was streaked with pastel colors and the day was beginning, but Cassie didn't care.

She didn't need sleep. No, she'd found bliss for the first time that she could remember. Not even her ex's texts would take that away from her. Her mother, on the other hand, would be a challenge. She and Andrew were scheduled to have dinner with Julia and husband number four tonight.

Bailey awakened and stretched from his comfortable spot atop Andrew's bedding, before trotting to the door.

With a moan, Cassie kissed Andrew one last time. "It's time for his morning walk."

"Let's get dressed." Andrew rose and stepped into his trousers. He was going commando, Cassandra noted with a twinge of excitement.

"You're going with us?"

Andrew paused in the process of buckling his belt. "Yeah. That's okay, right?"

Cassandra sprinted across the room and kissed his cheek. "I love that you like Bailey."

"Well, I like you more, if I'm being honest."

"That's okay. It's allowed." And it was. Because Andrew had passed the Bailey test, and that was a tough test to pass.

She returned to her room and got dressed in record time, fully aware that Andrew was watching her with his hooded gaze. Perhaps he wanted to reenact last night. It's what she wanted, but Bailey had to go, so they left on their walk instead.

Grabbing breakfast and coffees at a bakery along the way, they stopped at a park near Andrew's penthouse and watched the sunrise with Bailey as all three of them ate. It was empty when they got there. Cassandra had brought a tennis ball, and they played fetch. Or at least they tried.

"I had a dog when I was a kid. She was a golden retriever and she loved playing fetch." Andrew tossed the ball. It was close, but still far enough away where Bailey could get a small run in.

Bailey ran after the ball, bit it, turned to Andrew, dropped the ball, and ran back to them, leaving the ball behind. Andrew walked over to the tennis ball, picked it up, and brought it back, all the while explaining the process to Bailey.

"Okay, Bailey. Fetch," Andrew tossed the ball again, only for him to run, bite the ball, then drop it and head back to Andrew.

Andrew pointed to the ball. "Bailey, get it. Get the ball. You can do it." The look on Andrew's face was one of bewilderment.

Who knew a beagle could be so terrible at catching a tennis ball? Cassie had known, but Andrew never suspected it. Of that Cassandra had been certain, based upon the look of pure shock on his face while witnessing her beagle in action.

"Your dog can't play fetch to save his life, can he?" Andrew sat on the grass beside Cassandra as Bailey joined them. She laughed and secured Bailey's leash to his harness.

"No. He doesn't understand fetch," she answered. "But watching you try to teach him was very sweet."

He petted the beagle's head. "It's all right. You can't be good at everything. No one can."

Cassie couldn't help but smile. Who knew that the rich and famous Andrew Steele would spend so much time and effort encouraging a dog who wasn't his that it was okay to suck at fetch? Certainly not her, but there they were.

Andrew slid his arm around Cassie and kissed her head.

"Oh, I like that." Cassandra sighed, gripping Bailey's leash as she leaned against Andrew's chest.

"Would you like to know what I'm thinking?" he asked her.

She turned to face him. "Yes, please."

"That this is the definition of bliss." He had this dreamy, distant look as he watched Bailey, then returned his attention to Cassie. "Your dog is totally hopeless when it comes to fetch, but this is still the perfect way to start the day."

Smiling, Cassandra kissed him.

Bailey barked, and she tore her lips from Andrew's to find her dog staring at another, much larger dog, who was walking with his or her owner. As they entered the park, the other dog was panting heavily. The poor thing looked more like a potbelly pig than a dog, and he was plodding along slowly, as if each step was a chore.

Then he barked at Bailey, and Bailey barked back.

"No, Bailey. No bark." Cassie stood. "It's time we go."

Andrew followed suit as another round of *Bailey's Bark-Off* took place. Bailey had begun to tug on his leash.

The two dogs were having a staring contest, in addition to their bark-off.

"Bailey's holding his own. That's impressive," Andrew said, before heading over to their tennis ball.

The other dog barked and growled at Andrew. Bailey did the same back to the other dog. "It's okay, Bailey," Cassie assured him, though Bailey wouldn't stop growling.

He was stubborn on a good day, but today, he was downright lethal. Andrew must have seen it, too, because he picked up the tennis ball and brought it straight over to Bailey.

"Here you go, Bailey, it's okay." Bailey continued to growl and bare his teeth, until Andrew bent down and petted him. Then and only then did Bailey stop barking.

"That dog is dangerous!" the other owner shouted at them.

Cassandra ignored him, choosing instead to study Bailey with wide eyes. "Bailey was protecting you, Andrew. Not me."

With a look of surprise, Andrew bent down to pet Bailey. "Were you protecting me?"

Bailey licked him and wagged his tail. He then did his little butt wiggle thing.

"I don't remember much about dogs, but I remember that butt wiggle thing. That means the dog is happy to see you." There was an air of astonishment in Andrew's tone.

"It means Bailey loves you. And approves of you," Cassie added with a knowing grin.

Her dog approved of Andrew.

"Take that, Roth who shall not be named," Andrew said, before giving the beagle more pets. "Who's a good boy? You're a good boy."

Bailey wiggled and wagged his tail some more.

"You should be banned from this park. You shouldn't reward that dog for almost attacking another dog."

Andrew picked up Bailey and faced the other owner. "I'll have you know he's a beagle and very protective. Besides, your dog started it, and Bailey finished it. Oh! You know what? Bailey barked louder than your dog...than your much larger dog."

"I don't think that starting a fight with another dog owner is what we want to do today." Cassandra ushered Andrew away from the scene, as Bailey remained contentedly in his arms.

Once they were far enough away from the other dog and its owner, Cassandra said at last, "Apparently size doesn't matter, at least when it comes to a dog's bark."

"In a dog park." Andrew winked at her. "See what I did there? I rhymed."

Cassandra laughed. "You're incorrigible."

Andrew did his best to suppress a grin and wound up laughing instead. "I am. Seriously, though, did you see how Bailey handled that other dog? He was about to kick his or her butt."

Cassandra grimaced. "I don't think that's a good thing."

"No, it's great. Our little man held his own." Andrew petted Bailey some more. "I'm so proud of you."

This time Cassie was the one to laugh as they walked back to Andrew's penthouse. "No, it really isn't great, and it isn't funny."

Andrew feigned outrage. "So we get banned from one dog park. Who cares? We can buy another."

From his proud features, Andrew was truly impressed with Cassie's beagle.

"We can?" Cassie asked.

Andrew kissed her head. "We can. We're a team now. The three of us can do anything together."

For the first time since her wedding day fiasco, Cassandra realized that she was lucky that Jeremy had dumped her. Because this was where she was meant to be.

With Andrew.

And with Bailey.

Like Andrew said, they were a team now. She just wished Jeremy's threats weren't looming over her. Now she had something and someone to lose. And that made her fearful that Jeremy would make good on his threats.

Chapter 15

THOUGH ANDREW SPENT THE DAY IN HIS OFFICE, HE WOULD HAVE much rather returned to his bed with Cassie and do more of what they'd done the night before. Unfortunately for him, he had to go on the offensive and worked tirelessly planting seeds of doubt in the event that Roth was to make good on his threats to badmouth Cassie or their shiny new relationship.

Add to that, his usual workload of cultivating leads, sifting through tips, fact-checking, publishing binge-worthy celebrity news and gossip, and recording his own vlogs of breaking news and his day was jam-packed.

But the day had been rewarding. Andrew had never heard Cassie laugh so loud as when her dog had trotted to the tennis ball, bit it, turned, then dropped it again before trotting back to them. That memory alone was enough to ensure that he had a good day. Then there was the fact that Bailey not only accepted Andrew, but growled at a dog much larger than he was in an effort to protect Andrew.

He'd been overcome with emotion, to be honest. All because of a tricolored beagle, and even more importantly, because of Cassie. Because no matter how much success he'd amassed or how much wealth he'd accumulated, she had been what was missing—or rather who was missing—in his life. As corny as it sounded, it was true.

By the time they got in his convertible and drove to Manhattan, Andrew was more than ready to spend some more quality time with Cassie. Andrew had given Kyle the night off and he was looking forward to driving his favorite Selenite Grey Roadster to his favorite city with his favorite person, who tonight was wearing a body-hugging little black dress with a plunging neckline that made him all but hard just thinking of how he'd get her out of it.

"You seem very calm about spending the evening with my mother and number four. What gives?" Cassie studied his profile.

What had Cassie asked?

He adjusted his sunglasses. "Number four? Why don't you call him Luc?"

"I figured he was a phase, like numbers two and three." She wrinkled her nose. "With my dad being her first husband, none of the others ever measured up to him. At least not as far as I was concerned. My mother disagreed."

"I'm sorry." Andrew knew how difficult this was for her to discuss, and silently cursed himself for ever suggesting dinner with her mom. He'd tried to prolong it for as long as possible, but Julia had insisted on this night.

Taking her hand in his, he squeezed it. "To answer your question, I'm calm because I'm with you."

"Why, Andrew, you say the sweetest things when you want to." Her tone was teasing.

"I try." And he was trying harder than he ever had to ensure that he didn't say or do anything to ruin this thing with Cassie. Though in the past, Andrew had tended to get tongue-tied around her and blurt out what he felt, only to retract his statements shortly thereafter, he'd been doing exceptionally well ever since their argument during the *Househusbands* premiere.

It was there that he'd decided to voice how he felt. After all, why hide it? Doing so had messed everything up. Repeatedly. So, with that in mind, he'd decided to share his true feelings with her. He'd also decided not to hide anything from her, which was easier said than done because he still hadn't admitted that he may have misled her with his *mutually beneficial* sales pitch.

But did he really mislead her?

Ever since their breakup, he had missed Cassie, and he'd wanted another chance with her. The plan he hatched in Westhampton Beach had allowed him that second chance. In the end, wasn't that beneficial for him? Yes. As he thought more about it, he'd alluded to it. Andrew just never had the guts to admit how he truly felt.

Besides, he never said his business was hurting, just that *looks could be deceiving.* And that was true enough. Andrew had looked as if he'd gotten over Cassie, but he hadn't. Not really. Sure, he dated women when they were apart, but none were Cassie. No one ever measured up to her.

No one could.

By the time he handed his keys to the valet, Andrew was ready to make a minor admission.

"Hey." He pulled Cassie aside and leaned into her. "Remember when you asked me, or maybe demanded would be a better word, that I tell you that I don't care about you? And I couldn't."

She nodded. "How could I possibly forget that?"

"Yeah. That was memorable, but not in a good way." It was time for Andrew to course correct. "What I couldn't—or wouldn't say at the time, is that I *do* care about you. I always have. For all these years, I was never over you, you know?"

With a soft kiss, Cassie skimmed her fingertips along his jawline, causing his flesh to prickle in response. "That took a lot of courage."

He shrugged like it was no big deal.

"So, it's my turn for a confession. I wasn't over you either, not really. I tried to move on, and thought I had, but I hadn't."

Though Andrew hadn't expected such a confession from Cassie, he welcomed it with a relief that flooded him like a strong current.

Andrew kissed her one more time. It was his attempt to erase the past, to eradicate all of the time spent apart from one another.

With a sigh, Cassie leaned against him. "You make me breathless."

Then and only then did he trace the outline of her lips with the pad of his thumb, making sure that her nude lipstick was still in place. "What do you say we get this over with, then go home?"

"If that offer involves more of what we did last night, and more kisses like our last one, I'm all in." Her voice had taken on a seductive tone.

"That goes without saying. Especially with how sexy you look in this dress. It's reminding me of how sexy you'll look out of it." He winked at her. But for the first time, it was deliberate. "I meant to wink, by the way. In a flirty, 'you seem to anchor me somehow' way. I don't feel jittery with you anymore."

Cassie splayed one hand on his chest, then gripped his tie with the other, tugging him even closer to her. "After last night, I can say with all honesty that you have *nothing* to feel self-conscious about."

Her flirting was contagious. "You don't say?"

She kissed him once more. He would never tire of Cassie kissing him.

When she pulled away at last, Andrew moaned. "Why did I ever agree to this dinner?"

"Because you're a glutton for punishment?" Cassie offered him one of her sassy grins, then took his hand in hers. "What do you say we do this together? Get it over with and go home."

"Together." Andrew nodded as he led her into the upscale restaurant hand in hand. Once seated at a table for four, beside one another, he and Cassie flirted, talked, and had a drink while waiting for Julia and Luc, aka: "Four." Andrew just hoped he wouldn't slip and call the man by Cassie's nickname for him.

Leave it to Julia West to arrive forty-five minutes late and make a grand entrance to the point where everyone seated in the dining room was watching her. Then again, what did Andrew expect from the same diva who was a no-show to her own daughter's wedding?

"Hello, darlings," Julia announced with a flourish of her arms, as if she had just waltzed onstage in a regional production of some Broadway show. It was too much, even for him, and Andrew thought he'd seen it all.

Cassie stood and kissed her mother on the cheek. Standing stock-still, Julia waited in a prima-donna-esque pose, prompting Andrew to follow Cassie's lead. It was as if Julia was holding court, as if they were showing their affection for royalty, which Julia might well consider herself to be. Andrew wouldn't put anything past the woman.

"What a wonderful room. And look, we have such an important table, right in the center," Julia remarked as her husband held out her chair for her.

Luc remained stoic, in a navy suit and tie with a white rose in his lapel. Silent, and giving off a slightly eccentric vibe with the fresh flower in his lapel, Luc struck Andrew as someone who was used to Julia's theatrics, who had accepted her a long time ago.

With a smile plastered on her face, Cassie made eye contact with Four as he took his seat across from her. "Hi, Luc."

Andrew hid a smirk behind his hand, relieved that she remembered the man's name. He'd half expected Cassie would slip and call the man "Four."

"Hello. Nice to see you." Husband number four was a man of few words, just as Andrew had remembered. Okay, five words to be exact, but still...

By the time they'd ordered appetizers, and Cassie had ordered herself a second glass of white wine, Andrew watched as Julia scanned the room. He followed her line of sight, noting that eyes were no longer on her. In turn, she scowled as if disappointed that she'd lost her enraptured audience so quickly.

The public was fickle, as Andrew noted from his own experience with The Steele Dailies. People couldn't get enough news about a certain celebrity one day and would forget about them the next. Or become disillusioned with them, or just plain disgusted. Scandal or even overexposure would do that to even the most loyal fan base, or to the most rabid.

"So, tell me, Andrew. What made you seek Cassandra out again after you broke her heart so long ago?" Julia was nothing if not direct. She was also seated directly across from Andrew.

Lucky him.

Aware that Julia didn't know the truth about Cassandra being jilted at the altar, Andrew stuck with the cover story they'd agreed upon. "Cassie and I ended up in each other's orbits, and it was as if no time had passed."

"Where was this? And when?" Julia's scowl deepened, as did the lines around her mouth. "I never thought of *Cassandra* as being cruel, but dumping poor Jeremy the way she did, at the altar of all places, was downright despicable."

Julia stressed her daughter's formal name.

It was her battle cry.

With that came the realization that the tension and dislike between Andrew and Julia, at least on her part, was because of a name, or a nickname as the case may be—Cassie vs. Cassandra.

It was about control, or Julia's lack of it.

"I want details," Julia persisted.

"So do I," Jeremy Roth announced from behind Julia.

Dressed in a slim-fit suit, skinny tie, and a smirk a mile long, Roth exuded negative energy. Or maybe that was just the feeling he evoked from Andrew.

"Jeremy, this is a private dinner." Cassie's voice was low and lethal.

"I have an invite. From your mother, *Cassandra*. She always liked me." He chuckled, taking an empty chair from the table next to their group and pulling it over, before seating himself in a prime spot—at the head of the table between Andrew on one side, and Julia on the other, which was a good thing, because Andrew was certain that Cassie would want to be as far away from Jeremy as possible.

"Now, what were you about to say? Oh, I remember. You were about to provide torrid details about this love affair of yours. But, is it love? I'm not entirely sure." Jeremy's exaggerated grimace proved just what an actor he was. No wonder Cassie hadn't seen through him. Andrew was certain that Jeremy had deftly played the devoted boyfriend, then fiancé, while he was with Cassie until he'd decided to move on from her.

Andrew was equally as certain that things were about to get ugly.

"You invited *him*?" Though Andrew was sure that Cassie had tried to hide the pain that her mother's betrayal had dredged up, Cassie's voice still shook. It was slight, but Andrew caught it.

Judging by Julia's rattled expression, she caught it as well.

The unflappable and *it's all about me, Julia West* must have realized that she had crossed a line, or two hundred, by inviting Roth to dinner.

Andrew wished he was surprised at this turn of events, but he really wasn't. Throughout his life, the rich and snobbish had always stuck together and it'd been he who was continually the odd man out.

This situation was no different. Julia and Jeremy would stick together. What they would never understand was that Andrew was a scrapper who'd amassed a lot of influence. He would take them both on at once.

He was used to being outnumbered and coming out on top.

Though she was holding it together for her mother and Roth to see above the table with its pristine white tablecloth draped elegantly with expensive fine china and silverware, he felt Cassie's pain and it hurt.

A lot.

Cassie crushed Andrew's hand in a vise grip beneath the table. That, Andrew knew, was a small sampling of the intense pain she was feeling.

"You owe us an explanation, Cassandra." In all the time Andrew had known Julia West, he'd never seen her in a color other than purple. Tonight was no exception. She was garbed in what he was certain must be a violet designer dress with matching eye makeup. "You owe me an explanation."

"Allow me to get one thing straight. I don't owe either of you an explanation. As a matter of fact, I owe you nothing."

How she was keeping her cool, Andrew hadn't a clue. All he knew was that Cassie was staring down Jeremy like a pro and Andrew was proud of her.

"You do owe me an explanation, Cassandra. You're my daughter and therefore an extension of me, and what you do affects me." Mommie Dearest made it all about herself, as was her habit. Andrew remembered that about her. "Do you have any idea how humiliating these headlines about you have been for me? How could you have left poor Jeremy at the altar?"

Poor Jeremy.

Mommie Dearest did not just go there again, did she?

Cassie squeezed Andrew's hand in such a vise grip that he let out an "Ow—I—don't think we should be having this discussion here." He spoke more to Julia and Jeremy than Cassie and was rather proud of his quick save. No one in their dinner party seemed to have guessed that Cassie was currently squeezing the life out of him.

"Poor Jeremy," Cassie repeated, glancing from her mother to Roth, then back to her mother. "Poor Jeremy, is it?"

Her mother nodded. She'd suddenly turned mute.

"Huh. You want to know how I could leave poor Jeremy at the altar." Cassie turned to Andrew, then grinned before batting her long, curly eyelashes at him. Her tone was low, and seductive.

So was her touch when she traced his jawline with her forefinger.

"They want to know all the details about our relationship, and although neither of us owe them anything, I'd love to fill them in."

She smiled as she lessened her grip on his hand. And thank goodness she did. It had become extremely difficult to hide the pain Andrew was feeling. "Sure, Cassie. I'll let you do the honors."

Wasn't it funny what comes to one's mind at a time like this? Andrew came to the sudden realization that he had no endearing nickname for Cassie. Nothing but Cassie. His nickname for her. No sweetheart, no babe...nothing but Cassie. He silently put that on a to-do list as he handed the wheel to her. She was driving this ride from Hades and Andrew was just there for moral support.

"Andrew and I reconnected when I least expected it, and, while I wish I could say it was love at first sight for a second time, it was anything but. He got on my nerves, and I got on his like no one else."

"That's the truth." Andrew smiled at her. It really was the truth. "No one drives me as nuts as you do. It's what I love most about you, Cassie."

Love. He said *love.* And—*what was this...this feeling?* Andrew knew what it *wasn't.* It most certainly wasn't regret. No, he didn't regret his use of the word *love.*

He actually meant it.

He loved Cassie.

"I do... I love you." Andrew blurted it out, with a wink.

Oh, my—

Cassie kissed him. It was forceful, so forceful that his chair scraped the floor as she sent it back an inch or so. Then her kiss turned gentle. So gentle that Andrew was sure that this wasn't an act.

When she spoke, her whisper was hoarse. "I love you, too. Which is what I want you to remember as I light them on fire with my words," she whispered to him, turning to face her mother and Roth.

Holy hell, Cassie was sexy when she was enraged at her mom and ex-fiancé.

"So, here's the scoop. I love Andrew and Andrew loves me. *You…*"— she turned to her mother—"you must deal with it. Or not. It's your choice and after the stunt you pulled tonight, by inviting Jeremy here, I don't really care either way."

Turning toward Roth, her intense stare was fiery and unflinching. "As for *you*. You are a lowlife of the first order, and I'm glad we're over."

Roth opened his mouth to speak, but Cassie held her hand up in the charged air between them. "No. Don't talk. I'm not done yet. Did I say that he was a lowlife?"

Cassie caught Andrew's attention and he nodded, much too spell-bound for words. This was better than an action flick.

After returning her attention to Jeremy, she continued. "I realized something when I was with Andrew… I never loved you. It's always been him, and it always will be. What it won't be, what it will never be, is you. And I'm grateful for that."

"You were thinking of me, though. When you were with him." The shit-eating grin on Roth's smug face was one Andrew was itching to punch.

Though Andrew was more than ready to throw down in the fine five-star establishment like the reality television stars he covered on a daily basis, he refrained.

Instead, Cassie leaned forward and spoke clearly, for all at the table to hear. "Just once. And never again. With one exception—when I realized that I never truly enjoyed sex with you."

"What has happened to you?" Julia asked, her voice aghast. Gone was the diva, and in her place was a woman who was clearly shocked that her daughter had this much fire in her, and that her daughter was strong enough to take on two bullies like Julia and Roth at once.

It was clear that both expected to get away with making Cassie feel uncomfortable. What was also crystal clear was that it wasn't working. Cassie was strong and confident, and they couldn't touch that.

That's why Roth was currently clenching his jaw so tightly that Andrew could swear he heard the man's teeth grinding.

"What happened to me?" Cassie repeated her mother's question. "Well, Mother, that's a long story. Perhaps if you hadn't invited Jeremy here tonight, I would have told you. Had you asked me nicely, of course."

"This is your fault." Julia leaned across the table, pointing at Andrew as her mask of civility began to further slip.

"By all means, blame me. I never expected you to like me or approve of me." Andrew swallowed hard against the resentment that had been festering since Roth had dumped Cassie at her altar.

He pointed at the man, the same man who'd planned to humiliate Cassie, the one who was supposed to love her and care about her. "Just know that *this guy* isn't the person you think he is. If you love your daughter, you'll keep him as far away from her as you can. That's what I'm going to do."

"Really, Steele? Do you honestly think you have any real power?" Jeremy taunted him. "You were only invited to the wedding because of me."

"You?" A knot had formed in the pit of Andrew's stomach.

Jeremy smiled. "I knew the ceremony would be gossip-worthy and yours is the most popular gossip site, after all. As much as I hate to admit it, you are influential in your own way."

It was now clear that Andrew's suspicions about Roth had been correct. Roth had set Cassie up for a public fall. Roth, the man who was supposed to be respectable, who was supposed to be better for her than Andrew, *had* set her up on that fateful day.

Andrew had suspected it, which was why he'd felt no remorse about changing the jilted bride narrative and protecting Cassie.

One thing nagged at Andrew with Roth's admission: Why would he play that hand now? Here?

Was he hoping for a scene?

Andrew scanned the restaurant. No one was watching them. No one was filming them, and no one could hear their conversations above the usual restaurant noise. They'd gone this far without causing a scene, and Andrew wouldn't be the one to implode his and Cassie's relationship.

He made certain his voice was low, but dangerous. "Cassie made her choice, and it wasn't you. But, make no mistake, if you threaten to come after her again, I will come after you. And just know, I never make promises I don't keep."

"Did you say 'threaten'?" Four, formerly known as Julia's husband, Luc, spoke at long last. It was a dinner miracle. Andrew would have assumed he'd fallen asleep if the man's eyes hadn't remained open.

"Cassie made her choice," Jeremy mimicked, ignoring Four altogether. "Like she did when she created her company and decided to name it A Perfect Wedding? *A Perfect Wedding.* What a joke. It should be called A Perfect Wedding Disaster! She can't even pull off her own nuptials. Or hold on to her groom."

"Wait a moment. What did you mean by that, Jeremy?" Julia had raised her voice loud enough for everyone in the restaurant to stare.

It was the first time people's attention had been drawn to their table since Julia's arrival. Cassie hit all of her marks without ever raising her voice. That took guts, and it took control. Andrew's respect for her had grown tenfold.

"Jeremy, answer me." Julia's voice rose an octave higher, though Jeremy never answered her. Instead, the man's Cheshire Cat grin spoke volumes. Andrew knew it and so did Julia. At the very least she suspected that something was amiss, though Julia still had no idea that Roth was the one who called off the wedding to her daughter, or that Roth's intention had been to humiliate Cassie on that fateful day.

Andrew wondered how long Julia's blissful ignorance would last.

"Let's go home. I've had enough of being ambushed," Cassie said to Andrew before rising and looking straight at her mother as she tossed her linen napkin onto the table. "Thanks for dinner, Mother. Oh, just know that you will be paying for it. When it comes to restaurants, airlines, and hotels, Jeremy has developed a nasty habit of never offering up his own credit cards, or cash. Unless you make him, that is. How was our honeymoon hotel, Jeremy?"

"Fun. You should have been there." His comeback was swift. He grabbed Andrew's discarded menu and began perusing it. "What's for dinner? I'm starving."

"Great choice in that one, Mother." Cassie shook her head. "Bye, Four."

She walked past several tables where people were gawking and led the way to the valets, where Andrew handed his ticket over for his car.

"Cassandra, wait!" Cassie didn't turn to face her mother. "Cassandra—Cassandra—Cassie. Talk to me."

Only after her mother called Cassie by her nickname did she turn around at last. "You're going to be sorry you asked me to do that, Mother. I don't think you're ready for the truth, but that's exactly what you're going to get."

Chapter 16

AFTER A LIFETIME OF PLAYING BY HER MOTHER'S RULES, CASSIE had finally forced the woman to bend to her will. All by ignoring her mother until Julia West had no choice but to call her daughter by her nickname, Cassie, at long last.

What might have seemed trivial to some was in fact a huge victory. When it came to Cassie's mother, she never relented, never changed her mind, with this one exception. And with that, Cassie Benedict was here to stay.

It was past time that her mother accepted that fact. "How could you invite that man to dinner with me—with me and Andrew? I know you don't approve of Andrew, or me for that matter, but that trick you pulled is petty even by the low standards you've set for yourself."

"I'm going to pretend you didn't say that, Cassandra—"

"It's Cassie. And if you don't like it, then don't say my name at all."

Her mother took several steps backward, then sputtered. "Wh-why—why would you say such a thing?"

"Because in your haste to side with *poor Jeremy*, as you repeatedly refer to the rich boy you always approved of, you invited the one man who hurt me the most." Cassie took a step toward her mother, and whispered so only she could hear. "You invited the man who jilted me—your daughter—at the altar."

With that admission, she paused, allowing her words to sink in. "Do you understand now? That man in there hurt me. And while the timeline remains unclear, I do know now that Jeremy planned it. Heck, he knew he'd be bringing someone else on my honeymoon, that same honeymoon that I paid for."

Would her mother show Cassie even half the empathy that she showed to Jeremy?

"Why didn't you tell me?" was all Julia could say as she took another few steps away from the entry doors, as if she could outrun her past mistakes.

Cassie laughed. "Is that a joke? Why would I ever trust you enough to tell you? You'll do anything for PR, including hurt me in the process. You've proven that much, Mother."

"For heaven's sake, I called the paparazzi once on your eighth birthday and it got me a higher negotiated rate for that season. You benefited from it as much as I did. And you looked quite nice in the photos they published." Julia's lips formed a scowl.

"My birthday?" Cassie stared the woman dead in the eyes as her anger mounted.

She would no longer hide the truth.

Who had she been protecting, anyway? Not her mother. Certainly not her mother.

Julia West didn't deserve Cassie's protection. Not with what that woman had done.

Cassie's rage boiled to the surface until she confronted her mother, her tone low but deadly. "This has nothing to do with my eighth birthday, Mother. It never has. It's about my father's funeral. You remember him, right?"

A look of bewilderment clouded Julia's features. Her mother showed no sign of recognition. She had no idea where Cassie was going with this. Of that Cassie was certain as she continued.

"I'm sure you remember my father's funeral. I do. It's where I found out that you called the paparazzi and had them wait in the bushes, so they could get shots of me crying as my father's casket was being lowered into the ground. Then you pretended to mourn with me, so you would be seen in a favorable, and sympathetic, light, while negotiating a different contract than the one you were negotiating on my eighth birthday."

Andrew expelled a jagged breath. "Oh God, Cassie."

She turned to see Andrew watching her with sadness etched in his strong features. It wasn't the way she'd wanted him to find out, but now he understood Cassie's hatred for his chosen profession. Her mother had used her father, and in turn Cassie herself, as props in a graveside photo op for the tabloids in order to get what she wanted. That was the Julia West way, after all.

How many other times had Julia considered using her daughter to get an advantage? Cassie's eighth birthday, yes. That she knew, but were there things Cassie didn't know? Perhaps there were things she didn't remember.

Regardless, her father had always been there for her, had always protected her. And he deserved more. More than Julia, and much more than the drama she brought to his funeral.

"He was my dad; he was my everything and to you he was nothing but some extra on the set of *The Julia West Show*." Cassie swallowed hard, past the lump of emotion lodged in her throat.

The valet pulled up in Andrew's car and he sprinted to meet him at the driver's door. "Can you please take it around the block? Maybe once, if not twice? I'll make it worth your while and tip you double." When the man agreed, Andrew thanked him before returning his attention to Cassie and walking over to her, flattening his palm against her back in support.

"Say what you need to to your mother. We've got time." His tone was kind. Much too kind. Cassie was now causing a scene, and people were gawking at them.

But Andrew had bought her some time, and Cassie would take it.

Her mother raised her chin in the air. "I never knew that—"

"That what? That I knew what you'd done? That I saw through you?" Cassie's voice shook, though she didn't cower. No, this was her one chance to say her piece and she would do just that.

Without anger.

She spoke calmly, though how she did so, Cassie would never know. "I saw through you then, and I see through you now. You invited Jeremy here tonight to make a fool out of Andrew and try to get me back together with the guy from the wealthy family, the guy *you* approve of. Not based upon how he treats me, but how large his inheritance might be."

"I didn't know what Jeremy did—"

"You would have if you'd showed up for my wedding." Cassie didn't have time for her mother's excuses. And she lacked the patience for them as well. "You weren't there when I needed help, but Andrew was. And he cared enough to drop everything and show me support when my own mother wouldn't. Let's be honest for once, shall we? It was a choice that you made, right? Not to come home, I mean. You could have flown in for a day—for one day, for your daughter's wedding day—if you wanted. Right?"

Her mother stared at Cassie, and for the first time Cassie saw actual tears in the woman's brown eyes. This wasn't acting or overacting, as Julia's performances had tended to be in most recent years. This was shame, or the closest to it that Cassie would ever see from her.

"That's what I thought. Here's the thing: if you were a good mother, you would have been there if for no other reason than because Daddy couldn't be. He couldn't walk me down the aisle, and I can't begin to tell you how much I missed him." Blinking back tears, Cassie glanced at Andrew, who was watching her intently. He nodded, encouraging her to continue as the valet passed in his car.

Scanning her surroundings, Cassie noted that no one was looking at her. At least not anymore. They'd lost interest in what was going on between her and her mother.

It was time Cassie ended this.

Wiping her eyes, she laid it bare for her mother. She decided to use language her mother understood. "The bottom line is this: I love Andrew and you'll never approve of him. I honestly don't care if you do, and I'm certain Andrew doesn't either. If you want to garner attention for yourself by running to your favorite gossip sites and dishing about my failure of a wedding, do it. You be you, Mother. Just don't expect me to take part in any of it."

"Answer me one thing." Julia turned her attention to Andrew, walking over to him as a crowd exiting the restaurant veered around them and their drama. "Is this real?"

"I love your daughter. That's real." Andrew hailed the valet, who was driving up in his convertible. Reaching for Cassie, he held out his hand. "Are you ready?"

Cassie took his hand. "I am more than ready. Goodbye, Mother. Oh! Have a great dinner with Jeremy. You two deserve each other."

As Andrew escorted her to his passenger seat, then tipped the valet what she was certain was roughly four times what he would have usually gotten as a tip, Cassie looked at her mother one last time. Ever the actress, Julia picked up her chin, straightened her shoulders, and waltzed back into the exclusive restaurant with her head held high.

Nothing could keep Julia West down. Not even the truth.

"Are you okay?" Andrew asked as he slid behind the wheel and caressed her cheek.

All Cassie could do was nod. She felt exhausted. Emotionally and physically, so she changed the subject in a deliberate attempt to delay talking about her dad. "How about that bombshell that Jeremy dropped?

He's the one who invited you to my non-wedding fiasco. He planned to humiliate me and to have *you* be the one who published it."

"I had a feeling. That's why I didn't feel bad about flipping the narrative on him." Andrew met her surprised gaze. "What? Does it surprise you that I had my suspicions?"

"Let me see. Does it surprise me that my ex-fiancé would invite my ex-boyfriend to a wedding he had nothing to do with for the sole purpose of humiliating me in a brutally public way? Yes. I'm shocked. I never saw that coming. How did you know?"

With a deep sigh, Andrew's gaze softened. "Your ring tipped me off. He planned to break up with you and wanted to make sure he held on to the ring. It's currency to him."

Andrew was right.

She hadn't seen it. But she should have.

"That's why you asked me about the ring. About where it was, and if he paid for it." Cassie remembered that conversation on Dune Road all too well, as well as Andrew's question to her about who paid for her engagement ring. "I didn't see it because I thought he was being sweet."

"If I'd proposed to you, I would never have asked you to take that ring off." Andrew's eyes held hers, and in his smoky eyes, there was a raw emotion.

He meant what he was saying.

Cassie knew that much.

"You thought Jeremy had intentionally hurt me, yet you put up with my judgment about you, based upon your business." Cassie shook her head slowly as the realization dawned on her, with all its implications. "I'm sorry I was so wrong about you."

"Don't do that. There's nothing for you to apologize for. But since we're still talking, why didn't you tell me about your dad? Why didn't you tell me that's why you hated my business? I would have understood." He gripped the steering wheel with his free hand. "I probably would have given it up for you. I would have done anything for you."

She didn't believe it.

Not then. They were still young, and Cassie thought Andrew would choose his career over her. Without question. Now, tonight...That was a different story.

This Andrew would have chosen her.

She stroked his hand, suppressing tears. "Let's just go home. We can talk then. I've had enough of this restaurant to last a lifetime."

Andrew drew her closer to him and kissed her forehead before buckling his seat belt and putting his car in gear. As he pulled away from the restaurant, Cassie had never been so grateful to be on the road and headed to Andrew's penthouse. Not even on her disastrous non-wedding day, and that was saying something.

"Did you mean it?" Cassie expected Andrew to ask for clarification.

Instead, he grinned. "Yeah, I love you."

"I love you, too." She couldn't help but smile.

Somehow this horrendous evening wound up in the win column.

Chapter 17

THE DRIVE HOME MAY HAVE BEEN SILENT, BUT THE PENTHOUSE WAS anything but. Bailey met them at the door and barked, jumped, and wagged his tail to his heart's content. Andrew joined Cassie and her pup on an evening walk, while she savored the peaceful time with the one man, and one dog, that she cared most about.

Andrew's busy neighborhood was everything Cassie could have asked for. Between the views and proximity to both the carousel and Manhattan, it was perfect. It was easy to lose yourself in the magic and take her mind off everything.

By the time they made it back to the penthouse, Andrew offered to feed Bailey and give him fresh water while Cassie stood in front of the tall bank of windows in his great room, savoring his view of the Manhattan skyline.

At night, between the twinkling stars and the lights across the bay, it was as if Andrew had the entire sky and city of Manhattan at his disposal. Manhattan, while romantic, was nothing in comparison to this enchanted sliver of it.

She felt Andrew come up from behind her and was drawn to him, as he wrapped his arms around her waist from behind. Leaning against him, Cassie continued to study the skyline while he brushed her hair to the side, then kissed her neck. The scent of his cologne lingered, and she savored his musky scent.

"Do you want to talk?" His baritone was raspy.

Andrew had given her time to process what happened on this night.

It was only fair that she discussed what happened, and what she'd been keeping from him. "I owe you an explanation. Let's sit."

She led him to his leather sofa, then curled up in his arms. The view was still as glorious as before. The sofa was positioned in the precise spot with an unfettered view. It was deliberate. Cassie was certain of it as she nestled into the crook of Andrew's neck. It would be easier to confess if she weren't facing him.

"Now you know why I despised what you chose to do for a living." That was an understatement. What Andrew did for a living had disgusted her prior to their breakup and she didn't understand the appeal.

"I don't blame you for hating the paparazzi. What I don't understand is why you never told me." Andrew planted a kiss on the top of her head, then smoothed her hair, which she'd worn down tonight.

Cassie considered his statement. "I don't hate them per se, I just have no respect for them. And if I had told you, then what? What would you have done?"

"I would have looked at it differently. I might have even given it up."

"But that wouldn't have been fair. That's why I didn't tell you." It was one of the reasons she hadn't told him the truth.

But not the only reason.

"I'm only admitting to half of it, though. In truth, I thought you would have chosen your career over me."

Her confession hung heavy, sucking the air from the room.

"I couldn't have withstood that, not after losing my father just a few years prior to meeting you. So, I tried to ignore everything, which became much more difficult as you and Noah got closer to launching your business."

"You were unhappy, and I thought you were done." Andrew kissed her hair.

Cassie nodded. "I was prolonging the inevitable. We never would have worked back then. I was still too bitter about what my mother had done."

"You said that you don't respect the paparazzi. Did you mean them, me, or both?" There was an achingly desperate tone behind his question. One that caused Cassie to sit upright, turn around, and look him in the eyes.

After flattening her palm against his cheek, which was still smooth from shaving before they left for dinner, she said at last, "Them, not you. Never you. Especially not after watching you work, watching you fight for what you think is right. I now know that you wouldn't have flipped the narrative, or used it against Jeremy, if you hadn't suspected that he'd set me up. That same moral compass of yours would never allow you to stalk a grieving high school girl at her dad's funeral. And you would never allow one of your photographers to intercept that same girl on the way to her car."

"They did what?" He narrowed his eyes, which were dark and smoky in the dim recessed lighting.

Cassie remembered that day all too well.

"My mother held court at my father's grave, and I couldn't deal with any of her sycophants. Not anymore. In truth, I resented them being there, at the gravesite. Even her second and third husbands, or should I say ex-husbands, showed up."

There she was, a teenage girl who'd lost the one constant in her life, the one parent who'd been there for her.

She missed her dad even now.

Inhaling a ragged breath, the memory assailed her. It was still fresh after all these years. "It was a crisp, clear autumn day in New York. I slipped away and began walking to my car. One of the photographers stopped me and asked how I felt. I laid into the guy."

Yes, she had. Forever the good girl, Cassie harbored years of resentment and that photographer bore the brunt of it. "I unleashed on him. He was so rattled that he admitted to my mother's role—she'd even gone as far as telling the paparazzi that I'd cooperate with them and answer questions."

"Why would your mother do that?"

Cassie shook her head. "I don't think she ever expected them to approach me. Not there. I don't know. In the end, the photographer who did approach me felt bad, probably because I was crying uncontrollably. He apologized for my mother's scheme. She, on the other hand, has never apologized to me—not even tonight."

"I'm so sorry. That must have been devastating for you—then and tonight." He laced his fingers with hers. His hand was warm and strong. It made her feel like she wasn't alone anymore. She'd been alone since her father died, really. High school had been tough, and college would have been, if not for Andrew.

"My mother and I had a strained relationship already, and I had learned at a young age not to count on her. That day though, for a brief moment when she joined me by the casket, I started to feel like…well, like she cared about me. Until I learned that it was an act." She averted her eyes from him, choosing instead to study the soft leather cushion behind him. "That's when I learned to despise my mother, that's when our relationship deteriorated to the point of no return. By the time you and I met, she had moved on to husband number four, and I wanted as little to do with her as possible. I spent holidays at school and summers with Lauren. Whenever my mother and I did see each other, it was tumultuous. But somehow, she got along with Jeremy, which should have been a red flag for me."

"You handled him like a champ tonight." He tipped her chin up, until she faced him. "You set him on fire with your words and looked incredibly hot doing it."

His tone, and his eyes, were animated.

"Not just hot but incredibly hot, huh?" Cassie couldn't help but smile.

"Yeah, even though you did admit to thinking of him while you were with me. Please tell me that it wasn't when we were being intimate." He was teasing her now.

Cassie stretched, then leaned into him. "No, not while we were intimate. It was before, and only for a second, maybe two. Just enough for me to realize that I never felt anything even remotely like that with him. I'll have you know that you kept me preoccupied with other things."

Like his kisses.

Like his tongue.

Like…a lot of things.

Straddling him, she traced his firm, full lips with her tongue. Andrew's deep intake of breath told her this was what he wanted, as his hands trailed up her legs. He kissed her slowly, sensually, as his erection hardened between her legs.

Her dress had a short skirt, and Andrew slid his hands beneath it, then cupped her derriere before squeezing. His erection rose and became harder, then harder still with every kiss and his every caress. He peeled her thong down past her thighs and Cassie knew just what he wanted. That's why she kissed him once more before standing. As her eyes locked with his, she slid her thong down past her knees, then her ankles, then stepped out of the strip of lace.

Andrew moaned when she straddled him again, kneading her bare flesh as she rode him, teased him, and kissed him with all the love in her heart, and all her own desire for him, until he begged her for release. Then and only then did she unzip his pants and stroke his shaft, before sliding atop his erection.

His deep, throaty moan and hungry kisses were all the encouragement

Cassie needed as she gyrated atop him, riding his passion until he joined her in an intense climax. After their spasms had subsided, Cassie continued to kiss him, slowly and deliberately exploring his mouth and tongue with her own.

In their kisses, her heart was laid bare, as was his. Andrew's sensual kisses sent her senses reeling, and seemed more intimate than the act of making love itself.

He gave himself to her completely in his kisses.

As for Cassie, Andrew had become her lover, her best friend, and her lifeline. He had also become her true north. While it was true that they were both different now, Cassie would be forced to admit that theirs was a change for the better.

This Andrew revealed a vulnerability to Cassie that she'd never before known. And in his warm, strong embrace, Cassie found her home.

Lying on his sofa, wrapped in his embrace, Cassie stared out his panoramic windows.

"It's all about the view, isn't it?" she asked him.

"Yeah, it is." His tone was tender. Achingly so.

When Cassie turned to him, she met Andrew's eyes and realized that he'd been speaking about *her*. She was the view he couldn't get enough of.

"You are a smooth talker when you want to be." She placed her hand on his chest, atop the fine fabric of his shirt. She should have undressed him.

He shrugged. "I try. I really do."

For the first time, she knew that he did. "What's the saying about men being from Mars and women being from Venus? Because I think that applies to us, don't you?"

"We do have completely different ways of handling each other, and communicating with each other, don't we?"

"Yes." She just hadn't seen it, let alone understood it, until she'd gotten to know him this time around. While idly tracing his jaw with her fingertips, Cassie asked, "So. What do we do now that we're real, now that we're official?"

Andrew chuckled. "Try not to kill each other."

She couldn't help but laugh. "I think I can handle that. Would it be okay if I asked you for something?"

Offering her a naughty grin, Andrew teased, "You can ask me for anything."

"Though I'm not referring to sex at this time, that offer is tempting." With an arched brow, she got to her point. "I want your professional opinion on my website, my lifestyle blog, and my vlog."

"Oh, those I like. You have a great brand. The font, photos, everything is on point. What your site is missing is you." He rattled it all off in a quick staccato. Like he had been anxious to tell her. "Your social media footprint is on point, too."

"Okay, hold up. You've already checked out my platforms?" Though it sounded naughty, it was meant as anything but.

Honestly, Cassie didn't know what to think. She never expected Andrew to be interested in what she did, let alone be so interested that he'd have mental notes for her without being asked.

"Of course I checked out your socials and websites." He shot her one of his *who do you think I am?* looks.

Shaking her head, she muttered, "Of course you did. So, why don't you elaborate?"

"Well, you are your brand. You need to show more of yourself. Here..." He reached over to the end table and grabbed his cell, then repositioned himself to where she could see his screen. "A-perfect-happiness-dot-com. I like that name, by the way. It's a play on your business, but it's also a mood—because everyone's idea of perfect happiness is different."

How he got her, when no one else had ever tried, blew Cassie away.

This man was close to perfect.

"Here it is. Your home page is phenomenal. Great logo, and the branding is on point. I love the sepia. It's different enough from your business site, without losing the fairy-tale quality. I love that you've linked the two sites. But where are *you* here? On your vlog, sure, but short of those videos, you're not here. And you are exceptional. You are your brand. Own it. It doesn't need a complete revamp, but tighten it and make it more personal. Sell yourself and you'll be golden."

It was clear that Andrew had thought a lot about this. She recalled a prior conversation with him. "And you only kept up with me because my business catered to celebrity clientele, right?"

Andrew smiled. "About that—you've got me there."

"I know." She kissed him once more.

When their lips parted, Andrew traced lazy circles on her neck. It tickled her, to the point that she felt giddy.

"Are you truly grateful that Roth jilted you?" he asked, as his hand stilled.

"Absolutely. I would never have been happy with him. Even if you and I hadn't worked out our differences. He was a rebound guy, and he was the easy choice, or so I thought. Now that I realize he was using me, I have a different opinion of him."

Much different.

How had Jeremy been able to stay under her radar for so long? She'd thought he was decent, respectful, and respectable. Though he'd been different in the last six months of their relationship, she chalked that up to a combination of work stress and wedding stress.

While it was true that Jeremy didn't plan much of anything when it came to their wedding, he did seem stressed about it whenever she brought it up. It was clear now that something else had been going on. Something like him cheating. That might explain why he stopped having sex with her. He'd said he wanted to wait until their wedding night to have sex again.

"And the sex was bad. I liked hearing that tonight." Andrew's tone was teasing.

Cassie laughed. "I did say that, didn't I?"

"It was implied. Or maybe more than implied. But you kept your cool and handled it like a boss."

Bailey joined them on the sofa and yawned with a loud moan.

"Drama King is exhausted. Do you want to go to bed?" Andrew winked at Cassie. It was now their inside joke.

She no longer made him uncomfortable, she noted with a surge of happiness. "That sounds good, especially since I have a client appointment tomorrow. We're meeting at a venue uptown. My honeymoon is officially off my calendar, though I did enjoy spending it with you. Well, I enjoyed it when we weren't arguing."

He kissed her again.

These intimate moments were the ones Cassie had enjoyed most with Andrew. She always would, she supposed. With one final kiss, Cassie stood, as Bailey jumped off the sofa to follow her and Andrew into his bedroom.

Andrew's phone vibrated. "It's a text from Noah. Something's going on. Give me a second."

Nodding, Cassie sat on his bed, with Bailey on her lap, while Andrew called his business partner.

"Noah, what's going on?" Andrew tugged his silk tie, then with an exasperated sigh, he put Noah on speaker. "You're on with both of us now. Go ahead."

"Roth sent me an email threatening to expose what he called 'the lie of the century' as an exclusive with one of our biggest competitors if we didn't publish news that he and Bethany Phillips are engaged. As you know, she's the daughter of wealthy financier Neil Phillips. But first, how about you tell me how Roth knows that your relationship is a fake? That's got to be 'the secret of the century' he's talking about, right?"

Andrew expelled a deep breath. "That or the bride dumped the groom narrative—"

"Did my mother say something to him?" Cassie blurted for both men to hear. Would her mother sell her out to Jeremy of all people, after learning that he jilted Cassie at the altar? Probably. And though Cassie wasn't surprised, a rogue wave of disappointment washed over her.

Just when she'd thought that her mother couldn't hurt her anymore.

"No. Julia wouldn't do that, not after how you shamed her tonight. Besides, I just can't see Julia doing that. Not even she is that cruel. Roth might be fishing—he must be fishing. You didn't confirm it, did you, Noah?" Andrew asked.

"No. I'd never do that. But, on the off chance that he's got proof, I say we run his engagement story. We're in too deep, and we can't let him destroy our business." Noah's tone exuded *I told you so.*

Cassie couldn't allow Andrew and his partner to suffer for trying to help her. "How about I confess to everything? I'll say that I lied, and you only published what I told you. You'll both be off the hook."

"But you'll take the hit." Andrew loosened his tie and unbuttoned his top button. "No, Roth is bluffing. I know he is."

"How can you be so certain?" Noah asked what Cassie herself had wondered.

Dark circles were visible under Andrew's eyes, even in the dim lighting of his bedroom. He was exhausted. "I know guys like Roth. He's bluffing because he *likes* having something on me. The moment he gives this exclusive to another site, he loses his power. I'd make a sizable bet on the fact that he gets off on power."

Cassie placed her hand on Andrew's leg. "Why don't we discuss this in the morning? It's been an eventful night. We haven't even discussed the possibility that one of the valets or someone at the restaurant might say something about my argument with my mother outside."

"You were talking so low when you told her you'd been jilted that I barely heard what you said. Besides, I tipped the valets who were working with a lot of cash and specified that it was for all of them. I don't see them selling us out." Andrew sounded sure of himself. "I say we let things play out and see what happens."

That was a risk.

"I still think that I should come clean. I don't mind taking the hit." She was adamant.

"You were there tonight, Andrew. Is your gut really telling you that no one will talk?" Noah asked. "Your gut has never been wrong, as long as I've known you."

It was good to know that Andrew had great instincts. That must be one of the many reasons why he was so successful.

Andrew nodded. "Yeah. I'm sticking to my initial reaction. I say we hold off for now. Let's keep our eyes and ears open, Noah, and if there's one hint that I'm wrong—"

"I confess, which I'm prepared to do." Cassie wouldn't let this go.

"I'll think of another way," Andrew assured her. "But yeah. I'll prepare his announcement tonight. Respond to his email and ask for a photo of the happy couple. Once I receive it, I'll publish it."

Noah agreed, then bid them a goodnight, and Andrew disconnected the call.

Should they really wait and see? Cassie's gut told her not to.

"Andrew—"

"This whole charade was to save your reputation. I'm not sacrificing you to save myself." Andrew sat beside her and Bailey, cupping Cassie's chin. "I'm just as stubborn as you are. Maybe more."

He looked so tired.

Cassie wouldn't argue this any longer. "Let's put this on pause and get some sleep. We can double back tomorrow."

After nodding, Andrew removed his tie, then unbuttoned his shirt.

"I'm sorry for tonight. I shouldn't have—"

"What? Stood up to Jeremy and your mother?" Andrew bent down and kissed her forehead. "You said nothing wrong to Jeremy, and it was past time you confronted your mother about what she did at your dad's funeral. Besides, your mother inviting Jeremy tonight was beyond horrible. I don't blame you for anything you said."

But Cassie blamed herself. It was all she could think of as she listened to Andrew's soft breaths as he slept, and contemplated whether or not today was actually one for the win column.

The morning light brought a new day and new possibilities of both the good and bad variety. Though Cassie was hopeful, there was also a sense of foreboding.

She hoped Andrew's business wouldn't suffer on her account.

As for his intuition never being wrong, wasn't that the very thing that caused him to break up with her in the first place? This, in part, was why she'd already made up her mind to come clean. Andrew didn't yet know it, but she would come clean.

It was the right thing to do.

Besides, Cassie was done hiding behind their fake relationship. It was real, and she loved him. She'd sacrifice anything for him if it came down to it. Cassie just hoped that it wouldn't come to that.

Cassie got dressed and headed out with Bailey for a walk, breakfast, and to a flower market. It was time for her to return to the influencer scene, and she was ready.

Let the day begin.

Chapter 18

ANDREW WOKE UP TO A TEXT FROM NOAH DEMANDING THAT THEY
meet up. He showered, dressed, published the announcement of Roth's
engagement with the photo Noah emailed, and found Cassie arranging
flowers for her vlog in his kitchen.

"Good morning." She kissed him. "I heard you up and about. Guess
what I've been doing?"

Only after glancing at the greenery and flowers strewn haphazardly
on his countertops did Andrew answer. "You robbed Mother Nature."

"No." She feigned annoyance. "I went to a wholesale flower market
at the crack of dawn, and I've been recording my vlog for a while. But
now that you're here, I want to take a picture of us. For my site. I'm doing
what this genius media mogul suggested and making my site more about
me. I am my brand, after all."

He slid his arm around her waist and tugged her close to him. She
was wearing that sensual perfume again, the same one that sent his senses
into overdrive. "Tell me more about this genius."

"How about later? I see you're heading out."

He sighed. "I've got to meet Noah. Can I have a kiss for the road?"

"Come here, you." Cassie kissed him with those soft lips of hers.
Then she reminded him, "My camera is still rolling, so I will be publishing some form of that once I edit it."

"I've been forewarned, and I approve." He kissed her once more,
then headed out to meet Noah at a coffee shop down the block.

His partner wanted to talk. About last night, no doubt.

The sky was overcast with dark storm clouds as he exited his building. By the time he'd arrived at the coffee shop—a mom-and-pop joint, not a Starbucks, which was how Andrew preferred it—he heard the low rumble of thunder in the distance.

Upon entering the establishment, Andrew caught sight of Noah, who was already seated at a table with his laptop open. There were two disposable coffee cups on the table.

"Hey. Is that extra one for me?" Andrew motioned to the second coffee cup.

Noah nodded. "I want to hash this out. I told you that nothing would get in the way of our business, and guess what? Your stunt with Cassie is now getting in the way of our business."

"No, it's not. Our business is going great. We've got plenty of traffic and lots of irons in the fire." Andrew took a swig of his coffee.

His partner turned his laptop around to face him. "Look at this. This is the traffic to our site after you published the news about Roth being engaged. Traffic has decreased by twenty percent today. What will happen when he wants us to publish something else, then something else? How low will our traffic be then? No one cares about Roth or his bride-to-be."

That much was obvious.

"First off, I published that article about Roth less than an hour ago. Give it time. Next, my relationship with Cassie has increased our traffic by thirty-five percent, so even if those numbers you cited stand, we're still ahead. As for Roth, we made an announcement for him, and it didn't work out. We just won't publish anything else about him." Andrew swallowed another gulp of his coffee. He needed the caffeine. "I've got tips pouring in about all sorts of stuff that I'm following up on, not to mention the *Househusbands* cheating scandal news, that I verified and scheduled to post before I left home. I've now got proof that one of them is cheating with a costar. It's probably already sent our numbers skyrocketing. Try refreshing your report."

Noah did, and his eyes widened. "I processed my report too early, didn't I?"

"Yeah. Much too early and with too little faith in your business partner." Andrew traced the plastic lid of his coffee cup with his finger. "Listen, I'm juggling a lot, and would still be working right now if you hadn't demanded we meet up ASAP. In addition to the whole *Househusbands* scandal I mentioned, that's sending people in droves to us and seems to be evolving by the minute, Cassie and I have that event tonight at the Met, and a movie premiere this weekend. She always draws an audience for us. Trust me."

"What about you and Cassie? You haven't posted anything, and it shows in our numbers. You need to post another kiss again." Despite his sentence being formed as a question, Noah's harsh tone conveyed that he wasn't asking.

Andrew decided not to mention the on-camera kiss Cassie had recorded before he left to meet Noah. "Look, Cassie hasn't refused. I'm refusing. I'm not using our relationship to gain—"

"The business comes first. We both discussed it, we agreed to it." Noah wouldn't budge.

Andrew threw up his hands. "Fine. I'll discuss it with Cassie. Is that enough for you?"

"Yep. That's what I needed to hear. For now." Noah shut his laptop. "So, why don't you tell me what's going on with you two? Is this serious?"

"I suppose it is, yeah. I mean, I've carried a torch for her for years."

Noah fist-bumped the air. "I knew it. I didn't think you were over her. I mean, she was your longest relationship, am I right?"

"You are right, yeah." His partner was indeed correct. Even though Andrew had tried to make them work, his relationships post-Cassie had been few and far between. No other relationship lasted as long as his relationship with Cassie. Then, after a while, he stopped trying to make things work with anyone else, because Cassie was the one who got away, and it wasn't fair to any other woman. "I've never gotten over Cassie, you know?"

"No, I don't. I have no idea what that's like."

On that, Andrew was certain that his friend and business partner was telling the truth. He couldn't remember Noah being in a relationship beyond a single-digit series of months. He was a perpetual bachelor, and always would be, or so Andrew suspected.

"How does Cassie feel knowing that you did this all for her? Crafted this narrative and you got nothing in return? It was selfless, if you ask me."

Noah had no idea what can of worms he'd opened. Andrew was certain of it as he shifted uncomfortably in his chair. "She doesn't know, and she can't find out until I tell her."

"Excuse me?" Noah leaned across the table. "What do you mean she doesn't know? What does that woman think she knows?"

"About that…" Andrew swallowed hard, as his pulse pounded in his temples. "Cassie thinks it was mutually beneficial."

"And…" The look on Noah's face said it all. Andrew was in trouble.

"And nothing. I told her that my helping her would be for both of our benefits. She wouldn't have accepted my help otherwise."

"That was such a bad idea. Tell me you know what a bad idea that was."

"I know. Of course I know that, but it was the only thing I could do at the time." Andrew really had no choice.

Why didn't his partner get that?

"No, you did have a choice. You could have told her the truth. You didn't and she won't forgive you for that." Noah pointed at himself. "I'm terrible when it comes to relationships and even I know *that*. Why don't you know that?"

"I do, it just wasn't a priority at the time." Andrew's priority had been getting Cassie out of the way of any oncoming traffic that could have been headed her way and helping save her wounded pride.

Andrew had also wanted her to stop crying because, when she had cried in front of him on her non-wedding day, it broke Andrew. It had split his heart in half because the Cassie he'd known never cried. Not even once, which meant that she was really suffering. All Andrew knew was that he must make it right for her, so she wouldn't cry anymore.

"Here's a tip for you." Noah pushed his coffee cup aside. "If she finds out the truth, I suggest you don't use that reasoning with her. She may punch you. In fact, I wouldn't blame her if she did."

Andrew's head was pounding like a jackhammer. He could feel a migraine coming on. He hadn't had one since he was in college, but now one was forming. "I didn't exactly lie to her."

"True. You misled her."

In Andrew's mind, his racing mind, it still was an awful thing to do. "If you have nothing else to say, I'm going home. I've got work to do."

And he had a confession to make.

He must tell Cassie the truth. It was time—that's the one thing Noah had made clear to Andrew.

"You go home, and work on telling her the truth. That's what I'd do if I were you. Or maybe I would have told her the truth from the beginning." Noah drank another swig of his coffee.

"She wouldn't have gone home with me if I'd done that," Andrew reminded his friend.

"But at least you would have been honest," Noah countered.

With a heavy sigh, Andrew studied his coffee cup. "I hate you." His friend really could be a pain in the ass sometimes.

Noah smiled. "Somehow, I don't mind that. You're still my partner, and the guy I trust most in this world. So, just tell her, would you? I may not have the infallible gut instinct that you do, but I can sense impending doom. It's coming for you on two fronts: Roth, and Cassie. All because of one fake relationship, and a lie—sorry, a misleading statement."

"I did end up benefiting. We're together." Andrew cringed. "I did *not* mean that the way it sounded."

"I know," his friend sighed. "But it doesn't matter. You misled her and you know it."

Andrew did. He knew that, though he'd been in denial for far too long. Until things had gotten real with Cassie. Until her confession last night about her mother. Andrew saw her unfiltered and without armor for the very first time.

So, he'd known that he must tell her the truth, just like Andrew knew that he was imperfect and had said what he thought would make her decision easier on her failed wedding day. Because Andrew felt like he was the only person who could help Cassie, and he had helped her. The narrative had been flipped, but at what cost?

At the cost of Cassie, if she found out before Andrew told her the truth.

Though she might still dump Andrew when he told her the truth, he had to tell her now, before it was too late.

He tossed his cup of coffee in the garbage pail and headed home as the gray sky opened, pelting him with large raindrops. He hadn't brought his umbrella. Sprinting through the sheets of rain, he managed to make it home soaking wet, but quickly.

His penthouse was empty except for a barking Bailey, who ran right to him and greeted him with his excited butt wiggle. Andrew petted the beagle, then caught sight of a card standing upright on the island countertop beside the flowers that Cassie had arranged earlier.

I went to meet my client uptown.

Bailey's sitter is booked, and no change of clothes is needed. I'll meet you at the museum tonight.

-C

Andrew went into his office and worked for a while. Bailey joined him and was lying on the sofa, enthralled by the heavy rain pelting the large bank of windows. Though Andrew tried, he couldn't get Cassie off his mind.

After what seemed like an inexhaustible amount of time, he called Cassie at last.

"Hey, you," she answered. "My cab just dropped me off. I'm wearing my dress for tonight and am about to meet my clients. Did you get my note?"

"Wait, you're already dressed?"

"I didn't go full-on glam, but it will work for both my appointment and the event tonight. By the time I get done uptown, there's no way I'd make it home in time to commute back into Manhattan with you. How did your meeting go?"

"I don't want to talk about it." Andrew's head was still throbbing. "Tell me what you're wearing."

"Why, Andrew, do you want me to talk dirty to you?" she teased in that sultry voice of hers, taking Andrew by complete surprise.

"No. Not right now, maybe later, when you're not on your way to meet a client. But do tell me what you're wearing. I don't want to clash with you or anything." If he didn't feel a migraine coming on, Andrew would've answered differently and met her flirtation with his own.

"Oh, I'm good with whatever you wear. I'm in a neutral color today…ivory. It's silk, too. I wasn't paying attention to the weather and didn't know it might rain."

"Do you want me to meet you at your venue with the car?" Seeing her early would steady his frayed nerves.

"No. It would be too much trouble. You know how Manhattan gets in the rain." He could hear whistles for taxis in the background of her call. "It's easier if I take a cab and meet you at the museum. How about I meet you in the Great Hall?"

A surge of disappointment doused him. Andrew didn't think he could wait until after the event. He needed to tell her now, but he couldn't on the phone. "Sounds good. I'll meet you there. Text me when you're on your way."

Cassie agreed and disconnected the call. Though this plan wasn't ideal, it wasn't tragic, either. Andrew just had to get ready, get rid of his headache, and head into Manhattan. It would be several hours, but he would meet her and confess the truth.

Tonight.

Andrew would tell her tonight, after the event at the Met.

What could happen between now and then?

Chapter 19

CASSIE ENTERED THE HOTEL WITH PLENTY OF TIME TO SPARE, SO SHE took a moment to glance at her notifications. The article about Jeremy's engagement that Andrew had worked on last night, before bed, had been completed and published. She hadn't read it before.

Pausing to skim it, she first studied the picture of Jeremy and his new fiancée, both wearing beaming smiles beneath the headline "A New Lease on Love."

Cute.

Andrew had written a witty pun since the bride-to-be, Bethany Phillips, worked for her family's real estate division. The entire article, though short, was pure Andrew at his very best.

One would never be able to glean that Andrew actually despised Jeremy, or that good ol' Jeremy was a scumbag. He was portrayed in a positive light, though no untruths were spoken. Also, at no time in that article did Andrew ever say, or even imply, that Cassie had left Jeremy at the altar. That false narrative was nowhere in sight.

Call it Andrew's *look here, not there* strategy. It was on full display and judging by the comments already published, people had forgotten all about Jeremy once having been engaged to Cassie.

Smiling at Andrew's ingenuity, Cassie proceeded to the dining room, where her meeting was scheduled to take place. The swanky room was accentuated with crystal chandeliers and impeccable table settings placed atop pristine white tablecloths.

"Hi. I'm meeting Beth Mitchell and her groom—"

"Cassie. Over here." She'd recognize Jeremy's voice anywhere. She'd grown to detest that very voice since their failed wedding ceremony, and even more so since his antics last night.

"I'm sorry. Would you excuse me for one moment?" She smiled at the maître d', then proceeded to Jeremy, who was sitting with…What was she? Not his girlfriend, not anymore. She was officially his fiancée, of course. Cassie recognized her from the picture on Andrew's site. Jeremy had his arm around her like he was claiming his territory, while his smug smirk made Cassie want to slap him.

How had Cassie never seen this side of him? Not once while they were dating and never when she was engaged to him. It remained a mystery to her.

"What is it, Jeremy? I'm meeting a client and I don't want a scene like last night." Cassie sounded every bit as irritated as she felt. She didn't even bother to hide that fact.

"Oh, come on. Last night was hardly a scene thanks to you." Jeremy's smirk quickly morphed into a frown. "You never did raise your voice. Not even once. You took the fun out of it for me. I wanted to play."

"Well, this isn't a game, and I don't have the time or inclination to play with you." Cassie scanned the room in search of her clients. There was no other couple in sight.

"She's looking for us. Isn't *that* funny?" Jeremy's fiancée spoke at last. Her voice sounded rather breathy. Like a modern-day Marilyn Monroe. No wonder Jeremy was so taken by her.

Jeremy chuckled. "It will be very funny, once we tell her."

"Tell me what?" Cassie's heart began to hammer within her chest. She had a bad feeling about this.

Had Jeremy sabotaged her? No, she was early. Checking her watch, Cassie noted that she was still a few minutes early. Perhaps her clients were running late. Her cell pinged and she read a text from an unknown number.

Hi.

"What the—"

"I want you to tell her. Do it now so we can get started. I want to plan our wedding," Jeremy prompted his bride-to-be.

"I'm not planning your wedding." Cassie's eyes darted from Jeremy to his fiancée. They were both smiling.

Oh no.

Her clients weren't here, but Jeremy and his side piece were. Slowly, it was beginning to make sense to Cassie…

A client named Beth… Bethany, Jeremy's fiancée…

"What have you done, Jeremy? Did you schedule an appointment with me under a false name?" She stood stock-still with her hand on her hip, staring at them.

Jeremy remained silent, encouraging his fiancée to speak, while sporting a wide smile. He was enjoying this way too much for Cassie's own good.

"No. Not at all. My full name is Bethany Mitchell-Phillips, but my friends call me Beth. This is my fiancé. Aren't you, sweetie?" She blew Jeremy a kiss and Cassie thought she might retch.

Beth Mitchell.

Cassie's appointment.

While it wasn't quite a fake name, it was close enough as far as Cassie was concerned. The woman probably had someone else call and schedule the appointment with Cassie's assistant. In the hopes of what? Catching Cassie off guard? Ambushing her on what would be Jeremy's second ambush in a row?

No thanks.

"Okay, then. I'm out of here." She turned to leave but Jeremy grabbed her hand.

"Don't do that. Not yet." His voice was calm as he stood in front of Cassie, blocking her. He then released her and instead pulled out a chair. "Please sit. We've got a lot to discuss. Especially when it comes to your boyfriend. Or is he the love of your life? I honestly can't keep up."

She sat beside Bethany, who was a pretty girl, with straight blond hair pushed behind Chanel sunglasses. She wore them inside, on what had been a cloudy day. They must be decorative, worn to show off her wealth. *In that case, she might be the perfect woman for Jeremy,* Cassie thought.

Bethany deliberately positioned her hand in front of Cassie. To show off her ring finger, no doubt, and her flashy diamond…situated in a setting that was all too familiar to Cassie.

It couldn't be.

"Is that my ring?" Cassie blurted out.

Bethany held her hand in front of her face, admiring her shiny bauble. "No. We traded that set in for an upgrade. My set has a similar-shaped diamond, but mine is bigger. See?"

Jeremy's proud fiancée shifted, until her hand was in front of Cassie's face.

Upon closer examination, the thing still looked a lot like Cassie's ring, and she'd know. Cassie had worn hers for the past year. Perhaps Bethany's ring was half of a carat larger, but Cassie honestly couldn't tell the difference.

Still, she managed an "I do see."

Her former fiancé, also known as *the man she once loved and knew not why,* Jeremy Roth, patted Cassie on the back. "Now you're playing. See, we can still have fun."

"Ambushing me isn't fun, Jeremy." At least not for Cassie. She'd rather be anywhere but here. For Jeremy, knowing what she now did about him, Cassie suspected that yes, it probably was fun for him.

Upon sitting across from Cassie, Jeremy turned to his bride-to-be and kissed the excited woman. He was clearly enjoying this ambush and the attention he'd garnered by mentioning Andrew. What was equally as obvious was that his fiancée was a willing and rather eager participant.

What had Cassie ever done to Bethany Mitchell-Phillips?

Nothing.

The same could be said about Jeremy. She'd never wronged him in any way, yet he had planned her utter humiliation anyway. Cassie should have suspected that Jeremy would try something—even if she'd never have been able to imagine this.

The fact that Jeremy had Andrew announce his engagement meant that Jeremy wanted to drop a clue. Cassie just hadn't seen it. She'd been too concerned about Andrew's business, and not bringing him down with her.

Studying her nails, which were still blue, Cassie managed to look bored. She knew it would annoy Jeremy.

"Are we bothering you?" he asked.

Mission accomplished.

"Sorry, what were you saying?" Tipping her head to the side, Cassie studied the man she'd once thought she loved. Now she wondered what she'd been thinking.

"The last time I saw you wearing white was at the end of an aisle." He was trying to goad her.

"Is that so?" Cassie asked, feigning ignorance, knowing it would further irritate Jeremy. "I can't believe you remember standing at the altar. I'd all but forgotten."

Though her voice was calm, she was now sorry that she wore her elegant cream-colored silk dupioni dress with its exaggerated sleeves and corseted boning. Thank goodness she wore her strapless bra underneath. Though not needed, it was appreciated as Jeremy studied her intensely, his eyes roving at least twice over her décolletage.

"An altar. Well, we want one of those. Shouldn't you be writing this down?" he asked, when his gaze returned to Cassie's face at last.

She shook her head. "No. I usually record my appointments with my clients and play the recording back when I'm at my laptop, but that's not necessary because there's no way that I'm planning your wedding."

Only after turning to Bethany did she add, "No offense."

"None taken," Jeremy countered. "Because you will plan our wedding, and you will be Bethany's go-to person on our big day. You will also love every minute of it."

"And what makes you so certain?" She suspected his answer even before he opened his mouth.

"If not, I'll take Andrew down."

Yep, he was going there.

Son of a—

"Bethany's father isn't happy with how I've been portrayed on Andrew's site and he's about to call his lawyers. Papa Phillips says that I have a solid defamation case."

"And we agree with my father," Bethany chimed in. Gone was the woman's breathy voice. Instead, she spoke in a determined tone, with a grin that made her look like she was having fun seeing Cassie squirm.

Jeremy nodded. "Yes, we agree. But Bethany loved the layout for our wedding nightmare and wants you to recreate it for us."

"Only bigger and better," Bethany added with a mischievous glint in her eyes.

"I've seen firsthand how you hustle for your clients, and I want you to do that for my fiancée," Jeremy announced proudly.

In other words, Jeremy wanted Cassie to be his bride-to-be's bitch with a capital B. "Why would I do that, precisely? You want to destroy Andrew. You've made that perfectly clear. My planning your wedding would only be prolonging that and prolonging my own misery."

"Here's the thing." Raising his forefinger in the air, Jeremy continued to hold court. "In order for me to destroy Andrew, I'd have to humiliate you by letting everyone know the truth about who dumped who. Honestly, if it were up to me, I wouldn't think twice about it. But I'm in an untenable position."

There was the Jeremy that Cassie once knew. Enter the man with a vast vocabulary and the air of respectability. Now Cassie was reminded of the Jeremy he once pretended to be with her. It was amazing that he could fool Papa Phillips, as Jeremy called him, but Jeremy could be convincing.

Cassie would know.

She also knew that Jeremy was waiting for her response. Okay, she'd bite. If for nothing more than to get this over with sooner.

"What untenable position, Jeremy?" Her voice was almost robotic. Cassie wasn't about to give him any more satisfaction than was necessary.

"I can't do what I want because your mommy told me not to."

"My mother?" Cassie sounded every bit as shocked as she felt. "What does my mother have to do with any of this?"

"She actually threatened me last night, if you can believe it," Jeremy muttered as if hoping no one else would hear.

"I don't believe it." Not one bit. Julia West had never protected her daughter from anything. She just didn't put Cassie first. It wasn't in her nature.

"Well, you should believe it because that's the only reason I'm not destroying that man of yours." Jeremy's expression was serious.

Dead serious.

"Okay, let's say my mother did indeed threaten you. So what? How do I know that you won't still sue Andrew, or go after him in some other form?" How could Julia really keep Jeremy in line? No, it was too good to be true and Cassie didn't buy it.

She wouldn't allow Jeremy to destroy Andrew. Helping his father and their family business meant everything to Andrew and she couldn't allow Jeremy to take away everything Andrew had worked so hard to achieve. "Forgive me for not trusting you, but your word doesn't quite cut it with me anymore, Jeremy. What proof do you have? How do I know you won't renege on our deal? If I were to make a deal with you, that is."

Was she really entertaining the thought of making a deal with Jeremy? Had Hades frozen over?

Jeremy turned to his bride-to-be. "Darling, if you don't mind…"

"Not at all, buttercup." Bethany presented Cassie with three documents, spreading them out with care on the pristine white tablecloth in front of her. The first was a contract…a wedding planning contract, to be precise, naming Cassandra, also known as Cassie Benedict, as the consultant, Jeremy Roth as the groom, and Bethany Mitchell-Phillips as the bride, more specifically…

"This actually says 'happy couple Jeremy Roth and Bethany Mitchell-Phillips.' Wow." Cassie couldn't hide her astonishment.

Of all the nerve…

The second document was an NDA stating that Cassandra, aka Cassie Benedict, would not disclose anything about the relationships and/or breakups where applicable listed herein: that between Jeremy Roth and Cassandra, aka Cassie Benedict, or between Jeremy Roth and Bethany Mitchell-Phillips.

"This looks official, or as official as you can get without actually consulting an attorney." Her sarcasm was her only defense. Besides, the *happy couple* had definitely downloaded this online. Cassie was certain of it.

The third contract had already been signed. It was an NDA in which Jeremy Roth agreed not to disclose anything personal about Cassandra, aka Cassie Benedict, or their failed wedding.

"So, you're serious about this? You actually want me to plan your wedding and in return you, Bethany, and her father will leave Andrew alone? Really? Because I don't see any of that in writing." No, that wasn't in writing.

Cassie suspected that Jeremy was about to double-cross her after she acted as his bride's bit—bridal coordinator.

"May I speak for a moment, sugar?" Bethany asked sweetly.

Cassie suspected that Bethany was about to play good cop to Jeremy's bad cop.

"None of us are innocent here. We cheated, you lied, everyone was hurt. I get it." Bethany placed her hand on Cassie's arm. "But—and this a big but—I want a beautiful wedding, and Jeremy and I want to move on."

"Then why don't you use someone else to coordinate your wedding?" Cassie withdrew her arm. This was odd, on so many levels. Cassie just couldn't wrap her head around it, and her mind was working feverishly trying to discover all the angles and every pitfall imaginable.

Jeremy cleared his throat. "Just because I can't destroy Andrew by telling the truth for all the world to see doesn't mean I can't make you a little miserable by catering to my fiancée's every whim."

There it was.

The truth, at last.

"But if you don't want to help Andrew—"

"I didn't say that, Jeremy." Of course Cassie wanted to help Andrew. She just needed to ensure she did indeed help him, and not hurt him. "I don't want you to come after him. All he did was help me when I needed it. And when I walked in here today, I was prepared to announce that this whole thing was my idea, and that Andrew published what he did based upon my word. I'm still prepared to do just that."

"No. Don't."

He was too quick in his desire not to see her humiliate herself in public. "Why not? If you want to see me humiliated—"

"That's the thing. I don't want that. Because of your mom. If you don't believe me, call her."

The last thing Cassie wanted to do was call her mother after last night. Besides, doing so wouldn't help her trust Jeremy, now, would it?

"How can I trust you?" She glanced between Jeremy and Bethany. "How can I trust either of you? You lured me here under false pretenses, if not an entirely false name. That doesn't exactly invite trust. Besides, you could be trying to bide your time until you think of some other way to hurt Andrew."

Yes, that was Cassie's fear.

"Don't get me wrong, I'd be fine destroying Andrew Steele and *stealing*, for lack of a better word, all that wealth he's accumulated. Destroying his company and his reputation would be bonuses."

Cassie sensed a *but* coming.

"But Bethany's father is much wealthier than Andrew. And we choose to marry with Papa Phillips's blessing. All you have to do is plan our wedding for us."

It all ends with that one catch.

What choice did Cassie have?

"If I coordinate your wedding, and that's a big *if*, I want it in writing that you were dumped by me at the altar and that Andrew published nothing but the truth."

Bethany handed Jeremy a pen from her purse, and he scrawled those exact words on an expensive linen napkin.

Classy.

Before he handed it to Cassie, he paused. "I wouldn't be doing any of this if you and Andrew hadn't rubbed my nose in your relationship, last night especially. It was one thing when I believed this thing between you to be fake, but when your mother told me it was real, and that you're happy, at my expense…That was the last straw."

"My mother shouldn't have said anything." Why had her mother mentioned any of it to Jeremy? Julia had made it worse by inviting Jeremy last night, and by sharing details about Cassie's relationship with Andrew after they'd left.

He handed her the napkin at last. The writing was choppy, and messy, but there it was with Jeremy's signature. Just what she'd wanted.

"Are you satisfied?" Jeremy was growing impatient. "Because this is getting annoying."

Cassie had no choice but to agree. "We're using my contract, and my contract only. And you're paying for everything."

Bethany's lips upturned in a smile. "Actually, your mom is paying for it. She's so nice."

"You're blackmailing my mother." It wasn't spoken as a question.

Jeremy shrugged. "Blackmailing? No. It's a wedding gift. She's very generous. And she has her own contract with us."

"She'll be paying you directly," Bethany added. "She insisted."

"Well, aren't you perfect for each other?" Cassie unlocked her cell and pressed Record in her app. "Tell me, what kind of wedding do you want?"

"The exact same wedding as yours, only bigger, better, and more expensive." Bethany paused. "I was thinking of at least two hundred fifty guests, and I want more flowers, and maybe candles. Would a nighttime wedding be more romantic?"

Before Cassie could answer, Jeremy was quick to agree. "Yes, I think that would be great. I'd wanted something at night, but Cassie insisted on a daytime wedding."

Liar.

As far as Cassie was concerned, Jeremy and Bethany deserved each other.

Andrew, however, deserved none of this. And Cassie would have to tell him all about this shakedown when she saw him at the museum tonight.

The Met was her favorite museum, and she'd been looking forward to the event since he'd first told her about it. Now she dreaded it. Worse yet, her stomach was in knots, and it was all she could do to conduct the rest of the interview with her happy couple, asking them pertinent questions until they would be satisfied that she was doing their wedding justice.

In the end, Cassie thought she'd pretended to be adequately interested. All the while, she kept feeling her anxiety rise until it reached a crescendo. By the time she hopped into the cab, her hands were shaking.

It was her fault that Andrew was in this mess. Cassie knew that. When Andrew had agreed to a fake relationship, when he flipped the jilted bride script, Andrew had thought it would be mutually beneficial for them both. Instead, his business, his family, and his own lifestyle were in danger.

All because he helped Cassie.

She feared it wouldn't end at Jeremy and Bethany's wedding, either. Regardless of what Jeremy signed, Cassie didn't believe for one second that Jeremy would be satisfied until he'd hurt Andrew. The fact that Cassie was happy with Andrew would always grate on Jeremy's nerves. Of that, she was certain.

This whole thing was so much more than Andrew bargained for.

Would he ever forgive her?

Chapter 20

WAITING AT THE TOP OF THE STAIRS AT THE MET, ANDREW CHECKED his cell again. No texts from Cassie, no calls, and she was officially late. With the rain having dissipated, the storm clouds remained thick above, cloaking Manhattan in an early darkness. The Met was an imposing structure, but at night, when its grand exterior was illuminated, even he would be forced to admit it was impressive.

There was something about Manhattan at night.

Its cityscape, and especially its architecture, were breathtaking.

But not as breathtaking as Cassie, who'd just stepped out of her cab. Sauntering toward the steps, she was a vision in an ivory cocktail dress that hugged all her curves to perfection. She was sexy yet elegant, which wasn't an easy feat.

With her hair parted in the middle and pulled back, and her signature nude lipstick, she was a goddess. Andrew had never seen her look more beautiful.

Or more rattled.

He sprinted down the steps to meet her and before she could say a word, he kissed her. Long gone were their kisses for show. This kiss, like so many others since they admitted how they truly felt about one another, was real and it was epic.

Cassie clutched him tightly against her.

"You didn't text me. I was worried." He kissed her forehead. It was kind of their thing now.

"I'm sorry. I've been in my head the whole taxi ride here, and we were stuck in gridlock. Andrew, we need to talk." Her wide eyes and quivering lips told him something was terribly wrong.

Pellets of rain began to drop again, and Andrew shrugged off his jacket, placing it around Cassie's shoulders before escorting her up the steps and into the Great Hall of the museum.

Though crowded, they managed to find a semisecluded spot at one of the many white columns in the impressive structure. Because of the noise, they stood close enough to hear one another.

"What's wrong?" he asked, while his pulse hammered against his temples like a sledgehammer. He still hadn't gotten rid of his headache. It was getting worse with Cassie's unknown news.

"Jeremy and his fiancée...They were the clients I was scheduled to meet with. Bethany used her nickname for the appointment, and I had no idea that her last name was hyphenated. It was an ambush, and I walked right into it." Cassie took his hand in hers. "They want me to plan their wedding—"

"Well, that's never going to happen." Though his voice sounded calm, his nerves were taut, and rage was simmering beneath the surface.

Who the hell did Jeremy think he was? That man had the audacity to ask Cassie to plan his wedding to someone else, after dumping her at the altar. "You are not planning that man's wedding."

"Actually, I am." Cassie pulled out a napkin from her purse. She then handed it to Andrew.

"I don't get it." He stared at it, then flipped the linen around, and saw ink scribbled on it. "What...what does this say? 'Cassandra Benedict dumped me. Andrew...and truth.' That's all I can make out. Hang on. Is that Jeremy's signature?"

"Yes, his handwriting leaves much to be desired. It doesn't matter, though. What matters is that I had Jeremy write that I dumped him, and that you were telling the truth. It's your evidence if he ever reneges on my deal with him and decides to go after you. I know it's not perfect, but it's the best I could do at the time." She exhaled a deep breath before continuing. "That and agreeing to be Bethany Mitchell-Phillips's wedding planner."

"You're not doing that for me."

Cassie placed her palm against his jaw. It was cool and helped calm his raging temper. To think that Jeremy set Cassie up and forced her to work for him and the woman he was cheating on Cassie with? It infuriated him with a rage that was escalating.

"I would do anything for you." Her words were heavy with meaning and emotion. "I can't allow him to destroy everything you've created, everything you've achieved, because you were trying to help me. Besides, if your business was in trouble when you made that agreement, it certainly wouldn't survive a defamation lawsuit now, especially with what you and I both know."

If your business was in trouble… Andrew caught the emphasis on the word *if*. Was Cassie doubting him? She had every right to do so.

He had misled her, after all.

The bottom line was that his reasons didn't matter. He had to come clean. Now, before this went any further.

But first, he kissed Cassie once more. In that kiss, he gave her his heart and soul. He gave himself completely to her, with no reservations. Because she meant the world to him.

Cassie Benedict was the one, the only woman he'd ever cared about. She brought out the best in him, and also the worst. Some of that worst was on full display in the untruth he told on her non-wedding day. After pulling away from her, he rested his forehead against hers. Savoring her nearness, inhaling deeply in an attempt to remember everything about this moment. In case…

In case she didn't forgive him.

It was time to confess…

He clutched the lapels of his suit jacket that she still wore around her shoulders. "My business was never in trouble, Cassie," he whispered, refusing to release her just yet.

"What?" Cassie remained in his arms, as if she hadn't believed him at first.

He repeated himself. "My business was never in trouble. I implied it was, because I knew you'd never accept my help if there wasn't something in it for me."

"Oh, Andrew." Cassie took a step away from him and stared at him, with tears in her eyes. "Why would you do that?"

"Because I love you. Because I've always loved you and I hated to see you hurt." Andrew laid it all on the line.

"But you placed yourself in the orbit of Jeremy and he is coming after you with a wealthy benefactor to back him." Her eyes searched his. It was as if she was looking straight into his soul. "Do you know what that means?"

"I don't care what it means, because we're together again. That makes it worth it." He leaned into her. "I loved you then, and I love you now. That's why I did it."

"That makes it worse." A tear slid down her cheek.

He wiped it away with his thumb. "I'm sorry that I lied. Please forgive me."

Cassie blinked and more tears fell. "Of course I forgive you. But that doesn't mean it's okay."

What did she mean?

"Andrew, this is my fault. You sacrificed yourself for me, wanting nothing in return." She wiped her eyes. "And now Jeremy's coming after you. He wants to destroy you. Because of me."

Oh shit.

He *had* made it worse. A hundred times worse.

"Listen, it's okay. I can handle Jeremy. Just understand what I did and forgive me. There's nothing to worry about." He was trying to explain it, to minimize the potential of any damage to himself or his business because it upset her so much.

Too much.

He could see it. In her eyes, those mirrors to her soul, he saw anguish reflected and guilt, but Cassie had nothing to feel guilty about. "None of this is your fault, Cassie."

Her eyes filled with more tears. "Yes, it is. He doesn't want to see me happy. He knows that I love you, that this is real. And he won't be satisfied until…"

She covered her mouth with her hand.

Until what?

Andrew wrapped her in his tight embrace, clinging to her for dear life. Though he suspected where she was going, what she'd say next, he wasn't ready to hear the words.

"Andrew, you created this entire elaborate ruse because of me, and now it could destroy you. Your career, your business, your father, Noah, all of it, and they will be affected. All because of me."

He shook his head. "No, I won't let that happen."

"You have no choice. Even with the napkin, I don't know if Jeremy will stop coming after you. I don't think he will. You're successful, and he's an opportunist. If I've learned anything about him, it's that he'll chase money." Cassie nestled against the crook of his neck. "Knowing what you did, I feel even more responsible instead of less. This is all my fault."

"No. I got you back, which is what I always wanted, but never thought was possible." That was the truth, Andrew's truth.

"But as long as we're together, you're Jeremy's target. He doesn't want to see us happy." She clung to him for a moment, maybe two.

Andrew had lost track of time.

All he knew was that he refused to let her go.

"I can't allow you to sacrifice everything you've worked for because of me." Cassie stepped backward and away from him, breaking their connection. Her cheeks were red and blotchy now. "We can't be together. It will only put more of a target on you. As hard as it is to acknowledge, he'll back off if we're not together anymore."

Andrew couldn't believe what he was hearing. "So, you're going to break up with me not because I misled you, but for my own good. That makes no sense, Cassie."

"Now you know how it feels." She managed to grin, though a few more tears fell. "Did it make sense when you did it to me all those years ago?"

"No. And it still doesn't." He grasped her hand. "There's a way out of this. I just need to think."

A searing pain throbbed in his head, while the bright lighting in the museum was causing his eyesight to blur.

"What's wrong? You're pale." She cupped his chin, studying him.

"I've been fighting a migraine all day. I'm okay. I just want to go home." He looked at her. She was still there, with him.

Where she belonged.

Cassie wiped her eyes. "Let's get you home. You'll get into bed and I'll prepare a hot compress for you."

"Like you used to?" Andrew couldn't believe she remembered.

"I know what happens when you get a migraine, remember?"

He did remember. Cassie had seen him at his worst in college when his last migraine knocked him on his ass during finals. "Can we just go home, please?" With that one request, Cassie texted their driver and they left what was once a promising party.

Andrew held her through the car ride home, concentrating on her nearness for as long as he could. He just hoped it was enough to convince her to stay with him. His uncertainty wasn't doing his headache any favors.

When they arrived at his penthouse, Bailey met them at the door, gave one bark, then backed away as if even he sensed that something was wrong. Cassie excused herself and prepared a hot facecloth for his head. When she returned, Andrew noticed that she had changed into leggings and a sweatshirt.

She still looked beautiful.

Perhaps more so than before.

Once Andrew was in bed, he asked Cassie to stay with him. Did he need to ask her? He wasn't sure if she would have done so anyway, but he didn't want to take that chance. She got under the covers with him, and snuggled close, resting her palm against his chest.

Time passed, though he didn't know how much time. He wasn't keeping track. When Cassie spoke at last, her voice was hoarse.

"I understand why you misled me. I forgive you. Please don't forget that." She kissed his cheek.

How could he forget it? She forgave him. That's all Andrew wanted.

When Andrew fell asleep, Cassie was in his arms and Bailey was asleep at the foot of his bed.

By the time he awakened, his bedroom curtains were closed, and the darkness felt good. It was obvious that Cassie remembered how to care for someone with migraines, because she had closed the curtains throughout his penthouse.

His migraine had subsided, and while Andrew felt like he'd been hit by a truck, he was optimistic that he'd figure out a way to keep Jeremy at bay.

He looked for Cassie in his kitchen first, then in the bedroom she'd called hers when she first moved in. She wasn't there, nor was Bailey.

Andrew headed back into the kitchen looking for one of her notes, to no avail.

Based upon the time, she and Bailey weren't on one of their usual walks.

Anxiety coiled in his abdomen, along with a deep-seated dread that he just couldn't shake. It wasn't until he called Cassie, and she'd answered, that Andrew allowed himself to feel relief.

"Hi. How are you feeling?" Her tone was one of concern and caring.

He expelled a jagged break, grateful that she picked up. "I'm better. Thanks for taking care of me last night."

"I'm glad I could help. I closed your blinds or curtains and made sure the penthouse was nice and dark for you. I also placed a bottle of over-the-counter migraine relief on your nightstand, in case you need it." She paused. "Oh, I also stocked your fridge. So, you're—"

"Why does it sound like you're not coming home?" Though Andrew didn't want to hear it, he couldn't escape it, either.

Cassie sounded like this was goodbye.

Heading down his hallway, he entered Cassie's suite to find none of her things there. Not in the closet, or on the dresser. Bailey's doggie bed was also gone.

When Cassie failed to respond, Andrew made it easier on her. "You're not coming home."

"I'm not," Cassie whispered, her voice a raspy whisper. "I'm sorry."

His relief had been fleeting. "Cassie, please—"

"I'm so sorry. I didn't want to leave last night when you weren't feeling well. But I took what I could this morning. Bailey and I are staying in a pet-friendly hotel until I find a place of my own."

"Where are you?"

Cassie expelled a ragged breath. "It's better if I don't say. Seeing you will probably make it worse, and if you know where I am, you'll definitely come to see me."

"Don't do this. Please don't do this." Andrew couldn't believe that he was actually pleading with her.

There was a lengthy silence, then, "You're going to be okay. I've come clean. It will take the heat off you, Noah, and your business."

"I'm not worried about my business, Cassie—"

"I know, that's why I must protect you from yourself. Because you're not thinking of your business, but I am."

The combination of anxiety and alarm slithered again within his abdomen. "Don't do it."

"It's too late. I recorded a vlog admitting that I lied about dumping Jeremy. I posted it this morning on my platforms." She paused again. "You, Noah, your dad…You're going to be all right. Jeremy knows what I did. He's not happy about it but knows I'm to blame. And while I may be getting hammered right now by some of the #AndCass fans, it's nothing that I don't deserve."

"You don't deserve anything. We were in this together." Andrew shoved his hand through his hair. "Cassie, please come home. We can work this out."

"I meant what I said last night, Andrew. I do forgive you." Cassie sighed. "If I'm being honest, I suspected something was up when I all but interrogated you that day on the beach. I could have pushed harder for the truth—I should have, but a part of me… I think I was just so desperate for a way out of my mess that I didn't want the truth at the time. If that makes any sense."

It made a lot of sense. "Regardless, it's on me, not you. And it's also why you left, why you confessed, because you blame yourself." Of that, Andrew was certain.

Bailey barked in the background. Cassie spoke above the dog. "I've got to go. Bailey isn't used to it here, yet. Just… Andrew my love for you, it is real. I just won't risk hurting you or those you love."

If they loved each other, shouldn't they be together?

"But I love you, too."

"I know you do." Bailey barked louder, then bayed. "I've got to go. I'm glad you're feeling better."

With that, the call disconnected.

Andrew stared at his cell for several seconds, maybe a minute. He wasn't really sure how much time had passed, but it was long enough to formulate a plan, or at least the outline of one.

He was seldom without a plan, last night being the lone exception.

Yes, Andrew had another grand scheme.

And he wouldn't rest until he'd won Cassie back.

Chapter 21

CASSIE TREATED LAUREN TO LUNCH AT THE RESTAURANT ACROSS THE street from her hotel. In between bites of her salad, Cassie asked, "How are you?"

"I'm good. I've been traveling a lot, but my business is growing. It's what I wanted." Lauren owned her own cosmetics company and was expanding to at least one brick-and-mortar boutique. "My online sales are up, and my Manhattan flagship store will be open next year. How are you?"

"We're not talking about me—"

"Yes, we are. I'm worried about you." Lauren studied her friend. "I know cosmetics, remember? I modeled them for years before owning my own brand. You're wearing concealer, which is used for dark circles, which means you're not sleeping well."

"How do you know that?" Cassie placed her fork down on her plate. "Seriously, Lauren, you should be in the FBI. That's some cold-case-solving sleuthing you've got going on."

"Yet I didn't catch on to Jeremy's wrongdoings. Some agent I'd be." Her sarcasm wasn't lost on Cassie.

"I was engaged to the man. It's my bad and no one else's," Cassie assured her friend.

Lauren scoffed. "Jeremy is to blame. The blame rests solely on that man-child and no one else." Her tone had hardened, and it was down-right lethal, as was her glare. Cassie turned to see what her friend was staring at.

"Oh, not again." Surely, it was no coincidence that Jeremy was striding across the restaurant, heading straight toward Cassie. "Twice in two days? Seriously, Jeremy, I didn't see you this much when we were engaged. How do I get rid of you?"

Jeremy pulled out a chair.

"Nope. You're not joining us." Cassie grasped the chair. "Not again, Jeremy."

Only after rolling his eyes did Jeremy respond. "I need to talk, Cassie. What you posted is getting me into some serious trouble with Papa Phillips."

"Papa Phillips? Is this man kidding?" Lauren's sass was cranked to maximum, and she pointed to Jeremy. "Read the room. We don't care."

Jeremy scoffed. "You never liked me."

"I don't like anybody. But I will say this, my friend traded up. Now go, before I lose my appetite." Lauren took another bite of her Caesar salad.

"Can I just talk to Cassandra alone please?" Though Jeremy was asking this of Lauren, he continued to stare at Cassie.

People seated at tables nearby were starting to stare. One diner had her cell out. "Sit, but only for a moment, and do not make a scene. I'm pretty sure we're being filmed."

"Where?" Lauren peered around the dining room.

"White blouse to my right." Cassie sat back in her chair.

Lauren nodded. "Do you want me to make it go away? I can, you know."

"Who are you, an enforcer?" Jeremy's tone was condescending.

"I'll burn you for what you did to my friend." Lauren looked at Cassie, as if waiting for instructions.

"That would be a no to going over there. And it's a no to burning Jeremy, too." No matter how Cassie wanted to see that matchup between her ride or die Lauren and her ex-fiancé, that was a hard pass. "Jeremy, what do you want? I told the truth, and you have nothing to hold over me anymore. We're done."

As Jeremy tapped his foot against the table, it shook. Cassie planted her hand on his leg. "Stop. What do you want?"

"Can't you record another video? For me. Saying you lied about lying?"

"Seriously?" Lauren shook her head and dropped her fork on her plate with a loud *clink*. "This man can't be serious."

Sadly, Cassie was certain that Jeremy was indeed serious. "I won't do that, Jeremy."

"But I love Bethany." It was a whisper.

"What?" Lauren leaned over the table.

"Must I repeat myself?" Jeremy said to Cassie, who nodded.

"I love Bethany. Her dad isn't happy with me right now, after that video Cassie posted."

"Cassie told the truth. You did dump her at the altar." Judging by Lauren's raised tone, she wasn't intent on *not* making a scene for public consumption.

This was worse than a *Vanderpump Rules* meal. And Cassie was certain it would air in some form on social media, even if it was only a meme.

"You can't blame Cassie for posting the truth, but you might want to try it sometime," Lauren pointed at Jeremy then held her hands in the air. "That much is obvious to me, but you're another story."

"Tell me one thing, Jeremy. Why did you do it?" Cassie asked her ex, well aware that this was the last she'd see of Jeremy. "Why did you dump me on our wedding day, in front of all of those people?"

"It wasn't personal." His tone was calm and reserved.

Cassie leaned forward. "Yes, it was. It was very personal. What did I ever do to you?"

Jeremy sighed. "You still loved him. I knew that, even if you wouldn't admit it to yourself."

"I was marrying you."

"You didn't move in with me, no matter how many times I asked. And you bought that dog even though it hated me—"

"Adopted, not purchased. Bailey, not it, is a living, breathing canine." Cassie set him straight while Lauren nodded and gave her a thumbs-up.

"Fine, adopted. Still, I would have gotten rid of it for you."

Like Cassie would believe anything Jeremy said. Like she'd ever get rid of Bailey. "Bailey is a *he*, not an *it*. You really don't understand the concept of a pet, do you?"

Jeremy shrugged. "Fine. He doesn't like me, you made your choice, and I fell for someone else. I thought you and Steele would get back together and thank me."

"How did you think that I would ever thank you for humiliating me?" Cassie leaned forward, trying with great strength to control her mounting temper.

Was this man truly this clueless?

"Let's just say that I had hoped you both would get back together and that you would thank me." Jeremy paused. "Oh! Before you ask, that was before you embarrassed me in front of the world. After that, I just wanted to hurt you."

"At least you're honest about that." Cassie studied her ex. "I hope you find some happiness, Jeremy. Stay away from me and Andrew."

"So, you'll post—"

"Nope. Not a chance. Why don't you try connecting with Bethany's dad? Or better yet just say you're sorry and mean it." Cassie glanced at Lauren, who held her glass of club soda in a silent toast.

Cassie grinned at her friend, before returning her attention to her ex-fiancé. "We have a lunch to finish, and you're not invited. So, please leave, Jeremy."

Without a word, Jeremy did just that.

"Why do I get the feeling that he's got a plan B?" Lauren held her fork in the air.

Cassie arched her brow and took a sip of her own club soda and lemon. "Because it's Jeremy."

"Good point. You slayed him, by the way." Lauren paused before taking another bite of her salad. "Did he honestly think you'd be grateful that he dumped you so publicly?"

Only after pausing as she thought on it did Cassie admit, "Yes, he did and honestly, I am grateful. Because of him, Andrew and I reconnected, and I will always love Andrew. We may not be able to be together—"

"Why is that? Precisely." Lauren gave Cassie one of her know-it-all smirks. "What's stopping you from being together? I mean, the threat has now been neutralized, right? I mean, Papa Phillips, as Jeremy calls him, isn't supporting Jeremy's takedown of Andrew anymore."

Lauren had a point. Even Cassie must admit that, but were the things Cassie said and did enough to allow her and Andrew to get back together? Was her admission of guilt enough to protect Andrew? She glanced at her notifications. Cassie was still receiving hate DMs and those same people were siding with Andrew. If she was to get back together with Andrew, traffic on his site would suffer just from him being with her.

A text notification came through.

It was from Noah.

Meet me tonight. ASAP. Where are you staying? I'll keep it confidential.

Cassie tried to ignore the feeling of dread that washed over her as she texted him the name of her hotel before telling her friend, "First off, you watch too much true crime, and secondly, my breakup is, at best, to be categorized as TBD."

At least until Cassie had met with Noah.

Then and only then would she formulate a plan.

Chapter 22

After her lunch with Lauren, Cassie brought Lauren back to her room, where she needed some help repairing her image.

When she uploaded her initial video upon moving out of Andrew's penthouse, in which she admitted to lying about being dumped, and why, it felt strange to Cassie. Going public with something so personal felt inherently uncomfortable, but in this day and age of reality television and social media influencers, what was once private wasn't anymore. Not to her, and certainly not to everyone else who puts their lives under the intense and often brutal spotlight for all to see. Besides, she and Andrew made a very public show of their relationship, so she had no choice but to mark the end of it publicly.

Though her business had taken a hit, it wasn't as bad as she'd expected. True, she'd lost some future appointments, and a few endorsement deals, but most of her clients stuck with her, and Cassie didn't really need those endorsement deals.

Sure, it was nice, but her career had never been about making influencer money. It'd been about creating a business where she could craft happily ever afters for her clients. She'd never lost sight of that goal. As long as A Perfect Wedding was in business, and as long as Cassie delivered that perfect day for her couples and content afterward, she would be okay.

In addition to what she couldn't change, Cassie had gained an abundance of DMs and comments from people who could relate to what she'd gone through. As much as it pained her to admit, a lot of people could relate to being humiliated by someone they loved. Though it wasn't a club anyone would wish to belong to, even Cassie would be forced to admit that it was comforting to know that she wasn't alone.

Questions had arisen with her admissions, and it was time for another vlog. As difficult as her last one was, this one would be even harder to create. Because people had asked about Cassie's relationship with Andrew.

Was it real or fake?

They'd watched her relationship with Andrew unfold live and in color from their computers and devices. They had a vested interest, and she owed it to them to provide answers.

Cassie steeled her shoulders and took a deep, calming breath. Why was she feeling shaky, and much too vulnerable? Because she was about to admit all. At least, as much as she could without implicating Andrew.

"Are you sure you want to go through with this?" Lauren asked from the sofa.

Cassie nodded. "I have to. Many of these people who supported me during my relationship with Andrew still support me. They have questions."

Lauren headed to Cassie's GoPro. "Tell me when."

Nodding, Cassie instructed Lauren, "Let's do it."

Her friend pressed Record and gave Cassie a nod.

"Hi, everyone. This conversation is going to be tough for me today, but you've got questions, and I owe you some answers. You asked about my relationship with Andrew Steele. More specifically, you want to know if our relationship was real. The answer is both yes and no. You see, I had moved on, or at least I thought I had. I almost married someone else, after all. But as it turned out, Andrew hadn't moved on, not really."

When she thought about the early days of their fake relationship, Cassie was reminded about how real it felt. Their kisses, and his kindness.

He'd always loved her. She could recognize that now. It had been in everything he said, and everything she did.

"What Andrew and I had was real, though neither of us would admit to it, at least not at first. We fought it, and each other, a lot. I couldn't trust him or wouldn't. It was a choice at the time. I was still hurt from him breaking up with me when we first dated, and I was terrified of being hurt once again. So scared that I almost missed what was in front of me: the fact that Andrew had always loved me, and I'd always loved him."

Andrew helped Cassie through what had been the most humiliating event in her life, and the most difficult, second only to the death of her father, which she refused to address on camera.

Bailey jumped on her lap, and she petted the soft fur on his head, and his soft, floppy ears. Bailey missed Andrew and needed extra attention since they moved out of his penthouse.

Cassie felt the same.

"So, long story short, it *was* real. In the end though, sometimes, love isn't enough. I wish it had been. The one thing I can hope is something for each of you who are watching this, interested in my story… I hope you don't give up on love. Though I may not be fairy-tale princess material, I've always believed in happily ever after. In spite of everything that's happened to me, I still believe in it. It's what I want for each and every one of you. Believe in love, and don't make the same mistakes I did. Oh!"

Cassie paused as she was about to wrap this up. "One more thing I want to address: the word 'perfect' in my business. My sites and platforms are called the Perfect Wedding and the Perfect Happiness, but our 'perfects' are subjective. Nothing is without a flaw or two or more; we each just see happiness and weddings through a different lens. For me, perfect happiness isn't the same as it was last week or last month. I still cherish what I experienced, and I cherish that it was once mine. Hopefully, now I can experience a different perfect happiness."

Bailey sat upright, looking into the camera.

"For instance, I love, and am loved, by Bailey."

As if on cue, the beagle licked Cassie's cheek, then her lips. Lauren managed to stop recording Cassie's very personal vlog entry before the dog pushed Cassie backward. "Bailey. Stop."

Bailey didn't stop. "Okay, I surrender. I surrender."

Lauren laughed and so did Cassie. She couldn't help it.

"I'm going to the gym, then heading home," Lauren announced. "Unless you need me. Are you all right?"

Cassie nodded at her friend. "I'm fine. Go to the gym."

"It will get better. You know that, right?" Lauren hugged her friend. "You will feel better about everything."

"By everything, do you mean Andrew?" Cassie wouldn't get over him. Not this time. Because their breakup hurt worse the second time around.

"I mean everything, including Andrew. You miss him. That much is obvious." Lauren patted Cassie's shoulder. "I'm out of here. See you later."

Once she'd uploaded her vlog and posted it, Cassie opened her laptop and went straight to the document she'd been working on and continued where she'd left off.

She had been documenting everything that had happened to her since her non-wedding day in the hopes that it would help her process it. As it turned out, writing what had happened was her saving grace. She poured her heart out onto those pages, and it was cathartic.

She had no expectation of ever publishing it, but that was okay. Cassie still had a voice, and she'd use it until she'd gotten to express everything she felt.

Though she missed Andrew, Cassie couldn't allow herself to wallow in it.

Maybe someday, she'd share the document with Andrew, so he could at the very least know how much he meant to her. Yes, that sounded like a perfect plan as she typed, while Bailey snored softly on her lap.

There were endless blank pages and a whole lot of emotions that she'd been bottling up.

It was again time to be honest with herself.

Chapter 23

ANDREW RECEIVED THE NOTIFICATION WHEN CASSIE UPLOADED HER latest video and watched it immediately. At the very sight of her, his chest constricted until it was painful.

He missed her.

Too much.

The sight of her made his heart ache. She was beautiful. Heck, Cassie would always be beautiful in his eyes, though Andrew thought she looked a bit tired. Or maybe he was making too much of things. That was what he got for thinking of her constantly since she'd left.

Thinking of *them*, he silently corrected himself, because Andrew even missed the obnoxious beagle drama king more than he cared to admit. He couldn't help but wonder what trouble the beagle had gotten into lately, or more specifically if Bailey had had a bark-off with any other large dogs? If he did, it would have been at a different dog park…

A pang of longing assailed Andrew. If only he knew where they were. Maybe then he'd stop worrying about them. Or would he?

No. He'd never stop thinking about Cassie or Bailey. Not in a million years. He'd never stop missing them, either. Not even with the passage of time.

If one thing was certain, it was that this break from Cassie now was far worse than it had been years ago. Andrew appreciated her more now; he knew that what they had together was special. He also knew that Cassie was irreplaceable. He'd learned that the hard way after their first breakup.

At least Andrew could take some sort of solace in that fact that Bailey made Cassie laugh. If Andrew's plan to get her back failed, he'd know that she was loved and protected by one ferocious beagle.

"Hey." Noah bounded into Andrew's penthouse, and strode into the great room, where Andrew was seated on the sofa with his laptop. "You were right about the *Househusbands* scandal. This thing has taken on a life of its own, and we've got so many followers from it that I'm afraid they'll crash the site."

Andrew cocked his brow. "Well, I don't want to say 'I told you so,' but..."

"You told me so." Noah laughed. "Yeah, I know."

"What will you do without me?" Andrew gauged his partner's reaction, while Noah shook his head, as if dismissing his partner's statement as a joke.

"Clearly, I'd flounder without you, which makes it a good thing that I'll never have to find out." Noah placed his cell on the coffee table. "So, what did you want to discuss with me?"

Andrew shut his laptop and slid it onto his coffee table. "I wanted to discuss what you're going to do without me. You're going to find out sooner rather than later, so you'll need to step up."

"What are you saying?" Noah stared at Andrew. "This business is ours—yours and mine. We started it together."

Managing a grin, Andrew sighed. Yeah, they started it together. Two college kids who'd once plotted the rise of their empire did well for themselves, after all. "Our business is booming, but it doesn't make me happy. Not anymore. I miss Cassie, and I even miss Bailey. Man, talk about an admission. I miss a beagle with a raging case of drama king. If I have to give up the Dailies to get them back, I will."

Noah plopped on one of the chairs on the other side of the room. "There's no *if*. You've decided to do just that."

It wasn't a question, but Andrew nodded anyway. "I'm offering my half of The Steele Dailies to you. And I'm giving you a very good deal. Call it the friend and partner discount."

"There is no Steele Dailies without you." Noah tapped his foot, his annoyance showing. "You're the Steele in The Steele Dailies. You are the face of our business, and you were fine with it until…"

"Until I lost Cassie. The second time around." Yeah, that was true.

Though Andrew had missed Cassie before, his business had always been his lifeline. Not any longer. It didn't mean as much to him without her. And it failed to fuel his ambitions, not the way it used to.

"Look, I don't know what the future holds for me, I just know that the business doesn't mean the same thing to me anymore." Andrew studied his partner's reaction. From his tapping foot to his stern grimace, it was clear that Noah was pissed.

"What if she still doesn't take you back? What happens when you sell your half of the business and it's all for nothing?" Noah's tone was lethal, with a tinge of concern. "Do you know what this will cost you? Cost us?"

Those were all very good, valid questions.

Shrugging, Andrew considered his options. "If that happens, I guess I'll start over. I suppose I'll look for something that fuels my passion, or my ambitions."

That sounded unbelievable, even to Andrew's ears.

"I call BS." Noah sliced through BS like no one else. "You're trying to win Cassie back by sacrificing the only other thing you love, the very thing she's hated since you two were first dating."

Noah was right.

"Yeah. That's exactly what I'm doing. And it might not work, but I'm sure as hell going to try."

"Why are you doing this to me? I'm in this with you, remember.

We started this business together and have worked side by side in the trenches." Noah's tone was accusatory.

"Don't think I don't know that you're affected by my decision, because I do. I understand. I've got no choice though. I'm doing this because Cassie sacrificed herself for me—for us. By taking the blame for the lie about not being dumped at the altar, which need I remind you was the narrative *I* created—she sacrificed herself and her business. She sacrificed her reputation. Isn't this the least I can do?" As far as Andrew was concerned, this act was the least Andrew could do for misleading her in the first place.

The truth was that Andrew had made up his mind. He'd give up the Dailies to get Cassie back. Or even for the chance of getting her back. There was no guarantee that it would work, and Andrew might be giving up his business for nothing, but Cassie was more than worth that risk.

"This is foolish, or reckless, or both." Noah glared at him. "And you know that. You're more than willing to sacrifice everything, even if it accomplishes nothing. You're willing to sell us out, to sell what we built. This thing belongs to both of us. It needs both of us. I can't do what you do."

"You're selling yourself short. I hope someday you'll see that. You're not nearly as incapable as you pretend to be." Andrew leaned forward. "You don't approve of my decision, and I respect that. Just know that I'm not leaving you high and dry. I'll help you; I'll work for you for free. I just need Cassie to know that I would do anything for her—the way she did anything for me—even if it means I lose everything that I've worked for."

Noah scoffed. "This is a bad idea, Andrew. What's worse? You know I'm right."

"Maybe. But it's the only idea I can come up with, and I've thought long and hard about it." How could he convince his friend? "I don't take this lightly, Noah."

His notifications pinged. "Hang on. I've been waiting for a source to come through for me. No way…"

He read the text as Noah asked, "Is it from Cassie?"

"Nope. It's from Neil Phillips." Andrew handed his phone to his partner. "Guess who is planning to elope with Bethany Mitchell-Phillips?"

Noah read the text. "Roth."

"From the look of that tip line text, Neil Phillips isn't happy about it." Andrew grabbed his phone back.

This could be interesting…

"He wants your help. But what can you do for him?" Noah asked as Andrew reread the text from his tip line.

Only after considering it for a short while did Andrew come to his decision. "I mean, I should find out what I can do for him, right? It seems like the least I can do."

He dialed the number given though the tip line, and Neil Phillips answered on the second ring. "Mr. Phillips, this is Andrew Steele. What can I do for you, sir?"

By the time he hung up, Andrew had gotten the rundown on all things Roth-related. "Roth hasn't signed the prenup yet, and Neil knows that Roth is bad news for his daughter. He thinks they're going to elope, but his private investigators haven't found anything. He wants me to check with my sources."

"You're not an investigator, Andrew."

"No, I'm not." *But…* "Neil Phillips's private investigators haven't found anything. Besides, I do have sources, and a wide reach. Then there's the fact that helping Neil Phillips would stick it to Roth, and I want to do just that. He deserves it and then some. Not just for jilting Cassie at the altar, but for blackmailing her afterward. That was a dick move."

"You've made up your mind about this, too?" Noah combed his fingers through his hair, leaving it spiky. He did that whenever he was irritated.

"Look on the bright side. Neil is no longer financially backing Jeremy. Which means that he's no longer coming after me for the jilted groom narrative." Andrew grinned at his business partner.

"Good, then we're in the clear. You don't have to give up your half of the business." Noah stood, then threw his hands in the air. "Yep. That's good. Everything's back to normal. You scared me there for a minute."

"Just because Roth is out of the picture as far as Neil Phillips is concerned, Bethany Mitchell-Phillips is still an unknown factor with enough money to back Roth. And even if she were out of the equation, I've still got to do something epic to win Cassie back. And that means selling my half of the business to you." Andrew had thought about it long and hard.

That was his only option.

"I must prove that Cassie means more to me than anything, my business included," he explained.

Noah slumped back in his chair "Why do you keep harping on that? You may be ready and willing to offer yourself, and our business, as tribute. Don't expect me to just accept your decision."

Andrew stood and patted his partner on the back. "You'll be okay. You've got this. What did I say before? You're far more capable than you give yourself credit for."

The deep frown etched on Noah's face told Andrew that his friend remained unconvinced. He just hoped that Cassie took the news better.

Chapter 24

CASSIE ENTERED THE RESTAURANT AT EIGHT ON THE DOT. THOUGH busy, it was nowhere near the rush hour kind of crowd. Glancing around the room, she caught sight of him immediately.

Tall, dark-haired, handsome, and wealthy.

Yep, he was waiting for her.

The maître d' escorted her to the table, and she waved to Andrew's friend and business partner. "Hi, Noah."

Though she'd known Noah since he was assigned as Andrew's roommate in their junior year at NYU, she'd never been particularly close to him. To the contrary, Noah barely seemed to tolerate her back then.

"Thanks for meeting me." Noah stood, offering her a chair.

"No problem." Cassie sat and offered him a smile. "I must admit that I was surprised to hear from you today. What's this about?"

Cassie had been curious as to Noah's motives ever since he texted her with his request to meet. In all honesty, though, she had also been a bit concerned. "Forgive me for getting to the heart of it, but is Andrew all right?"

Noah paused, albeit briefly, before sitting across the table from her.

He failed to answer her, and panic seized her heart in a vise grip. "Noah, is Andrew—"

"It depends on your definition of all right."

What did that mean? She was about to ask when their waitress brought over two shots. "Oh, okay. Thanks. Um…" Cassie waited until they were alone. "Do you need a little liquid courage to get through this conversation, Noah? Because I'm good without it, though I'm beginning to get concerned. Is Andrew all right?"

Noah downed his shot like a pro. "Andrew doesn't know I'm here, talking to you. I didn't tell him, then I couldn't tell him."

"Is that code for something?" Talk about being cryptic. This guy wasn't making this any easier. Deciding that perhaps he needed more liquid courage, Cassie slid her shot across the table. "Here. Drink mine if you need it."

While it was good to know that this wasn't another ambush by Jeremy, Cassie doubted Noah's downing shots like water was a good thing. "You know what? On second thought, let me have this back."

Only after she'd slid the shot glass in front of her did she ask, "What is this about? Andrew and I are over, and I was more than a bit surprised that you texted me. Let alone offered to keep where I was staying confidential."

Noah studied her from across the table. "Well, I needed to talk to you before I texted you. Since I texted you, he told me something that I'm not okay with. I need...some guidance."

Guidance?

"From me?" How could Cassie be of any help to Noah? She barely knew the man. "If it's supposed to be between the two of you, perhaps you shouldn't tell me about it."

Cassie's unease was reaching a crescendo. What was this important secret? And if Andrew didn't want her to know about it, why was Noah meeting with her in private to discuss it? Her heart was beating at a frantic pace.

"Andrew has made me an offer. He wants to sell his portion of our business." Noah ripped the Band-Aid right off, without warning.

It threw Cassie completely off guard.

"Why would he do that? He loves that business. He built it from nothing and gave all of himself to it. His name is on that business." As she ticked off all of the reasons Andrew shouldn't sell his business, Cassie stared at Andrew's friend and business partner, who was currently avoiding her like the plague, choosing instead to avert his gaze.

She studied Noah's features, noting the dark circles beneath his eyes. This guy looked exhausted and wracked with guilt. Or was he concerned? Was something wrong with Andrew?

"Why are you telling me this? And why do you look so uncomfortable?" Cassie didn't understand what Andrew selling his stake in their business had to do with her. "What am I missing? More importantly, is Andrew all right? Don't make me ask you that again."

"Look, Andrew wants me to buy him out, and it's a good deal. He's being generous and has given me a great price." He looked her in the eyes at last, only to look away again.

What was he so upset about? It sounded like a win for Noah Carr. From everything she knew about him from the news and social media, Noah knew a good investment when he found one, and this would definitely be a wise investment.

"The thing is…Well, there are several things: the first is that I can't run The Steele Dailies without Andrew. Not really. Like you said, he's the name. Hell, he's the guy behind the whole thing, and I'll never be able to replace him." Noah reached across the table for the other shot glass, then studied it, again refusing to make eye contact with Cassie. "I'm the finance guy, and the real estate guy. I'm great when it comes to our bottom line, and our investments, especially in real estate. But my thumb isn't on the pulse of pop culture, let alone celebrity. That's all Andrew."

Cassie nodded, trying hard to keep up. "What does this have to do with me?" She now wished that she'd held on to the shot as she made eye contact with their waitress and ordered a vodka tonic. "Make it quick, please." She would need it STAT to get through the rest of this conversation.

"Noah?" She prodded him. "You're worrying me. What's this about?"

"Look, Andrew's my friend, not just my business partner." Noah paused, then downed his second shot.

Watching this man suffer was downright painful for Cassie, and she'd begun to think that something was seriously wrong. With him, or with Andrew, or both. She reached across their table and placed her hand on his. "Tell me what's happening. I'll help if I can."

"Isn't it obvious? I don't feel right about profiting from my friend's pain." He stopped speaking as their waitress dropped off Cassie's drink.

With a "thanks," Cassie took a large, unladylike gulp. The guy still wouldn't meet her eyes. At least the waitress hadn't ignored her.

"Noah, what's going on?" she prompted him again, imagining the worst. Was Andrew sick? In an accident? What? She was about to bolt and head to Andrew's—

"Are you willing to take Andrew back? Because if you're not, he needs to know now before he gives up everything for you." His tone was cold, hard, as was his demeanor.

Was she willing to take Andrew back? "Why are you asking me that?" It really was none of Noah's business. Cassie knew that.

"If you're not, then he's sacrificing his life's dream for nothing. That's not right, Cassie." Noah met her eyes at last. His gaze was fierce with determination. "Andrew deserves better than that, if I'm being honest."

"What do I have to do with his decision to sell you his half of the business?" Even though she suspected the answer, she had to ask, she needed to hear it from Noah.

"Andrew wants to prove to you that he can make that sacrifice for you, like you did for him by telling people that you were the source of the jilted groom narrative." Noah tapped his finger on the table. "He wants you back. If you're not willing to take him back, then you have to tell him. Otherwise, it isn't fair."

Andrew wants me back...

Cassie's pulse slammed against her temples. Andrew wanted her back. The knowledge sent Cassie's mind into overdrive. She hadn't seen him or spoken to him since their most recent breakup, yet she'd thought of little but him ever since.

"Does Andrew's decision have anything to do with Jeremy running off with Bethany?" Cassie had kept up with Andrew's site, of course. The fact that Andrew published an article asking for leads as to Bethany's whereabouts came as a surprise to Cassie, but also a relief. It meant that Bethany's father, Neil Phillips, wasn't going after Andrew, and it also meant that Jeremy was no longer a threat. He didn't have Phillips's wealth and connections at his disposal.

"Andrew offered me his shares before that news broke. I was with him when Bethany's father contacted him. That's one reason why I'm betraying his trust by coming to you." Noah placed his elbows on the table.

"One reason out of how many?" Cassie took another sip of her drink. She was on information overload, and her senses were reeling.

"I texted you before I knew about this, thinking I could help him. The guy misses you." Noah threw his hands in the air. "But now that he's willing to give up everything for you, I want to make sure that he doesn't do it for nothing. Andrew doesn't deserve that, Cassie. He's worked too hard."

With her mind racing in a million different directions, Cassie knew one thing.

She wouldn't allow Andrew to give up his business.

Not now, not ever.

So, with that in mind, she texted Andrew. We need to talk.

His response came through in less than a minute. Just tell me when and where. I'll be there.

Cassie typed, Your place. I'll be there as soon as I can, then thanked Noah and rushed up to her hotel room to pick up Bailey. She then ordered a car and headed to Andrew's place with one goal in mind...

Make things right.

Chapter 25

THE FACT THAT CASSIE WAS TRAVELING TO ANDREW'S PLACE CAUSED his nerves to prickle. He was wired, raw, and excited at the same time. He'd planned to contact Cassie the next day and ask to meet with her. The fact that she had contacted Andrew on that particular night accelerated his heartbeat until he'd swear it had skipped a beat or two.

It was a good thing that Andrew had prepared in advance. He'd already stocked up on the beagle's favorite doggie pâté, which was chilling in his stainless steel refrigerator just in case Cassie brought Bailey by. In addition, flowers had just been delivered in vases and were placed throughout his great room, his kitchen, and his bedroom—in other words, the places where they'd spent most of their time together. Not his guest room, because he never wanted Cassie to return there. Not to stay, and most certainly not to sleep.

They belonged together, by each other's side. Where he would support her, and love her, unconditionally. For as long as Cassie would let him. He just hoped she would feel the same when he offered him the best he had to give: himself. All of him—the good, the bad, and the ugly. But would she accept him for who he was, who he truly was deep down? Would Cassie want the geeky kid turned soon-to-be-unemployed gossip publisher?

Cassie was still the same quirky, fun, loving, and smart girl he'd first met, he'd first dated. She was just more of everything. And he loved her more for it. Andrew, on the other hand, had changed—what if she didn't like who he was now?

His cell notifications pinged with a text message from his doorman notifying him that Cassie was on her way up. Striding to the wall of shelving in his great room, he turned on his multimedia player and grabbed the remote. It was the same eight-in-one music hub with a turntable that had attracted Cassie on her first night at his place. It was also still preloaded with Cassie's favorite album on the turntable.

Once *The Stranger* played the first track, Andrew tossed the remote onto his coffee table. He had always loved Cassie's quirky taste in music, and the fact that she preferred vinyl records to Bluetooth or CDs had turned him into an eclectic guy when it came to his own musical tastes. Music, for the most part, sounded different when heard on a vinyl record. It was an indisputable fact as far as Andrew was concerned. She'd changed him for the better, and he could never shake her or her influence on him.

"What are you thinking?" She stormed in, carrying Bailey in her arms. Much like when Andrew had driven up to them on Dune Road. He was instantly struck by her spark, that vivacious energy radiating from Cassie's very presence.

It was a jolt unlike any other.

"What was I thinking when?" Andrew studied her, his heart filling with relief at the sight of her pink cheeks and tempestuous energy. She commanded the room.

And she sounded annoyed with him.

Were they back to that?

Cassie stood in his great room, setting Bailey down only after she'd removed his powder-blue leash that matched his collar. That poor canine needed a fashion intervention, as far as Andrew was concerned. Or not. The dog was pretty remarkable with his current flair for fashion. As he sauntered toward the large bank of windows with the glittering Manhattan view, Bailey rocked that powder-blue collar like a champ.

"Seriously, Andrew, what were you thinking when you decided to sell your portion of your business to Noah? That man's a mess and possibly a lush. He'll put that business *out of business* in less than a year." Cassie tossed the leash and her purse on his sofa like she owned the place.

Like it was her home, which he hoped it soon would be.

Andrew suppressed a grin. "'He'll put that business out of business,' huh? Well, if Noah does that, then it won't matter to me because *not my business* means it's definitely not my problem."

"You love that business, and you won't be happy when Noah Carr runs it into the ground. Trust me." Cassie stood a couple of feet in front of him and placed her hand on her hip. She then looked around the room, scrutinizing her surroundings. "This is quite the ambiance you've got going on here. Dim mood lighting, music, and flowers. Am I interrupting something? Are you expecting a date?"

Her breath caught in her throat. "I *am* interrupting something. Bailey and I probably should come back some other time."

She took a few steps back, her eyes wide while Andrew bridged the distance between them.

"Nope. Now is the perfect time for you to be here. See, I was going to text you tomorrow." Only upon sliding his arm around her waist did he continue. "I planned the mood lighting and music and flowers for you."

"But you had no way of knowing that I'd meet with Noah tonight. Or that I'd text you and stop by." Cassie narrowed her eyes. "Noah couldn't have made that whole story up. He told me that you didn't know. He—"

"He what?" Andrew asked, his voice low and husky.

"Noah said that you wanted me back. He told me that's why you wanted to sell your stake in the company." Cassie swallowed hard. "He also said you didn't know that he came to me."

"My friend was correct. On both counts." Of course Noah would go to Cassie behind his back. Andrew should have expected that Noah would contact her. He wasn't happy about Andrew's decision in the least.

With this information, Andrew came the realization that perhaps Cassie wasn't there to get back together with him after all.

Then again, she was still in Andrew's arms. She could have pulled away but didn't. Andrew would take that as encouragement and would be honest with her.

He had nothing to lose, after all.

So, he tugged her closer to him. "Here's the thing about me: I almost always plan ahead. After your text saying you were on your way here, all it took was a quick phone call to rush the flower delivery from tomorrow to tonight. As far as the music and lighting, I'd already planned that along with stocking your favorite bottle of wine in my wine chiller."

Cassie studied him intently.

"If you don't believe me, check my fridge. I even stocked up on Bailey's favorite pâté."

"That pâté you hate?" She grinned, leaning into his embrace.

"That very same pâté, God help me. That stuff is ridiculously expensive." Andrew feigned annoyance. "But Bailey's worth it. So, it's in my fridge for the drama king beagle, and that damn beagle only."

She flattened her palms against his shoulders, then roved up to the nape of his neck. Andrew was wearing one of his button-down dress shirts, no tie, and her warmth permeated the fabric. "Why is it in your fridge? I want you to tell me. Please explain it to me as if I didn't just ruin your surprise."

"I stocked up on Bailey's favorite pâté and did all of this because I miss you—both of you. And I was hoping you'd come home." He tugged her closer, then closer still, until…

Until her lips were close enough to kiss.

"I can't come home." Her green gaze was locked with his. "I won't come home if you go ahead with your plan sell the Dailies to Noah. That's a deal-breaker."

Her deal-breaker got the better of him. "Why? You hate that business."

"I did, once. But it's your life's work, and I'm not taking it away from you." Cassie traced his jaw with her soft fingertips. "Besides, I've gained a new perspective and have a newfound respect for The Steele Dailies."

The simple motion of her fingertips tracing his jaw sent his taut nerves reeling. "But I choose you, Cassie. I will always choose you."

"Which is why I won't force you to make such a sacrifice."

When he opened his mouth to object, Cassie captured his mouth with hers, probing with her tongue until Andrew granted her entrance. Only after stroking his tongue with hers did she pull away, though not too far.

"I love you. And I want you back. But I want you the way you are... the way you are now."

Their song was playing.

Cassie tilted her head to the side with a sultry grin. "Imagine...our song playing at this precise time. Did you plan that?"

"I wish I had, but even I couldn't have planned that with such impeccable timing." He kissed her forehead. "I think that means that we're meant to be. Only if you move back in with me, you and Bailey, that is. You are a package deal, after all."

"I thought you'd never ask." Cassie leaned into him, her signature scent filling his senses with yearning. "I do love you, Andrew Steele."

"I know you do. And I love you, too, Cassie Benedict." Andrew brushed a stray curl away from her face. "Which is why I've got to come up with something to call you other than Cassie."

"But that's my nickname...because of you."

"Be that as it may, everyone is calling you that now." Andrew had noticed that she'd changed her social media profiles to denote the change to Cassie upon moving out of his place. "And I need something that's irrefutably ours, that belongs just to us."

Andrew thought hard about it. "How about 'my love'? Because you are truly my love."

"It's perfect. And it might just be the only lovey-dovey term that Jeremy didn't call Bethany or vice versa during our meeting from Hades." Her expression was animated, and Andrew chuckled.

"Oh, you haven't heard the latest, have you?" Andrew couldn't hide his joy as he confided in Cassie. "I got word from Neil Phillips that my lead panned out. He found his daughter right before she was about to wed Roth in Vegas. He made her sign a prenup. Now the wedding is on hold."

"Oh, Bethany must be hurt. She really did seem to love him, in her own way." Cassie paused. "Jeremy must be livid. Either that, or he's unhappy. He crashed my lunch with Lauren today and claimed to love Bethany."

"Lauren and Roth in one restaurant… I wish I had seen that. Oh, wait. I did." Andrew's voice was husky. "Full disclosure, I saw a small bit of that conversation. Someone uploaded it to our tip line."

"I thought white blouse was recording us."

Andrew's brow furrowed. "White blouse. Is that code for something?"

"That's code for 'the woman recording us is wearing a white blouse.' Lauren understood what I was saying at lunch. Then again, she's into true crime, so when I start talking in code around her, she just gets it." She offered him a grin. "Sorry."

"Does Lauren still hate me?" Andrew asked, his tone teasing.

Cassie met his teasing tone with one of her own. "Only a little. As it turns out, she hates Jeremy more and called you an upgrade."

"Wonders never cease. Speaking of Roth, has he texted you since his whole Las Vegas wedding was called off? Oh!" Andrew's eyes widened. "Roth has two failed weddings under his belt. That's got to sting."

"I've got one under my belt and it stings." Cassie arched her honey-colored eyebrow. "And to answer your question—there was a question in there somewhere—I don't know if Jeremy has tried to text me because I blocked him after my second restaurant scene with him in as many days."

"Good. I'm proud of you." And Andrew was. Cassie had stood up to everyone who wanted to control her, which took courage.

He kissed her once again.

And, as his lips lingered, she sighed. "I've missed you."

Bailey scratched Andrew's pant leg, and he looked down at the beagle, who was holding out a paw to him.

"*We* missed you," Cassie said with a smile.

Andrew scooped up the dog and held him. "I missed you, too, Bailey. I missed both of you."

"May I make a suggestion?" Cassie petted her canine's snout. Once Andrew nodded, she continued. "Let's not break up ever again. It's not good for our little drama king. He's miserable without you."

"You've got yourself a deal." He kissed her forehead. "The same holds true for moving out. We're in this together. From here on out."

Their agreement was sealed with a kiss.

Andrew had never been so happy, or felt this…what? At home? Yes, and for the first time, he saw that home wasn't simply a place, it was a feeling. A feeling of contentment, a sense of belonging, all because of Cassie. His home was with her…

His home was *her*.

Yes, Andrew's home was a person. His person. His Cassie.

And she would forever be his love.

Epilogue

CASSIE WAS ECSTATIC WHEN ANDREW PRESENTED HER WITH TICKETS to a Billy Joel concert not long after she'd moved back in. That singer/songwriter had, in many ways, been the soundtrack to their relationship both the first time around and most especially the second time around. That's why those tickets had been the most thoughtful gift he could've given her. At least until they were seated in floor seats at the concert.

They sang, they danced, and they got swept up in the show.

When their song was playing, Andrew had slid his arms around Cassie's waist, then slipped a ring on her finger. An engagement ring. But not just any engagement ring. It was a custom-designed pink sapphire ring with diamonds. Knowing Cassie's affinity for gemstones and crystals with meaning, he'd chosen one that signified love, elegance, compassion, power, strength, and wise judgment because, as Andrew later admitted to her, Cassie possessed all those qualities in abundance.

After the concert, Cassie had asked Andrew what he would have done if Billy Joel hadn't played their song at the concert, knowing full well that the artist's playlist was proven to change on a regular basis. His response had been classic, confident Andrew: he would have proposed during another song. It could have been her second favorite, or third favorite, or he would have proposed after the concert. Because, regardless of which song was playing, their engagement would be perfect. It didn't have to be perfectly perfect, just perfect for them.

This man got Cassie, understood her heart, her vision, and even her brand. They understood each other, she knew beyond a shadow of a doubt.

With a beautiful new ring, and their Billy Joel tickets in a frame beside a picture of them together the night that Andrew proposed, Cassie and Andrew planned their wedding ceremony *together*. Because Andrew wanted to be a part of the whole process, and because Cassie couldn't deny him anything, let alone that.

Andrew may not have been perfect, and Cassie knew that she was as far from perfect as one could get, but they were perfect for each other. In the end, that's what mattered.

On the one-year anniversary of their first date, Cassie and Andrew rented the carousel for another evening. With the carousel illuminated in spectacular fashion, not to mention the Manhattan skyline, they exchanged vows. Lauren served as Cassie's bridesmaid, and Noah as Andrew's best man, respectively.

Andrew's dad, Stephen, officiated their ceremony along with Bailey, who wasn't encumbered with a Tiffany-blue-colored tutu this time around. No, the dog wore a pale pink collar instead and looked glorious.

The bride wasn't in white this time around, either. Instead, she opted for pale pink. And the groom wore a matching tie, while their precious canine bestie matched them proudly. A professional photographer was on the scene to record every intimate moment for the happy couple to cherish.

Julia West, actress extraordinaire, didn't show for this wedding, but Cassie did call her mother, who was filming yet another indie movie in Toronto prior to the occasion. Her daughter announced that Julia shouldn't break tradition and come to her wedding this time around. After all, Julia not showing for Cassie's first wedding had set a precedent, and Cassie didn't want to tempt fate. Her mother had readily agreed that Cassie and Andrew shouldn't ruin their winning streak. After all, inviting Julia and having her actually show up might have brought them bad luck.

With the carousel as their backdrop, Cassie and Andrew exchanged vows written by the couple.

"I take you, Andrew, to be the love of my life, and Bailey's dad. I trust that you will love me and our beagle with everything you are, and everything you have. Just as I love you. And…" She paused, beaming. "You're going to like this part. And, when Bailey gets kicked out of his next doggie park trying to protect you from a much larger dog, I trust that you will purchase a new doggie park just for us."

Their friends and family erupted in laughter, but in Cassie's heart she knew it to be true. All of it.

When it was Andrew's turn, he held her hand and squeezed it. "I want to repeat some of what I told you when you came home in front of those we love most in the world. I am yours, my love. Yours and Bailey's, because I can't remember a time that I didn't love you, and because my life would be awfully boring without you. And…I promise to buy us a thousand dog parks if I have to because you and Bailey deserve nothing less."

With a wink, Andrew kissed his bride, who was teary-eyed.

"I thought we'd agreed there would be no tears today." Cassie wiped her eyes.

Andrew held her tight. "I promised to try. But I decided that honesty is the best policy and followed my heart."

Cassie kissed him once again with all the love she possessed and Andrew dipped her in the most epic of wedding photo poses ever, with the carousel in the background.

"You know that my photographer got that shot," Andrew whispered in his bride's ear.

"That is the money shot, but we can never be too careful." Cassie leaned into him. "How about one more kiss? Just to make certain that your photographer did indeed get that shot."

Because Andrew could deny her nothing, he kissed his wife again, in that epic pose for the ages. Afterward, all members of the wedding party rode the carousel to their hearts' contentment.

"The second time is the charm." Lauren held Cassie in a tight embrace. "And I actually like the groom now."

Cassie arched her brow, smiling at her friend. "That must be what happens when the groom sticks around."

"I don't think so. If Jeremy had married you, I would never have warmed to him," Lauren laughed, though Cassie knew her to be dead serious.

Lauren and Jeremy never mixed. It had been the same with Bailey and Jeremy. The signs were always there with great big neon letters, though Cassie just hadn't seen them. In some ways, it was better that she hadn't. Because she and Andrew got back together at the most perfect time, in the most perfect way.

At least, it was perfect as far as they were concerned.

"Oh! I got a text from Jeremy." Lauren tipped her head to the side.

"Really? Did you light him on fire with your words?" Cassie joked.

Lauren's expression turned pensive. "He wanted me to wish you the best from him. And I think he might have meant it."

"No." Cassie hugged her friend again. "Are you growing soft? Are you learning to like Jeremy?"

"No. I don't like him. I don't like him. Don't make me." Lauren's petulant-child act was too convincing.

Andrew approached from behind and slid his palm around Cassie's waist. Her gown this time was formfitting, and it was the right combination of sultry and sophisticated, if she did say so herself. It was for this reason that she could feel Andrew place his palms on her curves. They were indeed the perfect fit for one another.

"Please tell me you're not talking about me." He sounded slightly apprehensive.

"Never." Lauren's expression was animated, while her voice was pure emotion. "At least never again. I like you now because you love my friend. She deserves that."

"I know she does. I won't forget." Andrew smiled. "Bailey would never let me."

"Neither would I." Lauren kissed his cheek. "Congratulations. Just when I didn't think anyone could possibly deserve her, you proved me wrong."

"Thank you for being my bridesmaid." Cassie hugged her friend one more time.

Lauren squeezed tight. "Don't make me cry. I'm wearing my waterproof mascara, but still, I don't want to tempt fate. That would be a horrible look."

"It's time for me to go, do you need a ride?" Noah asked Lauren, whose posture straightened.

"I could use a ride. Sure."

Cassie and Andrew exchanged a glance, a *what's happening there?* glance, before Noah kissed the bride's cheek.

"Congratulations." He smiled at her before shaking Andrew's hand. "I promise not to burn our company to the ground before you return from your honeymoon."

Andrew smiled at his partner. "I'll be checking in, just to make sure you don't."

He and Cassie watched Noah and Lauren walk in the direction of Noah's car.

"What was that about?" Andrew asked his bride. "The whole Noah-and-Lauren thing. Their interaction was…There was something going on, right?"

She was at a loss for words. "I have no idea."

With one glance, Cassie saw surprise emanating from Andrew's features.

"TBD," Cassie added with a sly smile as Stephen walked up to them with Bailey on his leash. She hugged Andrew's father. She was on a first-name basis with him now. "Thank you for officiating."

"It was an honor. Are you sure about me staying with you? I can head home. I mean—you should spend tonight together." His eyes widened. "That didn't come out right. Ah—"

"Dad. We're good. You will always have a suite in our penthouse, and you can stay with us anytime you want." Andrew hugged his father, who got a little choked up.

Cassie scooped Bailey up and gave him a kiss. "We'll be home soon."

Because Stephen had stayed with them so often, Bailey had gotten used to him. He would be Bailey-sitting tonight in what was once Cassie's suite. It was now a guest suite for Andrew's dad.

After Stephen and Bailey headed to their car, which would take them home to the penthouse, Cassie and Andrew sat on the same chariot as when they'd been there on their first date.

"We made it through our wedding without any drama," Andrew mused.

Cassie sighed, lacing her fingers through his. "Who knew that all it would take to actually get me through my own wedding would be the right man?"

"That and the fact that there wasn't an altar in sight." Andrew caressed her hand, tracing lazy circles with his thumb.

"No altar, but an ALTARnate ending." Cassie leaned into him. "See what I did there? The alternate would be spelled A-L-T-A-R-n-a-t-e..."

He laughed, "Yes, I see perfectly. And you are still, without a doubt, the quirkiest woman I've ever met, let alone married."

"Well, yes. I'm also the only woman you've ever married, so there's that, too." Cassie couldn't stop smiling. Andrew had that effect on her. He always would.

"You are my wife. Oh, that's another nickname. Wife," Andrew whispered in her ear. "Should I spell that one for you?"

She snuggled against him, her voice sultry. "Only when we're alone, but I must admit that one is my favorite."

"I knew it would be, *wife*." His smooth baritone was rich and brimming with emotion.

That voice…That voice was one that she'd never get enough of. It represented the intimate side of Andrew that belonged solely to Cassie and no one else. She treasured that fact as she captured his lips with hers and kissed him.

Once they were breathless, Andrew whispered to her, "I will never tire of your kisses."

"That's good, because you're stuck with me, and many, many more of my kisses." She snuggled beside him, reveling in his warmth and nearness. "Oh! I've finished my book."

Andrew kissed the top of her hair, which she wore in a low bun at her neck with a single pink rose. "I knew you would finish. How did it end? If you don't mind giving me spoilers, that is."

"In this case, I believe spoilers are required because it has the most perfect, most epic ending." She traced his lapel with her fingertip.

"I'm listening."

"The last lines are, quite simply: 'A jilted bride's road to romance isn't easy. But it's most certainly worth it.'" She held her breath, waiting for Andrew to respond.

"Was *your* road to romance worth it, my love?" he asked, pressing his lips against her hair once again, as if waiting for her answer.

"More than worth it. And our journey is just beginning," Cassie assured him, kissing Andrew once more as his wife.

Their road to romance may have been a rocky one, but they could agree on one thing: it most certainly was worth it.

**Read on for
more romance from Tracy Goodwin!**

Now available from Sourcebooks Casablanca

Chapter 1

AMELIA MARSH HALTS MIDSTEP, STRICKEN BY THE LAUGHTER AND squeals of a half-dozen children racing towards her.

"Incoming!" Grabbing her daughter and son, she wraps them in her arms, turning just in time to avoid the melee. One for the win column! Sure, those children appear to be sweet and innocent clad in their frilly dresses and formal ties, but she knows better. Amelia is a mom after all, and this is war—playground style. She's got the superpower of keeping her children in check. Like the Hulk/Bruce Banner, those powers come and go. Some days, Amelia is a master, while other days...well, not so much.

The playground is surrounded by trees and lush green grass; however, its pretty setting is *this* parent's nightmare. Kids of all ages shout, wrestle, and run like they're all on one heck of a sugar high. While she's scoping a group of younger boys wrestling in the kiddie play mulch underneath the jungle gym, Amelia's eldest tugs at her arm.

"Mom, can we play?" Her son, Jacob, asks, looking up at his mom with his signature bright smile. At ten years old, he is a charmer. What's worse? He knows it. One flash of his megawatt smile and he receives free cookies at his favorite bakery, or snags extra stickers at their local supermarket.

A little girl rushes past them, dressed in a pink tutu with a bunny tail that hangs haphazardly in the back. The child's faux tail bounces with every step she takes, and her bunny ears remind Amelia of their mission: today, they are attending their community Easter egg hunt and taking pictures with the Easter Bunny.

This is their first major outing since the big move back to Amelia's hometown of Houston, since her divorce, since their lives drastically changed. The last thing she wants is her children running around in the sweltering Texas sun, then taking pictures with some costumed cottontail while they sweat profusely with tangled hair or—worse yet—covered in mulch. She glances again at that same group of boys, who now have pieces of mulch stuck to their clothes and in their hair. The chances of more than one shower needed: likely. Drain-clogging potential: high. Just what Amelia's trying to avoid.

Crouching in front of her son, she ensures that her long skirt is covering her legs, then reaches for the hands of Jacob and his sister, Chloe. They're twenty-two months apart, the best of friends on most days, and bicker like nobody's business the rest of the time. "Why don't we take pictures with the Easter Bunny first, then you can run around. Deal?"

Jacob wrinkles his brow, considering his mom's offer. He's not buying what she's selling, and Amelia's glad that she didn't go all out like some other parents. Contrasting the once-pristine girls and boys wearing their best attire and ruining their special outfits, her kids are wearing clothes of their own choosing—cargo shorts and a polo shirt for Jacob, while Chloe wears leggings and her favorite ruffled shirt with a pink flamingo on it. No fancy shoes, either. Just socks and sneakers.

Picture-taking Marsh style is practical by necessity, because their family is cursed when it comes to family photos. Without fail, the better dressed her children are, the worse the picture. There could be fifty photos taken, and not one would include both of the kids smiling or looking at the camera at the same time. But, when they wear comfortable clothes—their favorite clothes—voilà! It's like a Harry Potter moment with magical smiles and happy memories.

At this community event, she seems to be the only parent with this mindset, seeing the abundance of children once dressed to impress now getting dirty, sweaty, and screaming louder than the audience at a Metallica concert.

"I promise you can play after—"

"They have cookies! Can we have cookies, Mom?" Chloe, her eight-year-old spitfire tomboy, points to a little boy eating a large cookie, then sprints toward the clubhouse, followed close behind by Jacob. When all else fails, cookies will do the trick and, thanks to a little boy covered in grass stains, a trail of cookie crumbs is leading Amelia's children away from the lure of a crowded playground.

"Save some for me!" she calls to them, walking close behind until they reach the pool clubhouse, also known as their community's "aquatic center." It's a fancy name for a small in-ground pool and a building with bathrooms.

Their subdivision of Castle Rock is a newer one, situated in the northern suburbs of Houston in a town named Timberland, Texas. Here, in what is known as the *Lush and Livable Timberland*, where natural pine trees that were once in abundance are rare thanks to the building boom, residents pride themselves on their thick green lawns and blooming flower beds.

Under the shade of the clubhouse and its covered patio, Amelia spies tables accentuated with spring-themed tablecloths whipping in the warm breeze, upon which plates of cookies with colored icing and cups of lemonade are arranged around stuffed-animal bunnies and Easter decorations.

She's traded sweat and dirt for icing and lemonade. Given the fact that her kids used to hate any and all imaginary figures in costumes, from Santa to the Easter Bunny to their school mascot, Amelia will take whatever photos she can get. Cargo shorts? Sure. Flamingo shirt? Done. Icing turning their tongues blue like Smurfs? She'll deal.

Such is the single mom in her. Always trying to please, to make the kids happy, and to find her own sense of satisfaction. Without her ex-husband, Daniel. It was his choice to start a new life with his mistress. Did it hurt? Yes. Because he walked out on their children and because he caused them pain. Though Daniel may have wanted out, he also wanted everything that he valued—their house, their money, their investments. What he didn't value are Amelia's biggest blessings: Jacob and Chloe.

Granted, she's no pushover. With the help of a brilliant attorney, Amelia fought for what her children and she deserved. When the divorce was finalized, it was time to remove her children from the situation and give them a chance to heal—near some of Amelia's best friends.

Today, she's on her own, with her children—who are scarfing down cookies like they haven't eaten in days. "Slow down, sweeties. Let's take a break from the cookies."

Mom rule number one: never let your kids overeat and throw up. As a matter of fact, avoid vomit at all costs. Gross, but true.

"Hello there." A saccharine-sweet voice and a terse tap on Amelia's shoulder grab her attention. "I'm Carla, from the community's management company. I don't believe we've met."

"Nope, not yet." Amelia would remember Carla, who is a sight to behold with teased red hair, full makeup, and a pristine pantsuit. How is this woman not melting in today's heat? In her light maxi dress and messy bun, Amelia is already perspiring, but Carla's heavy makeup remains flawless. Is she human or is heat endurance *her* superpower?

"Hi, Carla. I'm Amelia Marsh. These are my children, Jacob and Chloe." Her daughter waves while her son gulps more lemonade before flashing his signature grin.

Carla narrows her eyes, staring at Amelia's children, seemingly immune to Jacob's charms. In turn, Jacob smiles wider, arching his brow. With still no response from Carla, Jacob gives up and studies his feet, while Amelia gives him a reassuring pat on his back.

"Where's the Bunny?" Chloe asks.

"He's coming. How about you line up over there?" Carla points at the seating area where four carefully arranged lawn chairs remain empty, and a line has already formed, full of flushed and disheveled children. Parents are doing their best to right the damage done by playtime. *Good luck with that.*

Amelia's children look to her for approval, and she nods. Jacob smiles, his teeth blue from the icing. "That's my boy!" Amelia encourages him with a thumbs-up.

Mom rule number…who knows, since there are so many mom rules that she's lost count, but this is one of the most important rules of all: you can only control so much. Amelia has traded the messy, sweaty, grass-stained debacle for blue teeth. The glass half full theory is that the blue might not show up in the picture.

"Keep drinking, buddy." She smiles as Jacob takes another sip of his lemonade, then she turns to Carla. "What's the difference between the HOA and the management company?"

"The Homeowners Association consists of Castle Rock residents, some of whom preside on its board of directors. The management company, for which I work, handles the logistics, enforcing the bylaws—in other words, the community rules, and—"

"Collecting the annual dues," Amelia adds with a smile. Now she understands. "I know my dues are paid for the year. I took care of that at closing."

Studying Carla, Amelia notes that the woman has a half smirk/half grin plastered on her face. Just like her makeup, it isn't moving.

"I'm sorry about the letter arriving so soon after you moved in. But rules are rules, you know."

Amelia's catches the woman's exaggerated grimace. "Letter? I'm lost. Why would I receive a letter when I paid my dues?"

"Oh, no. You haven't read it yet." Carla gasps, her hot pink nails matching her lipstick as she covers her mouth with her hands.

"Nope, I haven't received it yet. What's in this letter? It sounds ominous." Amelia's humor falls flat on the stoic-faced Carla.

"There are rules."

"Right. You've repeated that. Three times, I believe. Possibly four." Shoving her sunglasses on top of her head, Amelia refuses to break eye contact with Carla, whose expression remains serious. "Rules like what, exactly?"

Carla shifts, then whispers, "Your gnome."

"My what?" Is *gnome* some sort of code word for one of her children? Amelia's head snaps immediately to her kids. Jacob laughs while Chloe chats with him, probably reciting one of her famous knock-knock jokes. The kids are safe, so her attention returns to Carla. "Did you say my 'gnome'?"

"Your garden gnome. The one in your front yard," Carla counters.

Amelia laughs. She can't help it. Carla's mock horror that this new resident finds her comment amusing quickly fades into impatience, her eyes emanating frustration and disapproval, the lines around them deepening.

Clearing her throat allows Amelia time to keep her expression neutral, her tone calm, and her snark to a minimum. "Do you mean my tiny, hand-painted garden gnome hidden within the bushes, flowers, and mulch that comprise a small portion of my front yard? You can barely see it."

Carla scoffs. "I see everything. It's my job to inspect the front yards. I drive by intermittently, so I can ensure our community remains up to the standards set in the bylaws."

Of course she does. The fact that Carla *sees everything* is a bit alarming.

Sticking to the topic at hand, Amelia explains, "My children made me that gnome for Mother's Day last year." Before the divorce. Before their move. It was displayed prominently in the front yard of their old home. That gnome represents her children's only request when moving to Houston: that she'd place it in their new front yard. It helps them feel at home.

"You must remove it, I'm afraid. Rules are rules, and some people's trash is others' treasure, so to speak." Carla grins, seemingly oblivious to the fact that she just insulted Amelia and her beloved gnome.

"Trash?" *Carla. Did. Not. Just. Say. That.*

Carla nods. "Not that I find your troll trashy, of course. Playing devil's advocate, the truth is that you may like it, but your neighbors may find it tacky. Besides, the ban is in the bylaws."

So, this woman has called her kids' gnome *trash*, *tacky*, and a *troll*. For any mom, especially Amelia, those are fighting words. "Who bans garden gnomes that you can barely see in their bylaws?"

"Your HOA. If you don't like it, I invite you to attend your next quarterly Homeowners' Association meeting. You just missed the last one, but I'll send out an email blast to all residents, signs will be posted at the entrances to the neighborhood, and an announcement will go up on the community website approximately ten days in advance of the next meeting." Applause drowns out Carla, and Amelia turns to see the Easter Bunny waving at the kids.

"Time for pictures! Have a good day." And just like that, Carla dismisses Amelia, sauntering away to schmooze with other residents.

Amelia blinks. *What the heck?* Gnomes are off limits, but bunnies are okay? She scans her surroundings which, like most front yards in her subdivision, are decorated with colored ribbons, bunny cut-outs, and enlarged egg décor. Yeah, bunnies on full display are fine, yet one tiny, beautiful gnome—the gnome that her kids made for her—must go? The same gnome that makes their new house a *home*.

The Easter Bunny high fives Jacob and Chloe, and Amelia makes a beeline to them, just as her daughter begins hiding behind her brother. Apparently, Chloe hasn't gotten over her fear of fake bunnies after all. This one is cute, sporting a purple suit jacket, a yellow vest, and a rainbow-colored bow tie. Though this event is held weeks before Easter, beads of perspiration trickle down Amelia's spine, causing her to pity the poor soul who drew the short straw and must wear a furry costume in this heat and sticky humidity. Hopefully, his or her costume has a fan.

"Hi, Bunny!" She smiles and high fives the faux fur paw of whoever is in the costume.

Nodding and swaying to the beat of Taylor Swift's "Shake It Off", which is blasting through the pool speakers, this rabbit is in character. Amelia needs to shake Carla off, since her blood pressure is still high from the woman's lack of tact and the accompanying ban notice. Over a gnome? Really? So, Amelia takes Taylor's advice, singing and dancing with her children in line. The Easter Bunny must be a Swiftie, too, because the person in the costume dances over to the chairs before taking a seat.

When it's their turn for picture time, Amelia hands her cell to a man standing next to Carla, who will take the picture for them. Carla... ugh. The sight of her after that catty "tacky" comment makes Amelia's heartbeat pound like an anvil.

Normally, Amelia would have let Carla's comments about the letter go. Who knows? She might have even removed her gnome. But Carla insulted Jacob and Chloe's art, even after Amelia explained the importance of it.

One simple, passive-aggressive comment is all it takes for her to decide that she can't let it go. Instead, Amelia may drive the kids to Target, Walmart, or both after they spend time at the playground and buy out their entire garden gnome department. If she's lucky, maybe they'll be on sale, and she'll display an extended gnome family on her front lawn. If the HOA wants to send her a letter, she might as well earn it.

As they approach the Bunny for their picture, Chloe hides behind Amelia's skirt while Jacob charms the fluffy cottontail immediately with a knock-knock joke. No matter which way Amelia turns, her daughter won't come out from hiding. Amelia half expects Chloe to hide *under* her skirt any minute. Every time Amelia moves, so does Chloe, taking her mom's dress with her. "Sit on my lap, Chloe. Let's take the picture together."

With Jacob on one side, and Amelia and Chloe on the other, they pose with the Bunny.

When the man holding her cell prompts them to smile, Amelia instructs her kiddos to smile, adding, "Say 'garden gnome!'"

"Garden gnome!"

It's official. The Bunny must think I've completely lost my mind.

On the bright side, the kids smiled, laughed, and took a great picture. Add to that the fact that Amelia's got a plan.

The HOA better look out, because this mom protects her gnomes at all costs.

Chapter 2

THANKS TO A BROKEN FAN IN KYLE SANDERS'S COSTUME, HE'S about to suffer heat stroke by rodent impersonation. It's not exactly the way he expected to go, but hey, if you're going to sweat to death, why not do so wearing a goofy Easter Bunny costume? Go big or go home, right? Sure, it'll be humiliating, especially when it hits the local news. And it would traumatize a lot of children.

Oh man! The kids...

In an effort to hide his demise from the neighborhood children, Kyle darts into the cleaning closet of the Castle Rock community's pool house, desperate to cool off. Struggling with the top of the costume, a muffled curse word escapes his lips as one of his pawed feet lands beside a bucket and a mop slams against his bunny forehead. It's Kyle against a cottontail costume, in a cage match, or in this case a closet match. His opponent—a bulky, furry rabbit costume—is a modern-day torture device that's currently winning.

Why did I ever volunteer for this?

Taking a step to the side, his oversized furry foot lands in the empty bucket. Still, Kyle manages to use his floppy tail to leverage himself against a wall. "The things I do for this community. Come on!"

Managing to free his face from the bunny head, Kyle tosses the thing onto a small table taking up too much space. He then rips the Velcro at his back and frees both arms, sliding the costume down to his waist. Drenched with sweat, he grabs his sports drink and takes several desperate gulps from the large bottle.

Though his foot may remain stuck, at least he won't die of dehydration. Limping over to the small table with the decapitated rabbit head, Kyle narrows his eyes, staring at the bunny's face which remains frozen in place, that wide, toothy grin taunting him along with its glossy eyes and fake wire-rimmed glasses.

Kyle mutters under his breath while placing the bottle on the table before attempting to yank his enlarged rabbit's foot from the yellow bucket. It still won't budge. Kyle once considered a rabbit's foot to be good luck, but in this cleaning closet of horrors, it's anything but.

Blood-curdling, high-pitched screams cause him to jump, as his eyes dart to the closet door, which is now open. Standing in the doorway is the cute mom wearing the casual dress who has covered her daughter's eyes, gaping at Kyle as her son yells, "The Easter Bunny isn't real! He isn't real!"

"I'm sorry!" It's all Kyle can manage. Repeating it louder, over the screams, doesn't do much.

I've traumatized this woman's children! I've destroyed their innocence. It's all he can think as his neighbor—Kyle doesn't know her name because they've never met—leads her kids into the closet and slams the door shut in an attempt not to traumatize anyone else's children, he supposes.

"Jacob, Chloe, it's okay," she says in a soothing voice, caressing her kids' shoulders. "This is the Easter Bunny's helper. Think about it. EB can't be everywhere at once, right?"

She wipes her little girl's tears as her son surveys Kyle with a skeptical expression. "You're the Bunny's helper?"

Sure, why not? Right now, Kyle would agree to anything that will calm the kids. "Yes, I am." He glances to their mom, who nods at him, as if encouraging Kyle to elaborate. "Your mom is right. The Bunny is busy painting eggs, making baskets, buying candy—"

"He buys candy? From where?" This little boy asks a lot of questions.

Kyle shrugs. "A candy store."

"What does he pay you?" the kid asks him.

"Not enough." It's the first thing that comes to mind. In truth, Kyle doesn't make a dime for this. He's a volunteer, donating his time so the community can save money as opposed to hiring a professional hare. He's also the community's Santa. Multitasking is his thing. Along with running his own business, he is the acting HOA board president, also on a volunteer basis, which means residents yell at him about the cost of their annual dues (in spite of the fact that the cost of dues hasn't risen once in Kyle's four years as president), letters they receive from the management company prohibiting decorations in their front yards and criticizing the height of their lawns, and all other concerns. Meanwhile, he sweats in a rodent costume on an eighty-plus-degree day for kids who don't belong to him. It's a thankless task. One he was reelected for, because no one was willing to run against him. There's only one poor sap in Castle Rock willing to torture himself, and he is currently being interrogated by a kid.

The boy scratches his head. "I want to drive a Ford F-250 when I grow up, have a Mercedes transit van, and a Tesla. My mom says I need to make a lot of money to pay for all of it."

Talk about a change of subject. "That's ambitious. You'll figure it out, though. You've got time." Kyle winks at him, hoping he's appeased the little boy's curiosity.

All he wanted was to cool off in a cleaning closet. Now Kyle is giving advice on a kid's future career path and vehicle ownership. This is way too much. Especially since it's cramped with the four of them in the tiny space, and the walls seem to be closing in. Or it could be Kyle's claustrophobia. Fun times.

"What's your name?" the boy asks Kyle, jerking him from his concerns regarding the confined quarters and heavy costume still covering the lower half of his body.

"My name?" That's an easy one. "Kyle Sanders. What's yours?"

"I'm Jacob Marsh, and this is my mom, Amelia Marsh. My sister, Chloe Marsh, is there," he points at the little girl, whose red cheeks are tear-streaked.

She nods. "Yeah, I'm Chloe Marsh, and this is my mom and brother."

"Got it." Chloe, Jacob, and Amelia. *Amelia Marsh.* A brunette with a killer smile, Amelia is luminescent, wearing minimal makeup and exuding a natural glow. Her dress is sleeveless and floor length, but when the breeze blows in the right direction, sandals that lace around her ankles attract Kyle's attention. She's left him breathless, or maybe it's the lack of oxygen in the cramped closet.

"Mom, I've still gotta pee." Jacob doesn't hold anything back.

Amelia steps forward. "We were looking for the restrooms. I'm sorry—um…"

"Kyle," he reminds her. "The men's room is one door down; the ladies' room is two doors down that way." Pointing to his left, Kyle stands stock still. With his annoying costume foot still stuck in the bucket, he isn't going anywhere.

"Right. Let's go, you two." Amelia opens the door a crack and ushers her kids out, before adding, "I'll be right back."

As she closes the door behind her, Kyle is left to stand in silence for what feels like forever. Just when he begins to think she's abandoned him, Amelia returns wearing a sweet grin. "Sorry, I had to make sure the bathrooms were single stalls, and that my children were safe behind locked doors. You look like you could use some help."

"Nope. Just chilling." Kyle places his hands casually on his hips, ignoring the fact that the rough interior fabric of his costume is causing him to itch. "This is how the Bunny's helper rolls."

Shaking her head, she laughs. "You're not rolling. You're trapped, from the looks of it. Here I thought rabbit's feet were good luck."

Kyle shifts his weight to his free foot. "I know! That's what I've been told."

"They lied to us. Unless..." Amelia smirks, tilting her head to the side. "The truth is that messing with a rabbit's foot *is* bad luck. I don't need any more of that. Perhaps I should pass?"

"No, please!" Kyle's plea is urgent. "It's not bad luck if the rabbit's foot is stuck in a snare and still attached to the rabbit. Besides, I didn't break a mirror."

"Duly noted." Amelia bends down, shoving a stray lock of hair from her face as she studies the bucket. "I was kidding, you know. I wouldn't leave you here, stuck like this."

"Good to know." Kyle exhales, watching her lips upturn into a wry grin. "You've got a sense of humor."

"So I've been told." Amelia reaches for the bucket and struggles to free Kyle's foot. "I've almost got it." She gives it another hard yank and Kyle's foot is free, though Amelia lands with a hard thump beside him.

Kyle offers his hand and helps her to her feet. Face-to-face, their eyes lock and he notices the gold flecks in her deep brown eyes. They're mesmerizing. He inhales, overcome by her intoxicating scent—a floral perfume with hints of musk. Those traits alone would make her attractive, but add the fact that Amelia just saved him from the ultimate humiliation, being forced to ask Carla for help...

Chills travel up his spine. He would never have lived that down.

"Thanks for coming to my rescue. Freeing me from a pail and convincing two traumatized children that I'm the Easter Bunny's helper takes skill."

She averts her gaze from Kyle's. "I did what anyone would have. Except a lot less gracefully."

"You're speaking to the guy who got his foot stuck in a mop bucket." Kyle raises his brow.

"I'm not one to judge." Her eyes shine with amusement and something more. *Is she flirting with me?* Before Kyle can fully ponder that thought, Amelia turns towards the closed door.

"In spite of your humility, I do owe you a debt of thanks." He offers her his hand, and she shakes it. Her skin is soft.

"Anything for the Easter Bunny's helper." She extracts her hand from his, then opens the door. "You okay?"

"I feel great." It's true. Kyle can't stop smiling. "Thanks again for the save."

"You're welcome. Now I've got to find my children before they do something not approved by Mom. Bye, Kyle." Amelia darts out the door, and Kyle peers around it in time to see her peek over her shoulder—long enough for him to note that her cheeks are bright pink as she studies his chest.

She just checked him out. One could argue that he's her man candy, and he wouldn't mind one bit, which is a first. Truth be told, Kyle checked her out, too—her ring finger, that is. She doesn't wear a wedding ring. Normally, Kyle would ask her out in a heartbeat. There's one problem, though—he doesn't date women who have children.

That one rule of his has never been so inconvenient, but it's a rule Kyle never breaks. At least not since its inception. Then again, he never thought he'd be wearing a bunny costume. Funny how life throws you a curveball.

A child cries outside the door and the jarring sound jolts Kyle back to his senses. *Don't go there.* Some rules aren't meant to be broken. For Kyle, this is a nonstarter—and for good reason.

Chapter 3

As Amelia watches Jacob and Chloe play on the jungle gym, she sneaks a peek at the Bunny posing for yet another picture. Who would have thought that inside that cute costume would be Mr. Abs for Miles? She could have gotten seriously distracted by Kyle's abs, had her kids not been screaming about the Bunny not being real. That brought her back to earth big time. As did Chloe's tears. And the fact that Amelia has no room in her life for... *What are they? A six-pack? A twelve-pack? All of the above?*

Whatever they may be, Amelia has no time for abs, or men. Nope, she is too busy making sure Jacob and Chloe are adjusting to their new life, new home, new routine. It's kind of nice to recognize that her divorce didn't kill everything inside her and that she can at least appreciate an attractive male specimen. Not that she is looking to get involved with one again.

A split second is all it takes for Jacob's laughter to turn into an exasperated sigh. "I don't want to play that game, Chloe!" he snaps at his sister.

Amelia's shoulders tense. She's on alert, ready to referee an argument or watch them work it out by themselves. Which will it be this time? Anticipation mounts as she watches Chloe halt midrun.

"Come on. Please?" When Jacob won't budge, Chloe sighs. "You never want to play what I want to play."

The tears will follow. Amelia knows it, as she takes a step forward.

"Don't cry, Chloe. We'll play it later, okay?" Jacob hugs his sister.

That's my boy.

Nodding, Chloe wipes her eyes. "You promise?"

Jacob smiles his famous megawatt smile, and all is forgiven as they kneel in the mulch and begin stacking pieces of it like they're Legos. Amelia's heart swells with pride and with love. There are times, many times, that the kids can't work things out without her, but this time… Well, this is a huge Mom victory and she savors it, watching her children smile and laugh. Probability of mulch in their clothes: high. And it's worth it.

Wails from the clubhouse grab her attention, and Amelia turns to see that Kyle has finished taking pictures with all but one of the children. This last one is young and won't stop crying as the Bunny rocks him gently. His poor mom clutches her cell, pointing the camera at the scene with an angsty expression, while Carla and the man who was taking the pictures earlier are nowhere in sight.

Glancing at her children, who are enthralled with the playground mulch, Amelia instructs them, "Stay here and be careful, please. I'll be right back."

Walking under the shade of the covered patio, she approaches the new mom. "How are you doing?"

"Not well. How do parents get good pictures? I don't understand." She walks over to the Bunny and Kyle hands the little boy with hair the color of spun gold over to her.

Rubbing his back, his mom, who is also a beautiful blond, grins, though her lips quiver. The child continues to cry as tears well in her eyes. Amelia can recognize a sleep-deprived woman when she sees one. Heck, she's been one many times over. "May I try?"

She nods and hands Amelia the little boy. Rocking the child, Amelia's expression is animated. "Look at how handsome you are. I remember when mine were this small."

Her reason for holding the young boy isn't because Amelia has a knack of calming children, or that his mom did anything wrong. It's because the young woman needed a break, and Amelia can relate. It's something she's experienced herself, along with the guilt that comes with the feeling. Between the little guy's time with his mom and Amelia, he has stopped crying. Though Amelia wishes she could take credit, the reality is that the little boy is exhausted, and costumed characters are kind of creepy.

"Hey, little one. I know you're tired, and this bunny is large, right? Looming over you." She's attempting to rationalize with a baby. Familiar territory, to be sure. "It's okay, though. Why doesn't your mom pose with you? I do that with my kids all the time."

The child watches Amelia intently, and so does Kyle—the Bunny's wide eyes ever present. The costumed head tilts to the side, like Kyle's caught up in Amelia's conversation with a child who is too young to hold up his end of the chat.

Turning to the baby's mom, Amelia suggests, "Why don't we switch. I'll take the cell and you can take this little guy. Maybe stand behind the Bunny. Holding him—the baby, not the Bunny. Obviously."

The young woman kisses her little boy on his forehead, then inhales a deep breath.

"We've all been there, you know," Amelia assures her, certain this is her first child. She recognizes how overwhelming it can be. "They don't warn us about the tantrums, or fear of Santa, the Easter Bunny, and elves. It should be in the handbook."

Amelia's last comment makes the blond laugh. The baby notices the shift in his mom's emotions and smiles.

"There you go. We've got a happy little guy."

Sighing with relief, the young woman whispers, "Thank you."

Tentatively, she approaches Kyle, who remains stock-still. Everyone is holding their collective breath, trying not to upset the little one.

"Ready?" Amelia whispers in an effort not to break the peaceful spell that's been cast.

Both the Bunny and the mom nod, then Amelia takes somewhere between ten and twenty photos. "There are some great shots in here."

The mom smiles, reclaiming her cell. "Thank you so much. Um, what's your name?"

"Amelia."

"I'm Sophie and this is Stephen. Hopefully, we'll see you again."

Amelia nods. "I'm on Royal Court. I have a tacky troll in my yard. Apparently, you can't miss it. Stop by sometime."

"We live a block away and walk down that street all the time. I haven't noticed a troll, but I'll look out for it. I love gnomes." Sophie is a smart woman with great taste, and Amelia likes her already. It's nice to have an ally in the neighborhood.

Though she has local friends, each of them live in different subdivisions. Amelia wonders if Sophie has a support system.

"What's your cell number?" She programs it into her iPhone and texts her name to Sophie's cell. "If you ever need anything, call me or text. I work from home, so I'm available."

Sophie smiles. "Thank you so much. Take care."

Glancing at Jacob and Chloe, Amelia notes that they've moved on to that Pokémon game with lots of hand gestures—the same game Jacob refused to play earlier. Chloe has been obsessed with this game, and Jacob humors her most of the time, or at the very least, more often than not. Amelia studies them, in awe of how well they seem to be handling all of the changes in their lives. As she knows from experience, looks can be deceiving.

"You're doing something right." Kyle's muffled voice is low beneath the costume, his presence all-consuming as he stands beside her. "They're great little people."

"Thanks." Though Amelia would like to think that it was his compliment which sent a shock wave through her system, she knows better. Still, she resists, pushing such thoughts aside. She shouldn't feel anything for Kyle, let alone attraction, because rebound relationships never work, and Amelia's not your casual sex kind of girl. She never has been. That's why she's only ever been with one man—her ex-husband. They were college sweethearts, marrying after graduation. Sex was something Amelia never thought she was very good at, and that was before he cheated.

Sure, Kyle's hot, but that isn't what currently has Amelia smiling. It's his kindness, the gentleness in his husky tone. And the fact that Kyle sees it, too…the genuinely good souls that are Amelia's children. It's validation, even coming from a stranger in a bunny costume.

Friend-zoning Kyle, Amelia claps him on his shoulder, noting the fur is matted. "Well done, Bunny."

Managing a thumbs-up, he waves and disappears, presumably into his closet. Where he'll remove his costume, and his abs will be on full display once more. Abs that Amelia must never think of again.

"Can you believe what her children wore? I mean she's single, but still. Can't she go to a thrift store and buy them proper Easter attire?" The voice is shrill, all too familiar, and middle-aged mean girl. As Amelia's learned, mean girls have nothing on mean women. Unsurprised, she recognizes that voice as Carla's. "What can we expect from someone who puts that monstrosity in front of her home? No taste whatsoever."

Following the soft sound of smothered laughter, she finds Carla taking a drag on her cigarette at the far side of the clubhouse.

"Carla, I'm glad I found you. I wanted to thank you so much for welcoming me to the neighborhood today." Amelia's voice is calm. She doesn't let people know they're getting to her. It would grant them power over her, and Amelia refuses to do so. Instead, she's well versed in her ability to shower them with kindness, knowing how it bothers them. She learned that art during her divorce, and it unnerved her ex-husband to no end.

Silence hangs heavy as Amelia slides her cell from her pocket and unlocks the screen with her thumb. *Camera app... Open.* "Let's take a selfie to remember this day. Shall we?"

On the spot, Carla nods.

"Smile, ladies." Amelia takes their photo—her, Carla, and Carla's friend, who Amelia doesn't know and doesn't care to know.

As she heads towards the playground, Amelia glances at the picture she just snapped. Carla has a cigarette in hand, standing beneath a sign that states in bold letters NO SMOKING. She must be breaking a bylaw, if not an actual law. Amelia plans to tuck that in her arsenal.

"Oh, Amelia!" Carla calls, causing Amelia to glance over her shoulder. "There's a community garage sale tomorrow. Benefitting a Houston animal shelter. I hope you'll donate." Carla's tone is sugary sweet.

"Absolutely. Count me in." Amelia plasters a smile on her face, all the while clutching her cell in a tight grasp, before marching past Kyle, who's now in a T-shirt and jeans as she gathers Jacob and Chloe.

"Are you okay?" Kyle asks, walking beside her as she unlocks the doors to her SUV with a remote key fob.

Waiting until her kids are inside and out of hearing range, Amelia mutters, "No, but I will be."

She hops into the driver's seat, turning her key in the ignition and blasting the air. Good thing she parked in the shade. Lowering the windows, Amelia allows the engine to idle as Jacob and Chloe snap their seat belts in place.

Kyle stares at her, his eyes wide. "What happened?"

Carla is a witch. Amelia bites her tongue, tapping her fingernail against the steering wheel.

Women like Carla don't hurt her…not unless they drag Amelia's children into it. That's the mistake Carla made, and it's a big one. Does she tell a guy she met in a cleaning closet about it? Of course not. Amelia knows nothing about him, except that he is a stranger who wears a bunny costume on a Saturday afternoon and compliments her children.

"It's nothing that you need to worry about." She manages a terse smile, but his narrowed gaze proclaims he isn't fooled.

That much is clear when he places his palm on her shoulder. "What did Carla do?"

Amelia stares at his hand, flattened against her flesh. No man has touched her, not since Daniel. Kyle's hand is warm and strong. Their physical connection causes Amelia's pulse to race.

Kyle jerks his hand away. "Sorry. I shouldn't have—wh—um—what did Carla do this time? She annoys most of us residents, you know."

"You live here?" Mr. Abs for Miles isn't a stranger, per se. He's a member of Amelia's new community. "Please tell me Carla doesn't live in Castle Rock, too."

"No, she doesn't. Why?" His dark brows furrow. Like he senses that Amelia is about to unleash psychological warfare upon Carla and her bylaws. Is Amelia overreacting? Probably. So, she inhales and exhales, first one breath, then two, followed by a third.

"Uh-oh. She's going Zen," Jacob announces from the backseat. Loud enough for Kyle to hear.

He turns to Jacob. "What does that mean?"

"Someone messed with the wrong mom," Chloe and Jacob say in unison. Amelia's children know her too well.

"Dad always said she should have been a lawyer." Jacob meets his mom's eyes in the rearview mirror.

"Yeah. He never won an argument. Mom is magical," Chloe adds.

Kyle scratches his chin, his smooth jaw tense. "Magical?"

"Logical," Amelia explains, clutching the steering wheel at the memory. "My ex used to say I am logical to a fault."

Averting her eyes from Kyle with that embarrassing admission, Amelia views her children through the rearview mirror. "Seat belts on?"

"Yes, Mom!" the kids answer in unison.

She knew the answer before asking, but used the question to distract Kyle, her new neighbor, from the words her ex-husband used repeatedly to intentionally hurt her. As if being logical and presenting a clear argument is an insult. Only Daniel would see it that way. Then again, Daniel had a warped sense of fidelity, honesty, and family.

"Thanks for helping the Bunny, Kyle." Placing her palm on the gear shift, Amelia waits for Kyle to back away before safely reversing.

And thanks so much, Carla, for putting things in perspective.

New home, new neighborhood, the same catty gossip. If only Amelia had listened when her husband was the talk of their old community. She wouldn't have been blindsided by his betrayal. But there's no going back.

Live and learn, that's her motto. What did Amelia learn? That Daniel did get something right: she *is* logical. It's time she researches some bylaws. But first, a respectful revolt involving some garden gnomes is in order.

Operation Game of Gnomes has begun.

Chapter 4

"MOM! WHERE DO YOU WANT THIS ONE?" JACOB HOLDS A MEDIUM-sized gnome in the air.

Amelia halts, carrying a larger one. They were in stock and half price. *Take that, Carla!* "Your choice, dude. Go for it."

Jacob places his gnome beside the tree in the middle of their front yard.

"Come here, you two. This is the last one…" Jacob and Chloe run to Amelia, and she gives her large gnome a Vanna White flourish with her hands. "Where do we put this guy?"

The children ponder her question, searching different parts of the front yard.

"Bunny man!" Chloe shouts, pointing to the street.

Amelia turns and sure enough, Kyle has parked his truck in front of her house. He's wearing the same T-shirt and jeans as when Amelia drove away from him earlier.

"Hi!" Jacob and Chloe say in unison before Jacob adds, "You drive a Ford F-250. What is your job? Wait…" Jacob reads the decal printed on the passenger door. "*Sanders Construction.* Is that your company?"

"Yeah, it is." Kyle smiles at him. "Maybe you can own one when you grow up."

"Do you have a Mercedes transit van?"

Kyle shakes his head. "Afraid not."

"Huh. I really want that Mercedes van."

"The Tesla, too," Chloe adds.

Placing her free hand on Jacob's shoulder, Amelia adds in a teasing tone, "Jacob is committed to his choice of vehicles. If he were to give you the complete list, it would tally at about two dozen and it grows almost daily."

"Ambitious." Kyle opens his passenger door and hands each of the kids a baseball cap with his company logo on them, before returning his attention to Amelia. "Can I talk to you for a second?"

"Sure. Why don't you two decide where we should put this last guy," Amelia suggests, realizing she's still holding a large ceramic gnome. Between the way she behaved before pulling away, and now the gnomes, Amelia is certain that she must appear to be a hot mess.

"I'm sorry about what Carla said." Kyle cuts to the chase, meeting her eyes. His are the color of moss and are surrounded by subtle lines when he frowns.

"You have nothing to be sorry for." Amelia leans in, so her children can't hear. "Carla insinuating that I'm poor, trashy, and can't dress my children properly had nothing to do with you."

Kyle stiffens. "Wait—what?"

"Oh. She didn't tell you about that?" *Oopsie.* "I thought that was what you were referring to."

"No. I was talking about Carla telling you to remove your gnome." He shuffles his feet, shoving his hands in the pockets of his jeans. "She actually said all of that other stuff?"

"Yep. So, why are you here, Kyle Sanders of Sanders Construction? My instinct tells me this isn't your average neighbor saying 'hi' visit." Her tone is teasing, but anxiety has coiled within Amelia's abdomen.

"Um. I don't know how to say this..." He studies the ground.

Her anxiety has now twisted into a tight knot. This can't be good. Funny how she immediately goes to the worst-case scenario. Once upon a time, Amelia used to be a glass-half-full person. Not anymore. Not since...

No matter how hard she tries, Amelia can't pinpoint precisely when it began. Perhaps it was the moment she discovered Daniel's infidelity, his secret life.

Hugging the gnome as if shielding herself from the onslaught of whatever Kyle's about to say, she waits with bated breath for him to say something, anything.

"I see your gnomes have multiplied. Is this some kind of convention?" His smile is tentative. Like he's not sure how she'll respond.

Amelia laughs. "'Gnome convention.' That's a good one. No, it's not a convention. Though I don't know what they do when we're sleeping. Isn't there some sort of folklore about gnomes coming to life at night, or was that in one of the Harry Potter books?"

Kyle shrugs, his smile widening as he waits for a real answer.

"Actually, I'm making a statement to our HOA, or is it our management company? One or both deemed a little gnome my kids gave me for Mother's Day as an eyesore. So, I'm protesting their bylaws."

"By breaking those bylaws in abundance. You think that's wise?" His eyes hold hers, and there's an intensity burning within his gaze. He's not judging Amelia, but there's something behind his question… Concern, maybe.

Glancing at her children, who are sitting in the grass out of earshot, Amelia whispers, "Look, I understand the HOA has a job to do, same with the management company. Here's the thing: my kids lost their dad, their home, and the feeling of security they once felt when my ex-husband walked out on us. That so-called trashy, tacky gnome was outside our home—the home my ex-husband now shares with his pregnant mistress. When we moved here, my children asked me for one thing—that I put that gnome in our new front yard. How can I tell them that the gnome they painted for me last Mother's Day isn't worthy of being in our front yard, according to some bylaws? Or that Carla thinks it's ugly? Or that I was in such a haze after their father's betrayal, during the divorce and our move, that I didn't read the fine print about a gnome hiding in the bushes being banned before I made that promise to them."

"Oh," Kyle mutters, exhaling an exaggerated breath. "You can't. Well, you could, but you'd break their hearts."

"Right? That's why I'm protesting." Placing her free hand on her hip, Amelia adds, "This neighborhood is teeming with Easter décor. Half the homes on this block have some form of the Easter Bunny in their front yards. How is my gnome different?"

"Theirs is for the holiday only. They are supposed to take their décor down after Easter, just like Christmas. It isn't permanent."

"Okay. Your clarification is noted and appreciated." She can use that to buy herself some time.

Kyle shoves his dark hair out of his eyes. It's black, and the contrast between it and the green of his eyes is striking. Enough to cause Amelia to stare, then look away, attempting not to stare. This guy throws her off-kilter, and she doesn't have the time or inclination to be off-kilter. Not for him, or anyone.

"You're going to think I'm the biggest jerk when I say this, but you can't keep the gnomes."

She meets his eyes again, her confusion heightening, simmering just below the surface. "Why not? If I do my research and make a compelling argument—"

"None of it will make a difference. The developer created the bylaws, and we're beholden to them. I can't make an exception for you, no matter how much I want to."

I can't make an exception for you…

There it is. The *I*. The exact thing her subconscious has been dreading since this conversation began.

"*You* can't?" Gripping the gnome she's holding with all her might in an attempt to center herself, Amelia's knuckles begin to ache. "You're one of them?"

One of them—that came out wrong, and much more accusatory than she meant for it to sound. "I mean, you're a part of the HOA?"

"Yeah, I am. The HOA board president, to be honest. I'm not proud of it right now, and I wish I could do something to help you." A crease etches deep within Kyle's forehead as his lips purse in a frown. "Believe it or not, that's why I accepted the board position. If it were up to me, I'd change the bylaws and let you have your gnome, but I can't. Not until the builders sell all of their inventory and we're free of them and the developer."

He studies Amelia's house, concentrating on the gutters. One of them is clogged. The fact that he noticed reminds her that she needs to hire someone. Great, in addition to upholding the HOA's gnome ban, Mr. HOA President is noting everything wrong with her property. She'll probably get another letter. Maybe two.

"I'm sorry," Kyle's baritone is brimming with sincerity. At least Amelia thinks it is. She's been wrong before, though. Hence her divorce.

"Don't be. Rules are rules. This is my fault. I made a promise to my children that I can't keep, unless I fight the rules. And though it may be a losing battle, I won't give up without a fight. I can't." That's the crux of it. Why Gnomegate will continue. Because she owes it to her children to at least try to keep her word. "So, these will be Easter gnomes by tomorrow. No violations here."

Kyle snaps his head from the line of sight of her gutter to Amelia. "I didn't mean—"

"Nope. You said it. You gave me the idea." Amelia raises her finger in the air. "No backsies."

Rubbing his jaw, which has become tense, Kyle mutters, "You're going to be a pain in my—"

"Swear jar." She interrupts. "We're kid-friendly here. You curse and it costs you money."

Expelling an exaggerated sigh, Kyle purses his lips before adding, "Backside. You're going to be a pain in my backside, aren't you?"

Amelia nods. "I expect that I'll be the largest pain in your…backside." She was about to curse, which would mean putting a quarter in the kids' swear jar.

If she had a dollar for every time she added to that darn jar, she'd be rich. Some would ask how that's possible when she doesn't curse in front of Jacob and Chloe. Well, Amelia goes by the honor system. Even when her children aren't around, if Amelia curses, the quarter goes in. That's typically how the jar fills.

As Kyle opens his mouth to speak, she waits for a retort. One that never comes.

"Would it help if I admit that I derive no pleasure from being a pain in your you know what?" she asks, half joking.

"No." One word. From Kyle, who is currently wearing a determined frown.

She softly says, "Sorry," to him, then proceeds to her front porch, where she places the large gnome directly in sight of the street.

Remembering what Carla said about the quarterly HOA meetings, Amelia breaks the heady silence between them. "Carla mentioned that I can take the matter up at our next HOA meeting. Expect me to be sitting in the front row, prepared to argue my case."

"You just missed one, I'm afraid. They're quarterly."

"She mentioned that. It gives me time to prepare." And prepare she will.

Kyle stifles a laugh. "Prepare? Holy…" His eyes meet hers. "Swear jar. Yeah. Never mind."

Based upon Kyle's tightly clenched jaw and the vein that is visible in his neck, this is torture for him. Amelia would find it cute if her gnome situation wasn't so serious.

"I'd expect nothing less." His words are precise, slow, and chosen with care. This guy is in control of his temper.

"Less than what, Mr. Bunny Helper?" Chloe asks, wearing the cap Kyle gave her as she and Jacob run towards them.

Chloe is faster than Jacob. It's the tomboy in her, combined with the younger sister who must compete with her older brother. It motivates her.

Reaching for the brim, Kyle adjusts her cap. "Let's just say that I'm sorry that I can't be more help with something. It's nothing for you to worry about, though."

"As long as you try hard, that's what matters." Jacob adjusts his cap to match his sister's. "Mom taught us that."

Exhaling, Kyle appears to be at a loss.

"Go inside, kiddos. Mr. Bunny has a lot to do, and you need to wash your hands, please." Amelia waits for the front door to close behind them. "So, what's next on your to-do list? Steal candy from kids? Issue tickets like the gnome police?"

Amelia's isn't using her usual snark, which is her defense mechanism. Instead, her tone is playful, since Kyle hasn't been a jerk in the least. Instead, he's gone out of his way to be nice when he didn't have to be, and she's attempting to cheer him up.

"Nope. I'm heading to the bookstore." He studies the gnome that started this mess, the one her children made for her. "There's got to be a book on dealing with a pain of a neighbor with an unhealthy obsession with trolls."

Gasping, Amelia chides him. "They're gnomes. All kidding aside, though, what I admitted to you about my divorce isn't common knowledge, and it's not easy for me to discuss. Had I known that you were on the HOA board…" She wouldn't have told him. There's no need to complete her sentence. He understands.

Why did she tell him? Because in addition to being the Bunny's helper, this guy seems genuine. Like someone she'd be friends with. Or more…if Amelia was ready, which she's not. Or maybe she could be, with the right guy. Regardless, Kyle isn't the right guy. Instead, he's on the opposite side of Gnomegate.

"My protest isn't personal." It's her olive branch, though not entirely accurate. Amelia confided in him, which she doesn't do much with people outside her inner circle of best friends. That's a lesson she learned the hard way. Even before Daniel. It was easy today with Kyle. That in and of itself should have been warning enough.

After clearing his throat and commanding Amelia's attention, Kyle shoots her a wide grin. "Just for the record, stealing candy and issuing gnome tickets are Carla's hobbies. Not mine."

"Well played, Mr. Bunny." Amelia pauses. This guy is charming. He's also her adversary. She refuses to forget that. "It's a shame we're on different sides of Gnomegate."

"Gnome what?" Kyle laughs.

Amelia shrugs. "It was between that and Game of Gnomes."

"You are a handful. Heaven help me." Running his hands through his hair, Kyle expels a deep breath.

"At least we share a sense of humor." Her tone changes, from joking to dripping with remorse, though he probably won't notice, so she adds, "I do regret that we're on opposite sides of this, but I'm not giving up without a fight."

"That's what I was afraid of." He turns, shouting over his shoulder as he walks to his truck, "I'll see you around, then. In the front row. Next quarter."

"Bye, Kyle." With a wave, Amelia enters her house and closes the heavy oak and glass door with a loud thud. Through one of the glass panels, Amelia watches as Kyle sits in his truck. He drives forward a foot or so, then his brake lights illuminate for a brief moment, as if he might park and return. He doesn't, though. Instead, he drives away.

Surveying the entrance to her new home with its polished cherry hardwood floors, her home office to the left accentuated with interior French doors, like most of the houses built by this builder, and a long corridor that leads to her kitchen, living room, and the rest of the house, Amelia thinks of the extended family of gnomes sitting in their front yard. When she considered taking on the HOA, she never thought that would mean taking on the Easter Bunny's helper. And Amelia never considered that she would regret that decision. For one brief moment, she does...until her children run down the hall.

"The front yard is so cool!" Jacob announces as Amelia sits on the hardwood floor. He hugs her, while Chloe climbs on top of her lap, joining in on their hug.

"I'm the bread," Chloe says of what Jacob calls their sandwich hugs.

"And I'm the tuna," Jacob adds.

Amelia giggles. "What does that make me?"

"The lettuce," Jacob replies, with a tone that conveys it's obvious.

Chloe nods. "Yeah, you're the lettuce."

Amelia squeezes them tighter. "Did you have a good day?"

"Yeah!" both children shout in unison.

"Decorating with the gnomes was awesome. Can we get some more?" Jacob asks.

Rubbing their backs, Amelia kisses her daughter, then son on the tops of their heads. "I think we've made our point with the ones we have."

"What point?" Jacob's curiosity leaves his ability to question anything and everything second only to his list of the different cars and trucks he wants.

"We're home." Two words. A sentiment Amelia doesn't fully feel yet, but she will. Once she's able to keep her promise to them about their gnome or, at the very least, try her hardest to do so.

After squeezing her kids in a tight hug one more time, she texts her best friends. It's a group text.

SOS. Need to whine. Pizza for all.

With that call to arms, her cell begins to vibrate. Amelia's group of friends have her back.

Oh, bring some Easter ribbon. Please.

One of her friends types back in record time. On it!

"I just thought of something." Jacob looks at his mom, then his sister. "We have a gnome home."

Chloe erupts with laughter. "A gnome home. That's funny!"

They both smile and Amelia tickles them, causing them to shriek with laughter until it fills the open floor plan.

Yes, they are home. This is just the beginning of their new chapter.

About the Author

Tracy Goodwin is the *USA Today* bestselling author of sexy sports romances and swoon-worthy romantic comedies. In addition, she pens sweeping historical romances, captivating MomComs, and vivid urban fantasies. Though the genres may be different, each story delivers her unique blend of passion, poignant emotion, humor, and unforgettable characters that steal readers' hearts.

A New Yorker who now calls Houston home, Tracy is the mom of two, a wife, the wrangler of two dogs, two cats, and lots of chaos. She's also a Funko Pop collector and loves singing carpool karaoke (even when alone).

Website: tracygoodwin.com
Facebook: TracyGoodwin.author
Instagram: @author.tracygoodwin
TikTok: @tracygoodwinauthor